A PLACE OF SECRETS

A PLACE OF SECRETS

A Northern Gothic Mystery

Shane Peacock

CORMORANT BOOKS

Copyright © 2025 Shane Peacock
This edition copyright © 2025 Cormorant Books Inc.
This is a first edition.

No part of this publication may be reproduced, stored in a retrieval system or transmitted, in any form or by any means, without the prior written consent of the publisher or a licence from The Canadian Copyright Licensing Agency (Access Copyright). For an Access Copyright licence, visit www.accesscopyright.ca or call toll free 1.800.893.5777.

The publisher and the author expressly forbid the use of this book in any manner for the purpose of training so-called artificial intelligence systems or technologies, and reserve this title from the text and data mining exception in accordance with the European Parliament directive.

 Canadian Heritage / Patrimoine canadien      Canada Council for the Arts / Conseil des arts du Canada

 ONTARIO CREATES | ONTARIO CRÉATIF    ONTARIO ARTS COUNCIL CONSEIL DES ARTS DE L'ONTARIO an Ontario government agency un organisme du gouvernement de l'Ontario    Ontario

We acknowledge financial support for our publishing activities: the Government of Canada, through the Canada Book Fund and The Canada Council for the Arts; the Government of Ontario, through the Ontario Arts Council, Ontario Creates, and the Ontario Book Publishing Tax Credit.

LIBRARY AND ARCHIVES CANADA CATALOGUING IN PUBLICATION

Title: A place of secrets / Shane Peacock.
Names: Peacock, Shane, author.
Description: Series statement: A northern gothic mystery ; 2
Identifiers: Canadiana (print) 20250165813 | Canadiana (ebook) 20250165848 |
ISBN 9781770867987 (softcover) | ISBN 9781770867994 (EPUB)
Subjects: LCGFT: Detective and mystery fiction. | LCGFT: Novels.
Classification: LCC PS8581.E234 P53 2025 | DDC C813/.54—dc23

United States Library of Congress Control Number: 2025934051

Cover and interior design: Marijke Friesen
Manufactured by Copywell in Woodbridge,
Ontario in August 2025.

Printed using paper from a responsible and sustainable resource, including a mix of virgin fibres and recycled materials.

Printed and bound in Canada.

EU RP   eucomply OÜ
Pärnu mnt 139b-14, 11317 Tallinn, Estonia
hello@eucompliancepartner.com, +3375690241

CORMORANT BOOKS INC.
260 ISHPADINAA (SPADINA) AVENUE, SUITE 502,
TKARONTO (TORONTO), ON M5T 2E4

SUITE 110, 7068 PORTAL WAY, FERNDALE, WA 98248, USA
info@cormorantbooks.com / www.cormorantbooks.com

"Three people can keep a secret, if two of them are dead."
Benjamin Franklin

"Man is not what he thinks he is, he is what he hides."
Andre Malraux

For Johanna, Hadley,
and Sammy.

1

The Body in the Basement and the Old Woman Upstairs

ALICE MORROW THOUGHT she was seeing a ghost. Sitting in her cruiser at the top of the snowy lane, nearly dozing off as the sun descended too early again on a January day, she saw lights come on in the farmhouse. That was impossible. There was no one there. Hugh Mercer had left weeks before. Left without a sound. Gone back to his wife, for all she knew. There hadn't been any tire tracks in the snow going up the lane the other two days she had come here either. Why she was doing this, she couldn't quite say. She had been here for hours this time, much longer than the previous days, just staring down at the house, seeing the white everywhere around her like blankets without warmth in this ugly northern beauty. Perhaps she liked to look at the shells of things rather than the real thing? The real thing hurt too much. The remnants of Hugh Mercer's stay here were enough: the house he had inhabited, the memories of him, the scent of him — they were enough. Just like the remnants of her first love, the love she had killed. She couldn't see that boy's face anymore. Her boy. Neither could she see Hugh's after just a few weeks. A tear fell onto her cheek, and she wiped it so hard it was as if she'd struck herself.

THE NEXT MORNING, she thought of asking Sal to go out and check on the house, but that would involve either letting her know that she had been there — three times — or revealing how much she cared for Mercer, and she couldn't have any of that. But she wondered about the lights. She wondered too about the lack of them in the other farmhouses she had vaguely seen dotting the quilt of snow in the valley. Grey dots in the near-black. People in the dark. They had either gone to bed early or hadn't felt the need for light. Would that happen many other places in the world?

It made her think too of the lights never coming on in another house just a few concession roads over on New Year's Eve. And that made her think of the body again. The one in the basement.

"That's why I'm here, near where Mercer used to live," she assured herself. "It's because of the body. I need him to help me make it make sense."

By mid-afternoon, she couldn't stand it anymore. She had his cell number, but there was no way she was calling him. Who knew who would be within earshot or perhaps even answer the call. She drove out to the farmhouse. By the time she got there, the sun was descending. When she reached the bottom of the lane, she saw his car sitting outside the garage, but it was hidden from any view anyone could have of his place from a distance. She smiled.

There was no sign of life inside, even when she slammed the door of the cruiser a little harder than usual. She marched up his front walkway and tried to make her footfalls as heavy as possible.

She smiled again as she recalled him saying that no one around here made any noise when they walked.

She knocked.

Nothing.

She knocked again. The lights came on in the second-floor window. She looked up and saw him, like a vision gazing down at her from upstairs. His bedroom. Even from the front door, even in the darkness, she could tell he was wearing his bathrobe at four-thirty in the afternoon. His hair, that full head of black hair with lovely streaks of grey, looked dishevelled. She wondered if he was naked underneath. Naked, just as she'd always insisted he be before they were more than a few steps into his room. She resisted the tingle that gave her. She resisted the image of him naked. A big man, an American, a homicide detective. An intelligent man. A man with feelings bursting to come out.

She could hear him descending the staircase. That made her think of the article she had read in an old *Time* magazine about how women's senses of hearing and smell are so much better than men's.

She didn't say anything when he opened the door. He had once said if a scriptwriter were writing dialogue between the two of them, his would be twice as long as hers.

I'm here to talk about the body, she told herself, *the body in the basement and the old woman upstairs.*

"Sergeant Morrow," he said to her.

"Detective Mercer."

"I didn't leave."

"I can see that."

He looked at her for a moment, stared right into her eyes. His eyes were soft in the falling light, and caring, and it scared her.

"Come on in and I'll explain why."

Her first instinct was to say no, but she went in.

2

Together Again?

MERCER DIDN'T TAKE her hand as they walked into the high-ceilinged room that served as both a sort of family room — though there hadn't been a family in this house for many decades — and a big country kitchen. Alice didn't mind the lack of apparent affection. In fact, she expected it, preferred it. It was their way.

The place was as bare as ever. Just the little table and two chairs in the kitchen. He pulled out one for her and sat on the other. The whole house was like this. Even in the living room, all that decorated the place was a bookshelf with a volume of the complete works of Shakespeare and a few other books he'd added; there wasn't a stick of furniture in the matching dining room either. The wooden stairs with their fancy banister led from the room they were in straight up to the four bedrooms leading off from the creaking upper hallway with its wide boards hewn more than a century ago from the forest at the back of this farm — three empty rooms and one with just his big bed.

She was nervous, and that made her angry with herself. Normally, she didn't give a damn about silences between the two of them, but as soon as they were seated, she felt anxious to speak, and then she listened carefully to every word she uttered.

"I, uh, I wanted to ask you something. Professional question."

"I need to tell you why I'm still here first."

"Just a few days ago, we found a body in the basement of a farmhouse about two kilometres from here."

"Nearly a mile and a half."

"Correct." She smiled in spite of herself. "There was an old woman —"

"She died in her basement?"

"No ... she was upstairs."

Mercer had looked like he didn't want to talk about this, but that information was almost too much for him. They both wanted to know the truth about things, and there was a truth somewhere in what she had just said that asked to be found. She could see him steel himself.

"Alice, I need to talk."

"Isn't that what we're doing?"

"I mean really talk. We never do that."

Alice swallowed. "I'm on duty. Thus, the outfit." She held her hands out, palms up in a girlish pose, and then placed them on her hips, which was a sight so far from who she was that it almost made Mercer laugh. And that was fine. She didn't care about how the police uniform made her look. The fewer stares from men the better. But she did know that he had been surprised at what she looked like the first time she'd taken it off upstairs. She knew that it intrigued him. And that reaction intrigued her.

"Can't take a minute?"

"A minute, Detective Mercer. I will start timing" — she looked down at her watch — "now."

"I'll need more than that. Bear with me."

"Shoot," she said, though her voice broke a little. Men often have a hard time looking into your eyes when they talk, unless they want something, want you. Then the look is greedy. But usually, you have to make them do it. You have to look at them until they look back. It sometimes seemed the opposite between Alice Morrow and Hugh Mercer. It certainly did right now. The look in his eyes was sincere and hopeful, and it terrified her.

"There are a lot of things I haven't been telling you."

"Oh? A liar, are we?"

"No. I haven't been lying to you. I've just been omitting things."

"And you're a man? What a surprise."

He smiled with an expression that said he loved her sense of humour. That concerned her too.

"I have to tell you some things about my past and my personal situation, things I should have told you long ago. Secrets, I guess."

"You don't have to. Your minute is ticking away."

"No. No, I do."

Americans were such open books. Even the men. She had never met a single man up here who had ever given away their feelings so cheaply. They were all hard to figure out in these parts. Not that she cared. She wasn't looking for a relationship. She'd had enough of that long ago.

"You know I have a wife."

"I do indeed."

"And you know that things have not been going well for us for a while, or at least I know you figured that out. But what I didn't tell you was that when I went back to Jersey a few weeks ago, I discovered that she had a new man in her life."

"Sorry to hear that ... I guess. But remember, I tailed you to your house down there, so I kinda know some —"

But Mercer was barely listening.

"I also discovered that she had been with him for a while."

"Oh."

"And they had actually been in our bedroom, together, when I dropped by to see her. Just coming back up the hall."

"*Together* together in the bedroom?"

"Yes."

"Oh."

"I can't tell you how that hurt." His voice had dropped, and she felt like she should reach across the little table and take his hand. But she didn't.

"But you've been with me," she said. "Together together, for a while too."

"Yeah. So, I guess that's kind of hypocritical of me, and I've known for a while that Christine and I were heading in this direction, but god, it still hurts."

She still didn't offer her hand.

"And they seem to be a couple, a real couple," he said, brushing his hand across the stubble of his unshaven face. "You and me, we're not."

"No," said Alice quickly.

"And there are kids involved, as you know. Our children. I'm not sure I've ever even mentioned their names to you. Stevie and Keith, both great kids, both away at college now, both not my biggest fans. I should have told you more about them before." He was looking down now. "They used to almost idolize me, Alice, but now they are embarrassed that I'm a cop. I'm embarrassed too, sometimes. When you think of the shit we do. The shit I did."

"You did? What do you mean?"

"I assaulted someone."

"You did?"

"Not long before I came up here. I was sure he was guilty, that he'd raped the young woman in the case we were investigating and beat her nearly to death, left her for dead. In fact, that's why my homicide squad was looking into it, because we were so sure she wouldn't make it. And eventually, she didn't. About Stevie's age, the girl was. We tried to take her victim statement in the hospital bed, but she couldn't speak. I'd seen so much of that horror. So, when I got my hands on him that night in the Bronx, in the rain, going through a terrible week with Christine, my kids not talking to me because I spent so little time with them, because I'm a cop, and I caught this suspect running from me, had him right in my hands, and I just ... I just snapped. I had my Glock out and in his face, right at his temple, and I was so angry I could have shot him fifty times. I can see his eyes now, looking up at me as I have him pinned, both my big knees in his chest and his arms wrapped under him. I turned the gun around and struck him. I nearly blinded him, smashed in part of his face." Mercer paused. "He didn't do it, Alice. It wasn't him. And my partner, he didn't report what I did, not a word. I pray every night that I will be forgiven, and I'm not a praying man."

Alice was silent. She couldn't believe that Hugh Mercer's eyes were reddening. Not crying. She wondered if he had ever done that or ever could. He had been so good on the Becky Prior case they had just worked on together, so strong and efficient. But his eyes were definitely different now, looking right into hers, or trying to. She was working hard to stay dry too, but not in sympathy with him. To her shame, she was thinking of herself, of her own trauma. This man made her do that.

"Thank you for sharing." Her hands were folded on the table, held tightly together. She glanced down at them now as if there were a police report there and she was about to read it. "The ... uh ... the woman upstairs ... in this house two kilometres from here? She died on New Year's Eve. *Then* we found the body ... in her basement."

Mercer reached across and took her hands. His enveloped hers. "I'm surprised I told you all that." His voice was steady now. "I was seeing a therapist in New York after the incident, and she told me to write things down, but you're here, someone I can talk to, now, and that felt better. I was alone here for Christmas and New Year's. I think you ... might be why I didn't go home."

Oh god.

"You just enjoyed the work we did together, Mercer, I mean the work work. And it sounds like there wasn't much to return to in the States." *Not much about the U.S. is appealing period, these days,* she thought. She pulled back her hands. "We are running tests on the body now."

Mercer actually grinned. "I see."

"Well, it's not really a body. It's just remains, a skeleton. Whoever this person was, he has been dead a long time. We are looking into how long."

Mercer cleared his throat. "How did the woman upstairs die?"

"Well, she was elderly. Very elderly. One hundred years old."

"Wow. That happen often around here? People live that long?"

"Sometimes. Not all that unusual."

"So, natural causes."

"Maybe. But after we found the body downstairs, we decided it would be a good idea to run some tests on her. Waiting for those too."

"I don't understand why you were looking around in her basement, though."

"It was because of the note."

"She left a note? You said probably natural causes. Not suicide."

"No. No, we don't think it was that. It wasn't that sort of note, not a confession of having done any harm to herself; it seemed to have been written a while ago, and it was left in an obvious place nearby, with her things, like it was there for others to read whenever she died."

"So, what did the note say?"

Alice took out her cell, found the photo, and handed the phone to Mercer. He looked down at the screen and read out loud. "There's a secret in my basement. Northwest corner, three feet from the north wall, four from the west. Dig. May this destroy my reputation forever. I deserve it."

"It was in an envelope."

"Anything on it? Addressed to anyone?"

"Oh yeah."

"To whom?"

"To me." She paused. "It just said ... *Alice*."

She tried to hide the way that made her feel when she said it out loud. She hadn't even known Evelyn Massey, not well at least. Her name had been written on the envelope in that shaky hand that very elderly people have, a hand that can look almost evil, as if the ink were dripping from each letter. And it had been underlined. Evelyn Massey had wanted her, Alice Morrow, involved in this, in investigating the corpse in the basement. She'd wanted her drawn into this mystery. *Why?* Sal had attempted to tell her that it could be any Alice and maybe they should be seeking someone else, but a quick bit of research revealed that Mrs. Massey had no relatives or close friends by that name. No, that envelope was not just for the police but for Alice Morrow directly.

She had stood there in the basement the next day and watched as the constables broke up the concrete and found the crate used for shipping farm animals beneath the surface. Under the circumstances, with her name on that envelope, she had felt forced to be there. And so she'd presided over the opening like someone facing punishment. The gasps. The smell. Then the sight of the six-foot, one-inch man — his skeleton, at least — jammed into the crate.

She hadn't needed forensics to know it was a man, or to see the broken-in skull, the two arms pulverized from the elbows down.

"I think I would like to stay tonight," she told Mercer, looking over his shoulder into the darkness outside his windows. Still, she wouldn't take his hand.

3

A Devil in the Details

SHE COULD NEVER stay all night with a man — though she nearly had once with Mercer — and she kind of liked the way it felt when she left them, lying there fast asleep, their bodies so done in, so exhausted by an encounter. With a woman.

Standing there as silent as possible, she took a moment to look at him before she left, police boots in hand and uniform dishevelled. She thought of the way it felt between the two of them. It wasn't like that with other men. She thought of him running his hands along her hips, tracing the tattooed letters, angled inward and so large they nearly reached her thighs: *A.M.* Her own initials, with hearts. He often appeared to want to ask, but thank god he hadn't. Not yet. She kept standing there, wondering if she should slip back in, warm beside him. But then she turned and tiptoed down the stairs without a sound. It was true, people from these parts were weightless, and moved about like phantoms.

She lingered in the living room for a few moments, looking around, but there was so little to see, so little of him, really. She opened *The Complete Works of William Shakespeare* and noticed he had bookmarked the tragedies and seemed to be working his way through them. A copy of *In Cold Blood* sat next to it and *The Girl with the Dragon Tattoo*, which intrigued her since she had read that novel herself just recently.

She left a note on the big kitchen counter, at first wondering if she should sign it with a crude drawing, maybe of a body part, his body part, then wondering if it should be a heart, but finally settling for one *x* and one *o*, lower case: *Come to the station in the afternoon. I will tell you more. We hope to have further news about the body by then. I really want you on board. Full cooperation this time. Promise. xo.*

SHE WENT HOME. Home to her parents' place. The last apartment she had rented, which she had lived in ever since she came back from police college more than twenty years ago, had been torn down to be replaced by condos. The first ones in town. She had planned to live with her parents for a few months, maybe a year at the most, and then move out again, maybe into one of those condos. Alone, she'd vowed. But that had been three years ago. It just felt comfortable being here, felt like she was back in time, way back before bad things started to happen. Having men over was awkward, so she only did it when her parents went out. She had no issue with having sex in her little bed, her teenage-years bed; in fact, there was something about it that thrilled her. And she could see that it thrilled the guys too. But she always kicked them out right after, found a reason to let them know they should be on their way. And she never dated a man twice; that scared her. Then Hugh Mercer appeared.

IT TOOK ALICE until after they'd finished their lunch at Connie's Home Style Grill to tell Sal. In fact, they had already left its welcoming interior, with its wooden floors and specials up on the chalkboard above the counter, and were moving along King Street Circle back toward the police station. They were trudging forward in the freshly fallen snow, their faces red from the cold even though they were only a couple of minutes out of the warmth in the restaurant. It was early January, and the weather was brutal.

"I, uh, went to see Hugh Mercer."

"What?" Sal stopped and looked at her. "You went down to the States and saw him? When? I know he's a bit of a looker and all but —"

"No. No, he's here. He never left. He's still living at the farmhouse."

Sal smiled. "Now, what would cause him to do that?"

"I don't know. Maybe he likes the weather."

"It ain't the weather, sweetheart. Where did you run into him?"

"Um ... at his place."

They had resumed walking, waving at folks, nodding. Most people offered friendly expressions, though some looked away when they saw it was Alice Morrow, and no one offered to chat. Sal stopped again.

"So, you just happened to be driving by the farmhouse, out there, oh, twenty minutes from town, and you just happened to drive down his sideroad and then down his lane and then happened to walk up to his door and knocked on it?"

"Sorta like that, yeah."

"So, just a how-ya-doing visit? Little visit to say hello?"

"Maybe a bit more than that."

"I thought there was a spring in your step this morning."

It wasn't appropriate to be in a relationship with a fellow police officer, but Mercer was not an official employee, Alice told herself. Sal just wanted her to be happy, anyway.

Alice started walking again, and Sal soon caught up.

"I told him about the Massey case too, thought maybe he would have a few thoughts."

"Well, we're going to need lots of those. I certainly never took old Mrs. Massey for a murderer. But what she said in that note, holy cow, that kinda freaked me out. Her hoping that the discovery of the body in her basement would destroy her reputation? Wow. That's basically a confession, isn't it? But then you consider the corpse ... somebody beat the heck out of that man. Pretty hard to picture her doing that. And then putting him in that animal crate and burying him under concrete? Man, that's a bizarre image. A crime of passion? Maybe. The emotions give you sudden extra strength? To me, that's the only way to account for the sort of violence in this. But why, exactly? If she did it, then why did she do it? What was going on back then? Had to be a little while back or she wouldn't have been even remotely capable of it."

They were talking quietly, using the ruse of sometimes raising their hands to their reddening faces to protect their skin against the cold, keeping their conversation private, turning slightly toward each other. Other pedestrians didn't seem to care anyway. Minding your own business was a sacred right here.

"Yeah, it's hard to believe it was her, but I agree, she kind of said it was. We can't just assume she did it, though, and narrow the case based on that. Maybe she's protecting someone? It feels like there's a whole world of secrets involved in this. A whole story from the past that we have to unearth."

"Just like we unearthed that body."

Sal's frozen mouth had made her last word come out as "booty." They both grinned under their gloves but then appeared a little guilty.

"If she did this, then she certainly wasn't who we thought she was," said Alice.

"No one is, especially around here."

They had arrived at the police station but had to stop for a moment to let several people pass in front of them, who all nodded slightly to the officers.

"I asked Mercer to drop by this afternoon."

"Should have given me some notice. I would have washed my hair."

They walked up the few steps and entered the station, a Victorian-era brick building right on the Circle. Alice remembered Mercer falling on his ass here on the ice, wearing those fancy New York dress shoes of his. He had better boots now. The man was learning.

Ranbir Singh was at the reception desk when they arrived. It was a job he was fond of. He looked down through the lenses of his glasses at his watch.

"You must have been enjoying yourselves greatly during the time allotted to you for lunchtime."

"Yeah, Ranbir, we get it," said Sal. "We're late. We like to enjoy ourselves. Sorry about that."

"No cause for sorrow," he said. "I was not referring to any abrogation of the rules of the police service. Not directly."

"We'll be in my office," said Alice. "Someone is dropping by soon. You can let him go straight back."

"Identity?"

"American man. Professional. You know him."

"Not Detective Mercer? I thought he went back to the home of the free and the land of the brave?"

"Just show him in, thanks."

Alice and Sal went through the door in the counter of the reception desk and were only a few strides toward the offices when they heard the outside door open and Ranbir's voice, raised in volume on purpose, greeting Hugh Mercer.

"Ah, my Yankee hard-boiled gumshoe! You're back. You cannot resist us ordinary people!"

"Yeah, real ordinary," said Mercer under his breath. "Hey, Ranbir. Is Alice here?"

He always speaks so frickin' loudly, thought Alice, *even when he's trying not to. American trait.*

"She and Constable Haddad have just arrived, after enjoying themselves at a lengthy lunchtime. I imagine they are listening. Ladies are always listening. Very clever, much more clever than us. My wife knows all about me and who I am, and I know nothing about her. Are you here to solve the case of the body in the basement?"

"No. Here to turn in my resignation."

"Eh?"

"Can I go through?"

"Of course." Ranbir buzzed him in.

Alice and Sal had stopped before they reached the office and turned to greet Hugh Mercer.

"Detective Mercer, so lovely to see you again," said Sal, coming forward and turning red when Mercer embraced her and gave her a kiss on the cheek.

"Mercer," said Alice.

"I'm here as requested," he said, "but not to join another investigation. I've learned to be polite from people up here, so I thought I'd come in and tell you in person." He paused. "I've had enough of being a cop. It made me into someone I don't want to be. I need to take some time away from all of that. This is a perfect place to change, it seems to me. I still have some savings I can use, but I think I'm going to try to get a job of some sort around here; maybe I'll farm a little in the spring, plant a garden, get some chickens and harvest the eggs. Been thinking about all of that. Thought maybe I'd see if I could help some organization here that helps homeless people too, something like that, people who've been abused by authorities, by the cops."

"Well," said Sal, clearing her throat, "that's lovely, I guess."

"You can't do that, any of that," said Alice. She didn't look upset. She said it as a matter of fact.

"Yes, I can."

"No, you can't. You can't work here. That would be illegal. And perhaps you've noticed that I'm a member of the police service in this town, as is Constable Haddad, so we would have to arrest you or at least deport you. You will recall that this is a different country. And if she didn't have the balls to kick you out, I would."

"Alice!" said Sal. She turned to Mercer and winked at him. "We'll just look the other way."

Alice's cell beeped, and she glanced down at it and swiped, then briefly read what was on the screen.

"And there's another reason."

Mercer didn't look pleased. "And what would that be?"

She handed the phone to him. "Read this. Out loud and with a little feeling. It's the preliminary report from the coroner."

He sighed and took the phone.

"The deceased," he read, "appears to be a young male in his early thirties, buried in the Massey farmhouse basement immediately following his death, which came as a result of a blunt force blow to the skull, though he also suffered from either prior or subsequent fracturing of his arms, perhaps tied behind his back at the time of death, which occurred about …"

He looked up at Alice, his mouth open.

"Go on, Mercer."

"… about sixty years ago!"

"Ho-ly," said Sal.

"Now, I'm guessing," said Alice to Mercer, "that you, like Constable Haddad and myself, have your doubts about whether or not the lady upstairs did this, if she was even capable of doing it, and if she did do it, then why and how, and why she left a note basically confessing to it, and if she didn't do it, then who did? Who in this kind, loving community about sixty years ago tied that rather large man's hands behind his back, beat the living shit out of him until there was no life left in him, and then buried him in a crate in a basement in a farmhouse, a place where Mrs. Massey lived for more than seventy years." She paused. "I'm guessing this intrigues the fuck out of you."

"Alice!" said Sal.

"Possibly," said Mercer, still looking at the screen.

"And I'm guessing you're un-retiring?" said Alice. "At least for a while? Until we go back through the mists of time and get some answers here?"

"And maybe deal with a current crime at the same time?" said Sal. "If we find out there's anything suspicious about Evelyn's death."

"Yeah," said Mercer, "maybe I'll un-retire just a little, for a while." He still had Alice's phone in his hand and was re-reading the text, shaking his head. She took it from him.

"Thought so."

"Though," said Mercer, "you're leaving something out, Sergeant Morrow."

"What's that?"

"We've got to figure out why Evelyn Massey put *your* name on that envelope."

Alice turned pale.

"Yeah, that too."

4

More

"OH!" SAID ALICE as her cell beeped again. "More?" She looked down at the screen and read aloud, "Evelyn Massey toxicology tomorrow." Disappointed, she glanced up and saw disappointment on Mercer's face too.

"Let's not get ahead of ourselves," said Mercer after a pause, "anticipating anything. Never wise. We have lots on our hands already, even if Evelyn Massey simply expired from natural causes. We have a victim of unknown identity who appears to have suffered egregious foul play, a murder evidently perpetrated at least six decades ago, so in the 1960s or earlier, and we have the house owner, who was alive and residing there at the time, apparently feeling guilty about it. We have to find out who the victim was, look at who may have disappeared around that time. And we need to piece together the scene down in that basement way back then. How and why it happened, exactly when. We need to see it in our minds, full of details. We need to find out who the victim's enemies could have been. We need to speak with Evelyn's relatives and friends, mine her past, that house's past. We need to penetrate a lot of secrets."

He stopped abruptly, as if realizing that he had been speaking for a while and that his voice was rising.

Sal patted him on the arm. "Welcome back, Detective Mercer."

"Temporarily," he said quietly.

"Let's go into my office and sit down," said Alice. "Mercer's right, there's a lot to chew on. We need a game plan or this will overwhelm us. We'll need somebody to help us with legwork too. This may be more than the three of us can handle."

She led them into her office.

"Like a cadet?" asked Mercer with a bit of a sneer. "Why don't we employ that child who helped us on the Prior case?"

They sat down, Alice behind her old wooden desk and the other two across from her. There was nothing on the desk's surface but a photograph of her parents, her laptop, and a small stack of files.

"He is not a child, Detective Mercer," said Sal. "I believe he is almost nineteen years old, though, yes, he doesn't have a large frame and is a bit fresh-faced, and sometimes he looks a little younger ... maybe fourteen or fifteen."

The office was almost bare, just a map of the little town and the countryside in the surrounding area on a corkboard stuck to the wall with pins all off to the side. The concrete walls were painted the same putrid green as the walls in the reception room and throughout the offices. The paint was peeling here and there. There would be no photographs displayed on the wall of suspects or people of interest as this case proceeded — this wasn't an American movie. Alice wasn't into that. She flew by the seat of her pants.

"Renaldo would do fine," she said, "but I have someone else in mind, a little better qualified and more useful."

"Oh!' said Sal, and the wrinkles on her forehead moved as she raised her eyebrows. She grinned. "Robbie."

"I saw your eyebrows elevate, Sal," said Mercer. "Who is this guy?"

"Just our newest constable," said Alice. "Took over from Ferguson. Young guy, early twenties. We got him quick — his family's from the area. I think he just went out yesterday for the first time on patrol with a partner. Seems like a nice kid, earnest, would be willing to do some extra work."

"Hunk," said Sal under her breath.

"Sorry?" asked Mercer.

"Oh, nothing. Alice and I will be looking forward to working with him. Very forward to it." She offered a high five to Alice and withdrew it quickly.

Mercer looked like he wanted to tell Sal that she was too old for that reaction. About three decades north of it. And that Alice was too. Anybody was, actually.

"His partner is an asshole, though," said Alice, "so hopefully we can keep him away from this." She glanced at Sal. "A young one too, just a bit older. Elwin Most?"

"Oh yeah." Sal rolled her eyes.

"Okay," said Mercer, "if we can tear ourselves away from our analysis of the mental and physical qualities of the youthful male cops on the force, let's —"

"The service," said Sal.

"Huh?"

"You called it the force," said Alice. "It's a service ... up here. We're the town and area's police service. Remember?"

Mercer paused and sighed. Alice loved it. It was fun to toy with him, and she and Sal could do it without much effort. She had read somewhere, perhaps in that same *Time* article, that men weren't as good verbally as women. It often seemed true.

"Okay," she said, "yes, enough of this girlish stuff. Let's move forward."

Mercer sighed again. "I didn't mean that."

"No worries," said Sal cheerfully.

"I wasn't —"

"Here are the things I think we should do first." Alice made sure she was speaking firmly and a little louder than usual, in the sort of voice that seemed to help put things on the proper footing when dealing with male colleagues. Not that Mercer was like them. Though he was, too. "Mercer has mentioned a few, at least in a general way. But here are my thoughts, to kick things off." She drew in her breath and began. "Since at this moment we have to consider Mrs. Massey's death not suspicious, we will concentrate on the demise of Mr. X in the basement. If the former becomes a concern, we will have to deal with that as well, a two-pronged investigation."

"Then we'll really need Robbie," said Sal.

"I believe she said one thing at a time," said Mercer.

"Right," said Alice. "Now, I don't think there's any DNA coming off those basement bones, though we'll maybe send everything off to the city and let them have another, longer look at it and see if they can come up with a miracle identification. But I think we have to function from the outset as if that's not happening, at least for a while. So that means our primary job is identifying the victim using more old-fashioned ways, then finding the means of his death, and then finally determining who did it. We will begin by looking into any local disappearances from, say, the mid-fifties to the mid-sixties."

"From Elvis right up to the Beatles," said Sal. "Drive-ins, beehive hairdos, and communist plots."

"Was there any town to speak of here back then?" asked Mercer.

Alice gave him a look. "No, it only burst into existence just before you got here."

"I myself have only lived in this community for thirty-one years," added Sal, "but I can assure you that there has been a vibrant town here at least since then."

"Vibrant?" said Mercer.

They ignored that.

"The town hasn't grown much since the Second World War," said Alice. "So you're looking at a place not much different in size. Not much different in atmosphere, either, or in terms of the people here. There are lots of families that go back many generations."

"I even married into one!" said Sal. "Foreign brown girl. It was a bit of an adventure. Kept my foreign name for police work too, which didn't sit well with some old-timers. More dark people around here now, though, and gaining!" She smiled.

"Thank god," said Alice.

"So, let's look into the disappearances from that time period right away," said Mercer.

"I'll do that before I go tonight."

"Didn't you tell me once, Alice, that there have been lots of missing persons cases around here over the years?"

"Well," said Sal as Alice nodded, "people want to get away sometimes. Maybe they have good reasons to get the heck out of here? And maybe they just want to cover their tracks when they go?"

"When I mentioned that, Detective Mercer," said Alice, "I wasn't talking about recently. I don't think we've had any missing persons cases during the time I've been with the service, other than the Elizabeth Goode and Becky Prior thing, of course, that you helped out on, and that was a temporary issue. How about you, Sal — you go back many more years than me in uniform. Can you think of any others?"

"Thanks, dear, yes, I'm old. But you're right, nothing in my time, no one permanently missing that I can recall. But yeah, it's a thing around here that folks talk about, how there used to be people going missing from time to time, back in the day. But I think that's just chalked up to a different era and it being harder to keep track of individuals back then. Maybe it's just sort of local legend too?"

"Is it women or men? Or children?" asked Mercer.

"Not sure," said Alice, "though if I had to go through what women went through in the old days, I think I'd check out of Dodge too."

"What we still put up with!" said Sal.

"Right on."

"Can, we, uh, get back to our game plan?" asked Mercer. "You didn't mention a husband, a Mr. Massey, Alice. I imagine he's deceased?"

"Yeah, long gone. Farmer. Died about sixteen years back, spent his last few years in a seniors' home. Not sure where he's buried, but we'll look into it. He and Evelyn were married for about fifty-five years."

"Wow," said Sal with a quiet whistle.

"So it's not him in the basement," said Mercer. "Maybe he did it, though. Or helped? Or did it and she knew he did it? That's the reason for the guilt?"

"I'll ask around about him," said Sal. "Or spend a little time with Robbie and ask him to do it."

"And the three of us," said Alice, "should talk to Evelyn Massey's children and her closest friends."

"Lifelong friends would be best," said Sal.

"Wouldn't they all be dead?" asked Mercer.

"Oh no, there's still a few. Can't kill them with a stick."

"Not really an appropriate way to put it, Constable Haddad," said Mercer.

"Sorry."

Mercer looked to Alice. "Mrs. Massey's children should be able to tell us who her good friends are and identify the ones who are close to her age, her generation at least, who knew her sixty years ago."

"I want to go back into the basement and try to reimagine the crime now that we have details about the blows the victim received." Alice scrolled through her latest phone message. "Yeah, they've got stuff here about exactly where the skull and arms were fractured, and what probable angle the blows came from. Let's look at the rest of the house too, and the property, figure out some scenarios on how this thing was done. It's an old house with an old barn, so I don't think anything major has changed there."

"How many children are we looking at?" asked Mercer.

"Two daughters. Both married and moved to the city. Successful in their own right. Apparently, they've stayed pretty close to their mother, visit often. They're living at the house for a while to tie up loose ends and attend the funeral."

"Can we see them now?" asked Mercer.

"Right now?"

"We'll need to call them first," said Sal.

"Why do that? Better to just appear. Maybe catch them off guard."

"Two ladies in their late sixties or so? They're not even suspects. Unless they did this when they were seven."

"Not call ahead? That wouldn't be nice," said Sal.

"Nice?" asked Mercer. "Nice? I'm not saying they did this, but maybe they know something that they'd rather keep hidden."

"That's possible," said Alice. "Let's compromise. I'll get Ranbir to call them once we're on our way. Let's go."

5

First Secret

TEN MINUTES LATER, the three of them were in Alice's police cruiser. Mercer's big frame was jammed into the back seat behind the screen, and the women were comfortable in the front with their seats pushed back a little extra for space. Alice was at the wheel, travelling well over the speed limit, as usual, and Sal was riding shotgun, the radio at her command, tuned in to a local station that didn't feature just current stuff. This time it was playing Feist's "1234," which they'd turned up to about volume level eleven. And they were singing along.

Alice avoided looking in the rearview mirror. She didn't need to. She could imagine Mercer's pained expression back there; she knew he dearly wanted to shout at them to turn down the music, or better still turn it off so they could hear any important calls from dispatch. Little did he know that she had her eyes on the light on the police radio — in fact, she had turned the light up as bright as it would go and would never miss it flashing to indicate an incoming message.

The snow had started to fall in big flakes, making the road slippery, no salt laid down on it yet, and Alice imagined that Mercer had his hands held against the back seat in case she suddenly went sideways. But the cruiser was low-set and equipped with snow tires acquired from a dealer she'd recommended to Chief Smith for all the police vehicles; he had the best "grippers" in town. "Never lost a customer," the dealer liked to say, "at least not many who weren't damned well at fault for their own fucking demise." *Turn into the skid*, she reminded herself. It was interesting, she thought, how the people around here didn't think of their lives as often being in danger, believing that they lived safe existences, yet the whole population put their lives at risk on winter roads for nearly half the year.

Outside, everything was white. Well, white and grey, with a little black here and there. They were well into the countryside now, among the rolling hills, and everything looked quaint to the eye, like God had melted a giant marshmallow over a huge toy landscape. A freezing toy landscape. Alice thought of the body in the basement, and of her own apparently benign colleague Leonard Ferguson helping Becky Prior abduct Elizabeth Goode and nearly kill her with a sledgehammer just a few weeks ago. She thought of the terrible secrets this whole polite country had, secrets that you heard about now on the news, and she thought of the other disappearances in this community right here over the years. Where had those people gone? Had they left on their own, or had they suffered some horrible fate? What had been done to that young man in Evelyn Massey's house sixty years ago; what agony had he been put through? All of these things had been done in this toy landscape by the benign people who lived here. The world outside the police cruiser's windows suddenly seemed even colder, the road more slippery.

Alice often wondered why Mercer had chosen to come here in the first place. Sure, he'd had to get away from his troubles back home. And the States wasn't a good place in many ways right now. But why here? And why this interest in her? Was it just temporary? Was it simply because he was hurting? Would it fly away like the large "birds flying across the sky" in Neil Young's song — geese, she always imagined, against an iron-grey background, living things in arrow formation, anxiously fleeing back south. *Helpless*. There was snow in New York City and in New Jersey, and it was certainly cold sometimes, but it wasn't like here. This area was known as a snow belt within a snowy area, especially out in the country. *Belt* was a good word for it. Alice never wondered, though, why she lived here, why she stayed. She knew exactly why.

About ten minutes along, a little past halfway to their destination, passing old two-storey brick farmhouses and falling-down barns and newer homes built closer to the county highway, they heard Mercer rapping on the screen behind them. Sal turned down the radio.

"Yes, Detective Mercer?" she asked.

"Alice, you said there were more details about the cause of death of the victim in the basement in your phone message. Any chance you could share them now? Might be good to have them in mind when were go downstairs to the crime scene."

A little passive-aggressive, thought Alice, but he had a point.

"Sure." She nodded toward her cell, which sat on the armrest between her and Sal. "Sal, read the bit after the bit I read."

"Okay," Sal sighed, "let's see." She paused as she found the message and scrolled down a little, her lips moving silently until she found the spot. "Here. Um … 'There appears to have been a single fatal blow, which struck the victim from behind at the back of the cranium rather than the top. The skull was cracked open at the peak of the wound from initial impact and then crushed wider toward the bottom, consistent with a downward motion, indicating the weapon used was likely sharp and heavy. It is impossible to say if the injuries to the arms occurred before or after the attack to the head. Those extremity injuries were numerous, indicating several strikes, splintering both arms from the elbows down to the hands. The arms were either pinned behind the victim during the assault or were tied there afterward.'" Sal stopped and shook her head. "Holy cow."

"An axe," said Mercer. "An axe wielded by someone shorter than the victim."

"An axe murderer!" said Sal.

"Ever deal with any of those, Mercer?"

"Oh yeah." He looked out at the landscape and didn't elaborate.

"What's all this stuff about the arms being pinned back?" asked Sal. "That's pretty friggin' creepy."

"Passion," said Mercer. "Like we've said: any time the blows are numerous and in the same area, that indicates passion. Whoever killed this man either hated him or … really loved him."

They didn't turn the music back on for the rest of the ride. Up ahead, they could see Mercer's place from the county highway, his house and barn appearing like a cute Lego model in the white distance. Then they shot by Del and Ebb Morton and Beth and Ben Morton's houses at the end of Mercer's long gravel sideroad. Soon they were past the road that led to the Goode place too, then the sign reading One Good Man For Hire outside Fred and Alma Freeman's home. As usual, all looked quiet at every one of those residences, no indication of the trauma the people living there had been through during the Becky Prior case … if they'd actually experienced any at all.

The Massey farm was farther away in the countryside, almost at the other end of the township. It was down a long sideroad, similar to the place Mercer was renting, but this spot had the look of a property that had once been prosperous, important in its community. Nothing terribly fancy, the way nothing was boastful around here, but with an orchard, what appeared to be the footprint of a big garden next to the lane as you came in, and a sprawling lawn that wrapped around the large house, which was brick and gabled and two storeys high with a wide front door and a brass knocker. A couple of hockey rink lengths from there stood the barn, a structure that looked like it wasn't in much use anymore, but in its day had been an ambitious building, massive and tall with a steel roof that was beginning to rust. There were three cars in the driveway.

Alice led the way up the front walkway and knocked.

"Her family was coming here on New Year's Day to spend some time with her. Both daughters and their husbands, a few grandchildren too, I think, who are grownups. But they got a call from someone that morning, a neighbour, saying that they'd noticed that Evelyn's lights hadn't come on at all New Year's Eve night. The family figured there was some reasonable explanation, that she had gone to bed early, perhaps. So they came earlier than they had planned that day ... found her in the kitchen."

Alice knocked again.

"She lived here alone?" asked Mercer.

"Yup."

"But she was one hundred years old!"

"Yup."

"The old girls around here were tough," said Sal. "Been through a lot. Put up big meals for full dining rooms of threshing crews, birthed and reared children, worked in the fields too, many of them, though I don't think Evelyn Massey ever did. I imagine she wanted to live alone, was fine with it. Heard she was in good shape right up until the end. There were always people checking on her, nurses, and hired help came by regularly to clean and other things. Neighbours often got her groceries. Not surprising around here."

The woman who finally answered the door had to have been one of the daughters, but she almost seemed too young. Alice would have put her at somewhere around fifty, but she knew that one of the Massey daughters was seventy and the other sixty-seven. The woman was wearing a black pantsuit, the sort of power suit a businessperson in the city might wear, though it appeared she had just put the jacket on over her white blouse to get the door. She pulled the entrance wide open, and they could see all the way through the big, bright country kitchen to the living room, where two other women were sitting near a long coffee table. Alice had seen Evelyn Massey's body slumped in a kitchen chair here when two constables had called her to come out to the house because her name was on the envelope that had been found at the scene. The basement, where she'd had to go after the note had been read, was an old country one, musty, clammy, and stone-walled, accessible only from the outside. It was the sort of cellar that even Evelyn probably rarely entered, except to store her pickles, jams, and stewed fruit in a little adjoining room down there. It had been full of cobwebs.

"Oh, the police," said the woman. "This is very short notice."

"Yes, sorry about that," said Sal. "Really sorry."

"May we come in?" asked Mercer, almost cutting her off.

"I suppose. We were having some private moments, going through old family albums. Come on right through. Shoes off, please. I'm Gloria." She turned and went back to the living room, leaving her three guests to remove their footwear.

"That's the oldest," whispered Sal. "She's seventy?"

Alice nodded. "Just turned. Attractive woman."

Of the two other women in the living room, Alice assumed the one who looked to be about Gloria's age was her sister, Gwen, though she too could have passed for someone around fifty, but more for the way she appeared to care for herself and dress than her looks, which weren't as striking as her sister's. The third woman was a much younger version of Gloria, obviously her daughter, likely in her late thirties or a touch past that and dressed just as tastefully as her mother and aunt, in a yellow blouse and black skirt with pearl necklace, as if she had just come from a meeting in the city. Her long blond hair shone as if it had been combed a thousand times. Before Alice's socked feet even touched the living room rug — one sock with a hole where the red-painted nail of her big toe poked through — she could smell perfume, a triumvirate of scents. She couldn't see an ounce of extra weight on any of the women, and it made her want to suck in her gut.

The two older ones had teacups in front of them, the younger a mug. There were three pairs of high heels lying on the rug nearby.

"Gwennie, Blair, this is the local police," said Gloria, "come to grill us about the mysterious note, no doubt."

Alice's preliminary research had told her that the two Massey daughters had both married well and lived in the city — Gloria had just retired from her job in the upper echelons of the school board, and Gwen was the owner of a high-end clothing store in a large city mall. There were three granddaughters, and this one, Blair, the eldest, was a marketing executive with a software firm and lived with her partner in the city. These three women were a formidable group. Alice looked down at the shining coffee table in front of the chesterfield they were sitting on and saw a stack of photo albums there. Blair closed the one they had been looking at and put her hand on top of it.

"Which one of you is Alice?" she asked, rather sternly.

"That would be me. Sergeant Alice Morrow."

"Why would my grandmother leave that note for you? It doesn't make any sense, and neither does the note."

"We have been telling Blair," said Gwen, "that, as far as we know, Mother didn't know you or anything about you. Well, I'm sure she knew one thing about you. Everyone knows that."

"Knows what?" asked Mercer. He glanced at Alice, and she saw that look in his eye, which he'd had before when local people had treated her coolly and almost with suspicion. She knew she was going to have to tell him why one day. He had been poking around about it anyway. Or did she have to? Some secrets are better left the way they are.

Alice turned red.

"Look," said Sal, "I don't mean to be impolite, ladies, but we will be asking the questions here today, not you."

There was silence in the room.

Not one of the three women had offered tea or asked their visitors to sit down.

"Well, I can assure you we are investigating that note," said Alice, attempting to keep her emotions in check. "And we can tell you for certain that it was written by Evelyn Massey, and we know that because we have other samples of her handwriting. And that note says, in so many words, that she is responsible for a body being buried in her basement ... a man's body."

"An individual who died some sixty years ago," added Mercer loudly.

Alice tried not to roll her eyes. Mercer loved to say dramatic things to the people they questioned, to reveal evidence suddenly, evidence not known to those individuals until the moment he sprang it on them. Maybe it was effective. Maybe it had helped get information out of people in the millions of homicide investigations he had been a part of down in the rotten apple in New York. Maybe it wasn't always such a bad idea. Or maybe it was just him being overly dramatic, American. Who knew? But it wasn't her style. And it certainly wasn't Sal's.

"Oh," said Sal, "that was a little sudden. But, yes, Detective Mercer is correct. We are indeed here to see if you have any thoughts about the aforementioned body ... you know, belonging to the man ... sixty years deceased ... the one right down there?" She pointed to the floor.

"No," said Blair.

"Do you care to expand on that?"

"No."

That caused an awkward pause as the police officers, all still on their feet, regarded Blair as she looked right back.

Gwen cleared her throat. "Won't you sit down?" she asked in a much gentler voice than she had employed until then, as if she had decided that taking another tack was advisable.

"Thank you so much," said Sal, and they all sat on the sofa across from the three women, the coffee table between them. Tea was then poured.

"Blair was quite close to her grandma," said Gloria, giving her daughter a firm pat on the knee. "We all were. She was as lovely a mother and grandmother as there was on this earth. Anyone can attest to that. Ask anyone who knows her ... knew her."

"We will," said Mercer.

"Good," said Blair, staring at him again. "Ask until you're blue in the face. She wouldn't hurt a fly."

"That note was preposterous." Gwen looked down and picked an invisible bit of lint off her pants. "She must have been out of her mind when she wrote it."

"You can't seriously be considering investigating Grandma for murder! Seriously?"

"*Was* she out of her mind?" asked Alice. "Any mental troubles? Did any of you see any indication of that?"

"She was fine," said Blair. "That note has to be a forgery ... or something."

"But the body was there," said Mercer. "Just as Evelyn's handwriting said it would be." He delivered the last line as if he were saying the final bit of dialogue in an episode of a Netflix crime series, not unlike one of those dark Scandinavian thrillers that Alice and Sal liked so much.

Alice didn't want to pile on, but Mercer had set a tone that might be capitalized on. "Yeah," she added quickly, "a man dead in a crate used to ship animals, several feet under the concrete floor of her own basement."

There was silence in the room again.

"I don't know anything about her past," said Blair suddenly.

"Why would you —?" began Alice and Mercer at the same time.

"Sorry," said Alice.

"Surely, my dear," said Sal to Blair, "you know something about your grandmother's past. That is a slightly strange thing for you to say."

"I mean I don't know any details. I don't know anything that you might be trying to find out about from sixty years ago. Maybe ... maybe someone forced her to write that note? Someone who had something to do with this man's death."

"Well," said Sal, "that is possible, I suppose."

"Perhaps you two, Gloria and Gwen, can answer that?" asked Alice. "Sixty years takes us back to the to early- to mid-sixties. What was your mother's life like then? What was going on? Could she have had any enemies at the time? Perhaps this death came about from self-defence?"

"Likely lots of women had to defend themselves, were forced to," said Blair. "Women were treated like cattle then. The patriarchy was in full bloom. Who knows what she experienced from men in those days?"

"Gwen? Gloria?" asked Alice.

"She was happily married by then. And my father was a gentleman," said Gloria.

"I didn't mean Grandpa," said Blair.

"Oh, I know, dear."

"We need to know more about Evelyn back then," said Sal. "Are there any photographs in these albums from those days?"

Blair's hand was still on top of one of the albums. And she didn't move it.

"She was a 4-H queen, and just lovely," said Gwen, and then she put her hand to her mouth, though she didn't leave it for long. She straightened her face quickly, removing the emotion she had momentarily let slip.

"4-H?" asked Mercer.

"Detective Mercer is not a country person," said Sal in a near-whisper.

"A beauty queen," said Alice, "agricultural beauty queen. 4-H is a club for country kids. You have pet cattle and goats and pigs, and you show them at fairs. They used to have beauty contests too. Lots of country kids were in 4-H when I was a kid. Some still are, I guess."

"They said she was the most beautiful woman in the county," added Gwen, "and Dad used to like to repeat that. He said she was not only the prettiest woman but made the best apple pies and was the best wife a man could ask for. He called her the best catch around." She dabbed her eyes with a tissue.

"Was he just a farmer? Or did he do anything else? He's been dead for sixteen years, right?" asked Mercer.

Gloria frowned at him. "Are you an American? I can hear an accent."

"Just answer the question, please."

"Yes, he passed away some time ago and was greatly mourned. He was a good man. A farmer, yes, mostly, but they said we had the best land in the county, that he had as good a business as any banker. One hundred head of beef cattle. Mom came from a poorer family, not far down the road here, and she made a good marriage when she married Dad. He was a hard worker, a churchgoer, a Rotarian. He was chairman of the school board in town for a while."

"She had some regrets," said Blair, who had been quiet for a while.

"Excuse me?" asked Mercer, leaning forward. "Regrets?"

Alice had seen this from him before. It was the shark in him. When someone said something that he could use, when someone slipped up, even just a little, he pounced.

"Whatever do you mean by that, Blair, dear?" asked her mother. She paused and then glanced toward the police officers. "I suppose we all have regrets of some nature. Let's look at a few photos." She gently took her daughter's hand from where it was still resting on top of the album and opened the collection to the first page. She flipped through a few pictures and turned the album toward Alice, Sal, and Mercer. They peered down and saw a beautiful young woman in a trim forties hairdo wearing a crown with "4-H" emblazoned on it, and across from that a wedding picture of a gorgeous bride next to a bland-looking man with horn-rimmed glasses, thick hands and fingers hanging down, his body squeezed into a tuxedo.

"What do you mean by regrets?" repeated Mercer, turning back to Blair.

"I'm sure she meant nothing," said her mother. "Nothing of consequence."

"Grandma and I used to talk, woman to woman, I guess you could say, and life wasn't perfect for her."

"Now, Blair, you —"

"No, Mom, we need to tell the truth. Grandma didn't do anything that these people are suspicious she might have done. I know that and you know it and anyone who knows her understands it. Anyone with a brain in their head does too. How could she? But if we pretend that her life was perfect, then we aren't really telling the truth. And the truth is what the police want. And what we want." She turned to Mercer and said bitterly, "We aren't sugar-coating anything. She didn't fucking do this."

"Blair, dear, no need to —"

"She told me one time that she sometimes wished she'd gone away, to the big city, maybe to the States, and discovered what was out there for her. She was very good in school, you know, but her father, he wouldn't let her go to university. I have to say, to be honest, I kind of hate him for that." Blair paused. "She told me once that she wondered about other men, other than Grandpa. She'd gone to a party once in the city and danced with some interesting guys. She said the way they spoke to her, the way they held her when they danced with her, kind of thrilled her. She said she wondered about that. Wanted more of it. She said her marriage was something she felt she had to do, that she had no choice. She loved Grandpa too, though, I know that."

"Did she ever have an affair?" asked Mercer bluntly.

"Mother?" said Gloria and Gwen at the same time.

"No," said Blair, "oh, no … no … she never said that."

"Are you certain?"

"What, are saying that I'm lying?" asked Blair with some heat. "Do you think you can push women around, Mr. Mercer? With those dumbass dramatic questions? A penetrating stare?" She locked eyes with him again. She didn't add "American." She didn't need to.

"No," said Sal, "no, I don't think he's saying that. Not at all. Not indeedy-do."

"Maybe we should go," said Alice, and she stood up and motioned for the other two to rise as well. Sal jumped up, and Mercer rose reluctantly. "I would like you, Gwen and Gloria, to provide us with a list of people who were your mother's closest friends. If there is anyone who knew her in the late fifties and sixties still around, that would be most helpful."

"Okay," said Gloria and Gwen at the same time again as they both got up quickly and smiled and motioned toward the door simultaneously.

"I don't know how or why that man died or why he was buried in our basement," said Blair, still sitting down. "It's a mystery that you will have to unravel. But I do know this: It has nothing to do with my grandma. It couldn't."

"Lovely to see you all!" said Sal in the silence that ensued.

"Oh," said Alice when they reached the door. "My partners and I would like to go down into the basement. We won't be long. We'll see ourselves out after that."

Mercer turned back toward the three women.

"We know now, by the way, that this man buried in your mother's basement was killed with an axe," he said, "his skull split as the result of a blow from behind ... and then the killer took the axe to this man's arms and hands. Just thought you should know."

Gloria and Gwen couldn't hide the shock on their faces. But Blair was more than shocked. She drew her hand up to her mouth to stop herself from crying out.

6

In the Basement

AS THE THREE of them walked around the garage to the basement entrance, Alice was thinking about Mercer revealing to the Massey women that an axe had been used as the murder weapon. *What a dick*, she thought. She also wondered if she should say something about it, chastise him a little.

"I'm sure you're wondering why I said that, about the axe."

"No, no, that was fine," said Sal.

"No, I'm sure I sounded a bit like a dick revealing confidential information."

"Oh, not to worry, Detective —" began Sal.

"Let the man finish," said Alice.

"I wanted to see their reactions to something shocking like that, something that horrified them and showed them in graphic detail how brutal this crime was, with their mother and grandmother as a suspect. And I got what I wanted, or what we wanted."

"Which was?"

"It seems to me that Blair is hiding something, something further, and her reaction was more extreme than her mother's and her aunt's. It told me I was right. We need to talk to her again, alone."

Alice tried to resist a smile. *Well,* she thought, *he may be a dick, but he's my dick.*

The entrance to the basement was behind the garage at the far side of the house. Alice led them around. It was a very old-fashioned way of getting to a basement, a country way, having to come outside, as you'd probably also had to do to get to the toilet in the old days around here. There were seven steep concrete steps and at the bottom an old wooden door with a latch on it. The door was narrow and less than six feet high. Mercer would have to crouch to enter.

"Kind of creepy," said Sal, who let the other two go first.

Alice unlatched the door and pushed it inward. The musty smell of an old country basement filled their senses. Dirt. Mould. Something like mushrooms and mice.

"A nice tight space to come up from behind someone," said Mercer as he stood in the confines of the concrete staircase. "A good spot for a woman to attack a man, if she could get a good swing in. He can't see her, and he can't get at her quickly even if he notices she's there. She'd have to know what she was doing with the axe, though, and have the strength to make one swing fatal."

"Yes," said Alice as she stepped onto the basement floor, "you wouldn't want to miss."

"Well," said Sal, "those old gals were supposed to be pretty strong back in the day."

Alice pulled the string on the light bulb hanging from the low ceiling, and the whole place became dimly lit.

The basement floor was nearly bare. There were big wooden posts here and there, and shelves against the stone walls with just a few things on them: snowshoes, ancient hockey equipment, lamps, and old toys. An old fan and a heater lay against a wall, and a blue furnace dominated the centre of the room. Cobwebs clung to the beams on the ceiling. There was another door leading into a smaller area.

"Fruit and jam cellar," said Alice, nodding that way.

"Wow," said Sal, as she entered and looked past the furnace toward the west end of the basement where the floor had been split open. "That's where it was, eh?" she said. "Where the body was buried?"

"Yeah," said Alice quietly.

They walked over and peered down at the grave-sized hole in the floor where the crate had been unearthed, and all three just stared at it for a while.

"Okay," said Mercer, "this isn't what I expected to see. And it's the first bit of evidence that Evelyn Massey may not be our murderer."

"What do you mean?" asked Sal.

"Do you think it makes sense that a woman, a housewife, back in the late fifties or early sixties, no matter how robust she was, would not only kill a fairly big man with an axe but then come down here and bust up this concrete, load him into a crate, and bury him underneath? I thought this was going to be maybe an inch of some sort of sealing on top, but this concrete is more than a foot deep."

"But it was sixty years ago," said Alice.

"So?"

"Well, breathe deeply, Detective Mercer. Smell that?"

"Earthy," said Sal.

Alice nodded. "Yeah, it still smells of dirt in here. This was an earthen floor once, maybe for a long time considering the lingering odour, *then* the concrete was laid over top."

Mercer raised his eyebrows. "So, you're thinking this man was buried in the soil here, just a grave dug in the dirt, and the hard surface went on afterward?"

"Maybe."

"If that's true," asked Sal, "then wouldn't whoever put in the concrete later on have had to do something with the soil floor first to prepare it? I can see the workmen not noticing that the surface was disturbed when they first saw it; it could have been all patted down and made to look nice, and anyone else who came in here, other than the murderer, wouldn't notice. But once you were putting in the new concrete floor and you were digging a little and levelling, wouldn't you notice that there was something just underneath the top here, a large crate for goodness' sake?"

"Hmm," said Mercer, rubbing the stubble on his jaw. "How deep in the soil was the body buried, Alice?"

"Not deep. Once they cracked the concrete a little, they could see it."

"Remember," added Sal, "we wondered if the husband might have been involved? Maybe he did it. That would explain some of this. Or ... maybe he put a nice hard concrete floor in down here just after his wife did it and confessed her crime to him. That way, he would have hidden things forever for her. But Evelyn, she couldn't live with what she'd done, or helped cover up, so she left that note."

"Okay," said Alice with a sigh as she looked down at the busted-up concrete, "before we go, we now have another question for Gwen and Gloria."

They moved toward the entrance, Sal out first, followed by Mercer and finally Alice. Just as she pulled the door shut, her cell beeped. She looked down at it.

"Toxicology report on Evelyn Massey," she said.

7

Two Ways to Stop Your Heart

THE THREE OF them stood at the top of the basement stairs as Alice looked down at her phone. "Let's see ..." she said. "Cause of death, heart failure —"

"So, natural causes," said Sal.

"... brought on by an excess of warfarin in the deceased's bloodstream."

"Warfarin?" Sal looked at Alice. "Isn't that what they used to use out here in the country to kill rats?"

"It's a slow-acting blood thinner, an anticoagulant, probably the most common heart medication for the elderly," said Mercer.

"But a rat killer too."

"Yeah. That too."

"Now I have two questions for Gloria and Gwen," said Alice, immediately moving away from the basement stairs toward the garage. Sal and Mercer followed and tried to keep up. Alice was around the garage and at the front door in seconds, it seemed. She used the knocker and wasn't gentle.

"Perhaps that's a little loud, dear," said Sal.

"They're two rooms away," replied Alice, "and they took their time last time. I still have to look into disappearances from sixty years back before I can go home tonight, and I've got curling at seven-thirty. I'm not going to wait around for those girls this time."

"I like it," said Mercer.

Alice was facing the door, turned away from him. She rolled her eyes.

The door opened.

"Oh," said Gwen, "you three again. I thought we answered —"

"Two more questions, madam," said Mercer, brushing past Alice and onto the mat. "Please ask your sister to step this way as well."

Gwen's face seemed to go a little pale. "All right," she said. She took a few strides toward the living room and called out, "Glor? The police have more questions." She turned back to Mercer. "Two, I believe." She looked toward the living room again. "Can you come this way for a moment?"

Gloria appeared, and Blair was quickly behind her.

"Oh," said Sal, "not you, dear, just your mother and aunt."

"No," said Blair. "I want to hear this. You can't stop me from being present."

"All right," said Mercer. "This is for all three of you, then. Do you have rats here now and have you had them in the past? And if so, do you and did you kill them with a deadly poison called warfarin?"

"I have no idea," said Gwen. "What a question."

"I think we had rat problems when we were kids, but Dad always took care of that," said Gloria.

"Your father?" asked Sal, and swallowed.

"Yes."

"Did your mother take any heart medication?" asked Alice.

"Yes. A blood thinner."

"Can we see it?"

"Blair, honey," said Gloria, "get Grandma's medicine. She kept it on the kitchen counter."

Blair quickly returned with it. Mercer reached out for it, but she pulled it back and handed it to Alice, who read the label out loud.

"Coumadin."

"That's warfarin," said Mercer.

Blair eyed him.

"We are going to take this with us," said Sal, "if you don't mind. And if Evelyn had one of those little containers with the days of the week on it so she could keep track of her dosages, we'll have that too, if you don't mind."

"Blair," said Gwen, "there's a container right next to where you found the bottle."

Blair went off to get it.

"One last question," said Alice.

"I thought there was just going to be two," said Gloria.

"Well," said Sal, "the first was a two-parter."

"Do you know when the concrete floor was put into your basement?" asked Alice.

"Um," said Gloria, "I can remember it just being dirt. It was pretty smelly."

"I don't," said Gwen.

"So," said Mercer, "that likely means it was laid in when you both were little. You, Gloria, were maybe around eight or nine? But you, Gwen, were probably about six or so, and that's why you don't remember?"

"I suppose, something like that," said Gloria.

"So, that means we are talking about ... sixty years ago?"

"What's this about?" asked Blair, returning and handing the pillbox to Alice. "I thought you'd asked all your questions."

"Thank you so much for your kind cooperation, all of you," said Sal. "We will get to the bottom of this, I can assure you all. Have a lovely day!"

Alice looked down at the pillbox as they stepped out the door. It was opaque blue plastic. She couldn't see into it. She gave it a shake. It was empty.

8
Disappearances

AN HOUR LATER, Alice found herself in a basement again, this time beneath the cells in the police station. It wasn't as damp and musty as the Massey cellar, but it was almost as frightening. She had sent Sal and Mercer home. Now she wondered if maybe that had been a bad idea. She moved between the rows of tall steel shelves, searching for the old missing persons files from sixty years back. She kept looking over her shoulder, behind her, and between the spaces in the shelves, hearing things — creaks, footsteps, rats. She had never met a woman who wasn't afraid of being underground in confined spaces. It was so shitty. So unfair. Like a lot of things.

She finally found what she was looking for and scurried back upstairs with it — a box of files that covered the 1940s through the 1960s. She didn't have much time. She glanced at her watch. Nearing five-thirty, and she still had to eat and then drive to the curling rink. She and Sal and Mercer had spent a little longer at the Massey place than anticipated — they had gone back down into the farmhouse basement a second time after their last few questions. They'd searched the shelves. No sign of rat poison anywhere. And that was where it would be kept. You wouldn't keep it upstairs.

"It seems like the excess of warfarin in Mrs. Massey's bloodstream likely came from her medication, and that's what stopped her heart," Mercer had said in the cruiser as they drove back.

"Well, the dosage container was certainly cleared out," said Alice.

"So, maybe it *was* suicide?" Sal had said. "Or someone somehow forced her to take too much medication."

"Or tricked her," Mercer had added.

Alice set the box of files down on her office desk and got out her cell phone. She searched for popular songs from the late 1950s for an appropriate soundtrack for this dive through the files, whipping past all the Elvis, Little Richard, Buddy Holly, Aretha, and Ray Charles, all that great American stuff, past Cliff Richard and the Shadows from the U.K. too, as she searched for music from home, from up here. There wasn't a lot, but she found a few things, most of it pretty sappy and wholesome, and then she found something she wanted to hear, something tougher. Ronnie Hawkins, a mix from his first album and another called *Mr. Dynamo*. She tapped, and a song burst on, the guitar crackling, then Ronnie's inimitable voice asking the question, "Who do you love?" He was growling and snarling like only he had up here in those days, unearthing the devil in us. Hawkins had come from the American south but had moved north to stay. In fact, he had lived not far from this very area until his death. The song sounded live and real.

She started going through the files, beginning with 1955, pulling them out and just glancing at them for now. The first couple of years had only a few folders, all of them thin, each missing person having been found shortly after they'd disappeared — runaway kids, old people who had wandered off, and a couple of wives who had obviously had enough for a while and needed to get away from their husbands and families.

"Likely just cause," she said to herself.

The first thicker folder came from 1958. She pulled it out and set it down on the desk on its own, noticing the *Unsolved* stamp on the outside. There was another thick one from 1959 stamped *Unsolved* as well, and that surprised her a little, but then there was another one for 1960, another for 1961, and another for 1962. She set them down on top of each other as she pulled them out.

"Oh my god," she said, "that's five. Five in five years!"

She turned back to the box and kept searching, but all the other files from the sixties were much thinner, all the cases solved. She put them back into the box, leaving the five unsolved cases on her desk, turned off Ronnie Hawkins, who was launching into "Bo Diddley," and took the box back to the basement. As she paused at the top of the stairs, after she flicked on the light, she heard a sound below, like a footstep.

"Hello?" she called. "Anyone there?"

There was no answer, no sound. She chided herself for being ridiculous, for still being spooked by the fact that her name had been on that envelope, for being a girl — well, not for that, that was even more ridiculous, but for allowing the whole being-alone-in-a-confined-space thing to get to her again. It was likely just a shelf creaking down there — this whole building creaked. She adjusted the box, balanced it in under her left arm, and put her right hand on her gun.

She kept her hand on the weapon going down the stairs, feeling ridiculous about it. Walking along the aisle toward the missing persons section on the shelves, her footfalls echoing in the room, she glanced to the sides and behind again. No one. She found the spot and replaced the box. Then she opened the 1970s and 1980s box and quickly looked through it, forgetting to keep vigilant for intruders. There wasn't a single unsolved file in the box, and when she glanced through the 1990s, there were none either. She didn't bother with any after that since she knew that no one had gone missing and not been found since she'd been with the police service. Most of that information would be online anyway.

Her fears returned as soon as she closed the lid on the last box, and she walked out of the basement and up the stairs with her hand on her weapon again, feeling like a jerk.

Back at her desk, she glanced at the time and decided to just take a cursory look through the unsolved files. No more time for Ronnie Hawkins; it would just affect her concentration. Maybe she could simply see if any of the people in these folders were young men, a touch north of six feet tall. The first page of each file was a copy of an 8" x 10" photograph of the person in question. That would make a quick look through things easier.

She opened the 1958 file and stared at the photograph. A woman. About forty years of age. Not their man.

She opened the 1959 file, and it made her gasp. A man. An attractive one with tousled, slightly curly light hair and nice eyes, likely somewhere in his thirties. She turned to the next page. She looked at the description and found a height. Five feet ten inches. It was almost a disappointment. Not their man.

She opened the 1960 file. Another male, but this time a boy, really. Looked to be somewhere in his teens, anywhere from fifteen to seventeen, she guessed.

She opened the 1961 file. Another man, distinguished looking but far too old. She peered down at the name. A doctor.

She opened the 1962 file. A woman, young, middle to late twenties, studious-looking in her very dated glasses.

And that was it.

No six-foot-one-inch young man. It almost made her angry, and that didn't seem like a very good reaction.

She got up, glancing at the clock again, seeing that she would just have time to whip home, get out of uniform, grab a sandwich, and head to the curling rink. She got to the door and decided to take a quick peek at that first file again before she rushed out, the one with the woman about her age, maybe a bit younger. Looking at the file had upset her. A woman lost. It seemed wrong to head out into the night without even looking at her name. She deserved a name.

Alice walked around to the back of the desk and opened the first file again, stared at the photograph for a moment, and then turned to the next page, where the missing person's name was always noted.

"Violet Massey," it read.

9

The First File

BY NINE O'CLOCK the next morning, Alice had all three of them — Constable Salma Haddad, Detective Hugh Mercer, and young Constable Robbie Trew — in her office lined up in chairs in front of her with the stack of missing persons files on the desk between them. Alice had phoned Sal right after curling to bring her up to speed, and then Sal had had the pleasure of calling in Robbie for a little one-on-one consultation to give him the latest information. Only Mercer was a bit out of the loop, and the joy that gave Alice and Sal was almost incalculable.

It had been a strange morning already. The sun was out, and it actually felt warm on the streets. Snow was melting and water was trickling down from buildings, primed to become big icicles when reality came back. The weather report was for two more days of weirdly warm weather. Only Mercer was wearing a thick coat. Robbie was in short sleeves.

"Detective Mercer, this is Constable Robbie Trew, who will be helping us out on the Massey case."

Robbie, who was about the same height as Mercer, well-built

with dark hair, blue eyes, and an engaging smile, stood up and reached over Sal, who was sitting between them, to extend his hand to Mercer. The American cop took it, though perhaps not quite as enthusiastically as it had been extended.

"We have some news to share with you, Detective Mercer, pertaining to the case. Dramatic news." Alice looked at Sal and Robbie. "Wouldn't you say?"

"Yes," said Robbie.

"Oh, indeed," said Sal.

"We?" asked Mercer. "All three of you?" He glanced at them, lingering a bit on the earnest face of the station's newest boy recruit, and then back at Alice. "*All* of you already have this information?"

"Yes," said Sal, "and you don't. Our deepest apologies, just the way the logistics worked out last night and this morning."

"But we're telling you now," said Alice, poker-faced.

"How kind of you."

"And when I say news, I mean that in plural. A couple of dramatic things that have intrigued the three of us" — she paused for effect — "the last of which is an absolute barn burner."

"Do tell."

Alice cleared her throat. "The first is that there were five unsolved missing persons cases in this area between 1958 and 1962."

Mercer leaned forward, his pride vanishing at this intriguing news. "Really?"

"Really."

"And what else? What else?" He had that look in his eyes again, the one Alice had seen many times during the Prior case, the impatient expression of someone in search of the truth, someone hoping there was justice to be found somewhere. But it was also a look of fascination, a puzzle solver's glint in the eye.

"The first missing person, who vanished in the summer of 1958, is, or was, a woman named ..." She paused for perhaps a little too long. "Violet Massey."

"Wow," said Mercer, moving to the edge of his seat. "Relation?"

"Sister-in-law," said Sal. "Evelyn's sister-in-law."

"Harold Massey's older sister," said Robbie.

Mercer glanced over at him. "Thanks for adding that."

Alice opened the Violet Massey file and turned it toward Mercer with the photo looking up at him. A plain-looking woman with a short, tight hairstyle and dated horn-rimmed glasses looked back at him. Her prominent jawline resembled her brother's.

"Unmarried, an old maid as they unfortunately often said in those days," said Alice, "born 1916, forty-two years of age at the time of her disappearance. Employed as the head librarian at the public library and part-time as the bookkeeper for her brother's farming business."

Mercer stood up. "We need to search the Massey property now, maybe dig up the rest of the basement."

Alice motioned for him to sit down.

"I'll have Robbie and a few others look around the farm, discreetly."

"Discreetly? We need to do an immediate and thorough search of the entire property. Use ground-penetrating radar."

"Isn't that that thing they used for all the —" began Sal.

"We don't have that. It's too expensive. At least for now, at least for the level of evidence we have at this point."

"All right," said Mercer, sitting back down and looking a little sheepish, as if suddenly remembering where he was again, working with a small northern police service that had a grand total of fourteen officers in their employ. "Let's gather more evidence then, just our little group. And we need to look at this Harold Massey guy. I think it's fair to say that he's growing as a suspect."

"Robbie," said Alice, "can you look into that? Search Harold Massey online and in our databases and see what you can find, if anything. Ask around about him too. That might be more fruitful. Just get us a basic portrait. I think I've heard his name in the past, and Gloria said he was prominent in some ways in the community. I'm guessing you know people who knew the family."

"I do, Sergeant Morrow."

"You don't need to call me that. Alice will do."

"All right, Alice. Thanks for including me in all of this. I'll go out to the Massey place and look around too, about the possible buried remains. You said to do it discreetly?"

"Yeah, we'll call the Massey women and find out what their schedule is over the next little while, in case we need to talk to them further, and then let you know when they won't be there. Just do a preliminary search, look for likely places where bodies might have been disposed of. I know it will be tough in the snow, but something might strike you as suspicious. This was 1958, so it's unlikely you'll find anything obvious now, but just get the lay of the land for us. It may be a bit of a reach, maybe just a coincidence that a Massey disappeared too ... at about the same time ... Sorry if we're sending you on a bit of a wild goose chase. Bring someone with you."

"Oh." Robbie's shoulders sagged.

"Are you reluctant to do that?"

"No, it's just that my partner ..."

"Elwin Most?" asked Sal.

"Yeah ... he wouldn't be any good."

"What do you mean?"

"He's ... uh ... sorry to say this, but he's kind of a, uh ..."

"A jerk?" asked Sal.

"An asshole," said Alice.

"I'm glad you said that, not me. He's a little my senior in terms of service. But, yeah, he's pretty opinionated, pretty old-fashioned.

We were moving some homeless — unhoused — people from the encampment in the park yesterday, which I just hated doing, just makes the cops look like bigger doinks than we often are. I mean, where are these people supposed to go? And my partner was kind of nasty with the folks in the tents and said all sorts of things to me about them being lazy and thinly veiled racist stuff — not so thinly veiled, actually. Crap about Indigenous people too. Just tossed that in. Doesn't he know my mom's from Jamaica? Doesn't he know that kid who is working for us, the cadet, Renaldo, is Anishinaabe? And Most flies a flag on his truck! Supposed to be patriotic! What kind of hypocrisy is that? Is that really caring about your fellow citizens in this country? He needs to keep his mouth shut." All of that had come out in a bit of a torrent, Robbie speaking faster as he went along, his voice rising a little.

"Agreed," said Mercer quietly.

"I don't want to be stuck out on the land with him, walking around, hearing his opinions. He's going to be speculating about the sorts of people who commit murder, and I don't want to hear that. It's bad enough in a cruiser."

"Okay," said Alice, "this is kind of overtime stuff anyway. Take someone else."

"How about Ranbir? Sergeant Singh."

"Good choice."

"Maybe Renaldo too," said Mercer, and he was serious. "Good kid."

Robbie smiled at him and nodded, then got to his feet.

"No, no," said Alice, "sit down, Robbie, I'd like to go over the other files with all three of you right now. All of you need to know what we are dealing with here."

"But I thought you said on the phone," said Sal, "that none of the missing people fit the description of the body in the basement? Didn't you say that you just happened to notice the Massey woman's name? Why would four other missing people have anything to do with this?"

"Serial killer," said Mercer.

"What?" said Sal. "Here?"

"We have to consider all possibilities," said Alice, grim-faced.

Sal squirmed in her chair. "Old Mrs. Massey killed five people?"

"Or Harold Massey," said Mercer. "Big, strong guy, looked like he had hands on him like an MMA fighter in that photograph in the family album."

"He was a farmer, hard worker. The Masseys? Really? Here?"

"You already said that," said Mercer.

"No one is drawing any conclusions. Just let me quickly go through the files while I have you all here. You're probably right, Sal. There's probably no connection, but we can't ignore these other files, not when these disappearances happened within so short a time period and are unsolved, and we have a body, a mutilated body in a basement, murdered and buried at about the same time."

"Maybe," said Robbie, "people used to look the other way when things happened around here, dark things, but we can't afford to do that anymore."

"Okay," said Sal quietly and shrunk down a little into her chair.

"All right," said Alice, "next file: 1959." She opened it.

10

The Other Four

"THIS ONE GAVE me a bit of a start at first," said Alice, holding up the photograph of the young man in the 1959 file.

"Whoa, he's a looker," said Sal, then turned a little red. "Sorry."

"No," said Robbie, "you're right, he looks like a movie star, like Brad Pitt or someone."

"James Dean," said Mercer.

"Yeah," Alice said, nodding, turning the photo around and staring at it, "1950s, same hairstyle, same beautiful face, same slightly naughty look, like he's a rebel, got a secret or something. Could be James Dean himself." She kept examining him. "Hmm, wish I knew what that secret was." Then she shook her head. "Under six feet, though, so not our Massey basement dweller."

"Name?" asked Mercer.

"Caleb Carruthers, age thirty-three at the time of his disappearance."

"Next file," said Mercer.

"Give me a second." Alice sighed, set the Carruthers file down, and picked up the one under it.

"September 1960. Just as the days were getting darker." She held up the photo to show a teenage boy.

"Oh, man," said Robbie.

"Yeah. Sixteen years old. Vanished without a trace. Charlie Eaton, lived in town here, student at the local high school."

She set the file back down, picked up the next one, opened it, and held the photograph up for the others to see. It was of a middle-aged man, probably in his fifties, distinguished looking with slightly thinning hair, a moustache, and glasses. He looked out from his photograph as if there were no mysteries in the world. Boy, was he wrong, thought Alice. "Dr. Albert Johnson," she said. "Practiced in town."

"I remember, when I first got here, doctors used to make house calls," said Sal. "That seems like a long time ago now. He probably did. Looks like a decent sort."

"Yeah, well, whatever he did, he vanished in the summer of 1961, disappeared from our community and into thin air."

"Dear me," said Sal.

"Last one?" asked Mercer.

Alice gave him a bit of a look. She had rarely met a more impatient man. She picked up the 1962 file. "Shirley Ezinicki," she said and turned the photo toward them, a young woman in her middle to late twenties in a beehive hairdo and lipstick, wearing horrible cat eye glasses.

"Glad those styles have gone out," said Sal. She paused. "Sorry. Inappropriate. Bad timing."

"She was a teacher," said Alice, "taught at the local elementary school in town. Hadn't been here for too long."

"That's it? Five of them?" asked Mercer.

"As far as we know. I think that's enough."

"But no six-foot-one-inch man in his thirties."

"Maybe they got the other guy's height wrong," said Robbie. "This Caleb Carruthers guy? He's about the right age."

"No, I doubt even here they'd get something like that wrong in a file like this," said Mercer. "And the height difference is just too much."

"We'll ignore that first comment," said Alice, "but you're probably right. I'm sure you are."

"Do you think there's anything that connects all of these folks, sir?" asked Robbie, turning to Mercer.

"Just call me Hugh, Robbie, and no, not that I can see, other than that they are all from here, that's a pretty tight area. And, of course, Violet Massey, she's connected."

"Let's ask the Massey daughters about their Aunt Violet," said Alice. "And maybe even about the other four missing people, see if that turns up any connection."

"I'll call them when we're done here," said Sal, "and I'll find out about their schedules while I'm talking to them. I'll let you know, Robbie, when you and Ranbir might go out there. And we need that list of their mother's old friends. They should have that together by now."

"Should we be doing a deeper dive on some of the other four missing people too?" asked Robbie.

"That would be spreading our investigation thin," said Mercer, "especially when we don't have any concrete evidence, yet, to put all these problems into the same drawer. We already have a lot of things to look into. But maybe we could try to dig just a little into one of them, and if we found anything there, even anything minor, then maybe it would be worthwhile looking at the others."

"I'd suggest this guy," said Alice, turning the photograph of Caleb Carruthers toward the others again. "Mr. James Dean. The rebel without a cause. He's first on the list chronologically, and he's a young man, just like our skeleton in the Massey basement. That gives him a connection, however slight, right off the bat. If he just grew a few inches, he'd be our guy."

"Okay," said Mercer, "good idea."

Alice turned the photo back toward herself and regarded Caleb Carruthers again. "He looks familiar for some reason. Like I've just seen him recently or something."

11

Blair's Confession

SAL WANTED TO make her phone call to the Massey sisters, and Robbie had to meet his partner in a few minutes, so when Alice made her strange comment, which silenced the room, they both excused themselves, got up, and left, Sal with a look of anticipation and Robbie with a sigh as he faced his day with Elwin Most.

Alice and Mercer were left alone. She was instantly worried that he might want to talk more about their relationship. She wanted to get out of this intimate space, go somewhere else, have a more businesslike conversation. Her mind was racing with the possibility that there had been a serial killer in the community. But she wondered if that could be true. Like Sal had said, *here*? That wasn't the sort of thing that happened here. Ever. There must be another explanation. She needed Mercer to help her even more now. She was sure he had been up against this sort of thing down south, maybe more than once. Could he help her connect the dots? Line up these disappearances somehow?

"Ever have something like this happen in New York? Or is that a stupid question?"

"Like what?"

"A ... uh ... a possible ... serial killer?" *A mass murderer.* It was hard to even say it out loud.

He sighed and looked away. "Yeah."

There was silence again for a moment.

"Shelter Café? One of those pumpkin spice lattes has my name on it. Literally will, actually. We can dive a little deeper into this and wait for Sal's report. I'm sure she's on the phone already, won't be long."

"Sure."

They emerged onto King Street Circle into the surreal warm day, Alice heading through the door first, taking off her police jacket almost the minute she felt the sun, Mercer choosing to keep his fleece coat on. As Alice swept her jacket over her shoulder, her phone came bounding out and hit the sidewalk, thankfully into a still knee-high, though wet, snowbank.

"Shit," she said and bent over to pick it up. Mercer nearly ran into her and placed his hands on either side of her hips to stop himself from knocking her over, gripping her for an instant.

"Whoops," he said.

"Yeah, right," she replied as she stood up and laughed.

They stepped away from each other, and she looked down at her phone. "Someone's called me. I had it on airplane mode while we were meeting." She checked who it was. "Blair Massey-Khan."

"The granddaughter."

"Bingo."

"Call her. Now."

They stepped back from the sidewalk and leaned against a building. Blair picked up after the first ring but didn't speak. Alice turned her phone on speaker and lowered the volume a little, placing the cell between her and Mercer.

"Hello?"

"Sergeant Morrow?"

"Speaking."

"I ... I have something to tell you, something I should have told you before. About ... about Grandma."

They could hear cars passing on the other end of the line and that quality of reception unique to car Bluetooth.

"Do you want to say it over the phone?"

"No. I'm heading back to the city now. Just left."

"Well, I'm walking over to the Shelter Café on King Street Circle. Do you know it?

"... Yeah."

"Do you want to drop by? We could talk there."

"Uh ..." Four or five cars must have passed. "Sure. I'll see you in about ten or fifteen minutes."

"Thanks, Blair. This is the right decision."

Blair didn't say anything and hung up.

"Well, that's more than a little interesting," said Mercer. "I knew she had a secret."

"The only person on earth who does."

"I mean she has one about *this*."

"I knew what you meant."

They started walking again. King Street Circle was a full circle, around and around, with just a few spoke-like dead-end streets and two escape routes: King Street East or King Street West at the two midpoints in the circumference on opposite sides. Alice and Mercer approached the west side and were about to cross the street, Alice still in the lead. A car seemed to appear out of nowhere, driving close to the curb, heading right for her.

"Alice!" Mercer pulled her back. The car sprayed her with slush and headed out onto the circle, not a word from the driver, not even a "sorry," the most used word in town.

"Asshole!" said Mercer. "Take his licence plate number."

"No," said Alice, "no, it's okay."

"What do you mean? It's like he was coming at you on purpose!"

"Let's go. We have bigger fish to fry. It was an accident. He just didn't see me."

There it was again. And right in front of Mercer again: a nasty reaction to her. The driver had known it was Alice, had intended to do what he did. It wasn't that everyone reacted like this, but quite a few didn't mind spraying her with slush or greeting her with disdain or scaring the heck out of her. She probably deserved it. That was why she was doing all of this now, why she had come back to town to live and work when really she should have gone somewhere else. That was why she couldn't be with Mercer. She might be happy in a real relationship with him. He might be happy with her. It was better, though, to just find a guy every now and then. Make love. Well, not love. She was punishing herself.

It was obvious that Mercer wanted to talk more, but she stayed in front of him and walked right up to the counter as soon as they got into the café, keeping quiet as she moved, his boots pounding on the plank floor behind her amidst the fairly loud crowd inside. Well, loud for here.

The owner, Jonathan Li, was behind the counter and greeted the two of them sheepishly. He'd been an unreliable witness in the last case they'd worked on.

Alice got her pumpkin spice latte, Mercer ordered the same, and they found a three-person table off to the side. The spot was perfect for more criminal investigation talk. But Alice could see a look in Mercer's eyes, his thoughts still on the car that had nearly hit her, so she excused herself and went to the washroom, hoping Blair might be there when she returned.

But it was still only Mercer, looking up at her as she approached with a dangerously caring and sympathetic look on his face.

"It was just an accident, okay?"

"But I've noticed a few other —"

"I don't want to talk about anything you've noticed that doesn't have to do with this case, Detective Mercer." She took a sip of her latte.

Mercer sighed. "Okay." He took a drink too but then tapped his fingers on the table and frowned as if he wasn't willing to entirely change the subject. "We haven't talked about why your name was on the envelope."

Man, he was good, she thought. Like a dog on a bone. He hadn't added, "I'm wondering if it's related to why some people treat you a certain way around here." He didn't have to. He knew she knew what he was saying.

"That's because it's a dead end. I didn't know Evelyn Massey. She must have simply been aware that I was a police officer."

"But why you of all the officers in town, *especially* if she didn't know you? Why not just put Chief Smith's name on the envelope, or someone else whom she actually knew with the force —"

"Service."

"Service." He paused. "I think we need to start looking into connections between you and —"

"Oh!" said Alice. "Here's Blair!"

Blair Massey-Khan entered the café with trepidation, holding the door slightly open as the charming little bell tinkled to announce an entry and poking her face around it to survey the situation and seek Sergeant Morrow's face. When she found it, she pushed the door all the way open and walked in her high-heeled boots in a direct line toward her goal, barely noticing people she passed, almost knocking a young waitress's tray to the wooden floor. But she stopped abruptly a couple of strides from Alice, noticing for the first time that someone was sitting across from her. That American male detective.

"I thought you'd be alone."

"Well, I'm not conducting this case by myself, Ms. Massey-Khan."

Blair looked at Mercer and then back at Alice.

"You can choose to stay, or you can go. I can't force you to do anything."

"But," said Mercer, "we know now that there is something you haven't told us about your grandmother ... and that could lead to all sorts of suppositions on our part."

Blair paused again. Alice pushed the table's third chair back with her foot, grinding it on the floor. Blair thought for another moment, then sat. She didn't take off her coat, toque, or gloves, nor did she make a motion toward the counter to order anything. She obviously wanted to get this over with.

"Grandma ... Grandma and I, we used to talk a lot. I think I told you that."

"Yes," said Alice.

"And ... and a couple of times she mentioned ... she mentioned ... that ... she felt frustrations in her life ... as a woman ... as someone who was given little choice."

"You already told us that too," said Mercer. It was apparent to Alice that he wanted to add, "Cut to the chase," but he didn't, and she was thankful for that. Best to let Blair take her time. She had come here to tell them something new, after all.

"Her marriage to Grandpa wasn't arranged, it wasn't remotely like that; they loved each other. But in many ways it might as well have been. Grandpa had a good farm, good prospects. His family had a pew in the church and never missed a Sunday. He and his family, going back many years, were highly respected in the community. So, when he expressed interest, Grandma knew what she was expected to do. It took a while, but she eventually married him. And he was a good man." Blair sighed. "She was a beautiful woman, the most beautiful in the county."

Alice nodded.

"You told us that too," said Mercer.

Blair didn't even look at him. "She had lots of suitors. Apparently, she had one particular guy who really liked her, with whom things might have gone pretty far. But that young man didn't have what Grandpa had. And he wasn't a stable sort either. I ... I think Grandma loved him, maybe never stopped. Tears came to her eyes when she talked about him." Blair appeared a little teary too. She sighed, looked up at the ceiling, then looked down again. "And ... and ..."

"Yes?" asked Alice.

"After she was married ... just once ... she had a lover."

"When was this?" asked Mercer, leaning forward.

"I don't know, exactly. She only mentioned it once, and she seemed to feel horribly guilty about it, which I don't think she should have felt at all. When she told me, she swore me to secrecy and really started crying, sobbing. It was horrible. I felt so sorry for her."

"You have no idea when it was?" asked Mercer.

"Well, I think my mother was little, and Aunt Gwen was alive too. That made Grandma's guilt even greater."

"And what happened to this man? I assume it was a man?" asked Alice.

"Yeah, it was a man. I don't know what happened. It sounded like they were together for just a short while and then ... I don't know, it was like he disappeared."

Alice could feel the little hairs rise on the back of her neck.

"Thank you for telling us this, Blair. I know that was hard."

"Yeah," said Mercer, "but is there anything else you can tell us? Did she say anything about the man, anything at all? His name — even a first name — his habits, where he was from, his occupation?"

"I think he was an actor," said Blair, turning to Alice, the tears standing in her eyes.

"Why do you say that?" asked Alice softly.

"I don't know. She didn't actually say it, but it kind of sounded like it. She said he was 'in' something. I don't remember exactly what she said, but it was like a movie or a play title or something, but she didn't go on, she didn't really say much at all about it, just blurted it out and then stopped and wept. It didn't feel right to ask her more. I figured she would tell me more later. But she never did."

Alice was staring at Blair Massey-Khan. She had never met her before yesterday. Blair was about half a decade younger than her, had never been in trouble with the police, and didn't know people whom Alice knew. And yet, this younger woman looked familiar to her. It was her face. That pretty face, almost as pretty as her mother's, looked familiar.

"I've got to go," said Blair suddenly, standing up. "I have some meetings in the city this afternoon." She turned but then looked back at them. "I was brought up by a good family, and I had a good grandmother and grandfather too. But I was also brought up to be honest, to tell the truth, to be honourable. My grandmother would expect that of me. And I know the truth will exonerate her. That's why I told you this. But know this ... my grandma would never have done anything bad, anything evil, anything you suspect her of!" She glared at the male detective.

"We'll keep in touch," said Mercer.

"Goodbye," said Blair to Alice. She fixed her hair, carefully wiped her eyes with her gloved hand to not disturb her makeup, and left quickly, the sound of her boots on the floor sounding above the murmur of the patrons.

"Did they shoot any movies here in the late fifties and early sixties?" asked Mercer as soon as she was out of earshot.

"Don't know. They do now from time to time. Our town looks so ordinary, I guess, so it plays ordinary very well on-screen. Maybe like American towns used to be? And cold, which is perfect for darker things. We're good for, you know, bad-things-happening-to-everyday-people-in-boring-places kind of stories. And we don't charge the American movie companies much. Money talks, especially for them. I don't know about back in the day, though. If anything like that happened, I think it would have been a big deal."

"We need to check for that in the old papers, and for any out-of-town theatrical companies that might have been putting on plays here."

"They used to do that in the town hall. There's a theatre up above the offices. A beautiful old building, classical style. The prince of Wales opened the main part in 1860, says so on the plaque anyway, came in on the brand-new railroad. They still put on plays up there, but just local things."

"We're looking for a six-foot-one-inch actor, Alice."

"Yup. But why would she kill him?"

"Why *wouldn't* her husband kill him?"

And why would Evelyn Massey want me to know about all of this? thought Alice. *Me.* Mercer was looking at her like he knew what she was thinking. She hated that. He often did it. Never in her entire life had she known a man who could do that. Certainly none of her "dates" could.

Sal rescued Alice from Mercer's sympathetic look by entering the café at full gallop, a look of victory on her face.

"Yes?" said Alice as Sal approached, sweeping her police cap from her head and depositing it on the table. But Sal held up her hand and turned to the waitress who was passing. "Fatima," she said, "I know we're supposed to go up to order stuff, so I'm so sorry for doing this, but would you mind bringing me one of those spice pumpkin lattes like the two other officers here are having, and a slice of banana bread?"

"Sure," said Fatima and smiled. "No problem."

"And," added Sal, "one of those pure chocolate or devil's chocolate or whatever the heck you call them brownies too."

"Coming up," said Fatima.

"Thank you, my dear." She turned back to the other two. "A girl's gotta eat."

"So?" said Alice.

"Got the list of Evelyn's old buddies. A couple of them almost her age are still alive!"

"Excellent," said Mercer.

"And apparently Blair has left for the city and —"

"She was just here," said Mercer.

"She what?"

"Her grandmother had a lover," said Alice, "probably an actor. This was when her daughters were little, so about sixty years ago, and Blair described him as kind of disappearing."

"Really?"

"But you were saying?"

"Oh! And both Gloria and Gwen are leaving today too, probably are gone by now. So their place is wide open for us! I was in touch with Robbie, who was glad to dump Elwin Most, and he'll swing by the office and pick up Ranbir, so the two of them will be heading out to the Massey place soon."

"Good work, Sal."

"Things are melting," said Mercer, looking toward the window. "Perfect day to be poking around out there."

"Like God's revealing the devil's deeds," said Sal.

"Well," said Alice, "I have to go. Got a lunch date, then some personal stuff, booking off for the afternoon. I will see you two tomorrow morning; we'll go over the list of friends and get onto them, and hopefully Robbie and Ranbir will have something for us. Text me the list when you get a chance, Sal."

"Personal?" asked Mercer.

"Yeah, personal. Bye-bye."

Alice didn't have a lunch date, nor did she have anything personal to do in the afternoon. She'd just go home and eat, maybe take a look at the list and make some interview plans whenever Sal sent it. Then she'd likely just watch something on TV tonight, maybe another crime series. She had a couple on the go. The American ones were ridiculously fast-paced and looked like all the roles were played by models, and you could just shut your mind off. She really didn't want to get into Mercer's personal questions right now, maybe ever. Best to try to keep him to professional stuff. She wanted to be with him from time to time. She needed that. But it had to be on her terms.

MERCER AND SAL were left alone at the table. Her latte, banana bread, and brownie came soon.

"So, Sal, why do *you* think Alice's name was on that envelope?"

Sal had a mouthful of banana bread, so she waved him off for a second. "Hand me that serviette," she mumbled through her chewing.

"The what?"

"The napkin."

He handed it to her, she wiped her mouth, and then she stared at him.

"I have no idea. And I'm not poking around in her private life."

"Though you know stuff about it, about her past."

"I indeedy-do. But I'm her friend. My lips are sealed."

Mercer sighed. "Just like everyone else around here."

12

Another Body

ALICE ATE ALONE at her parents' place, even though they were both home, taking her meal with her up to her room. She sat there at her little desk eating and trying not to look at Luke gazing out from the wall directly in front of her. But he was staring at her. She had placed the photo there not only because it was her favourite image of him but so he would do that — gaze at her forever. Alive again. His eyes were happy and affectionate, yearning for her as always, and now endlessly. She looked back and smiled. He was so ordinary, and that was what had killed him, why she had killed him. How could anyone be so wrong?

She had Sal's text in front of her, the list of Evelyn Massey's friends, but she couldn't look at it, couldn't concentrate.

She turned away and glanced around the room. It was so small. You couldn't swing a cat in here. Now there was an old saying. She hadn't changed anything in more than twenty years. The three posters fanned out on the wall, centred by the Tragically Hip, the same scary Tom Thomson print, the same bedside table supporting all the books she was reading, often dark stories. There was an

Emma Donoghue there now and a Henning Mankell. The same little bed. Luke had been here so many times. And in that bed with her. She remembered the way he'd trembled. She could still feel his skin and smell it. Her victim.

It was important for her to stay in this community. Be ordinary. Take her lumps. Seek justice.

She didn't do anything for the next few hours, just lay on the bed and thought. But slowly her mind turned to the Evelyn Massey case, to the justice that needed to be sought there, for all those people who'd disappeared. Then she started thinking about Robbie and Ranbir out there with the Massey property all to themselves. She sat up and looked around for her phone.

When Mercer answered, he sounded groggy.

"Asleep, Detective?"

"No, ma'am."

"Thinking?"

"A little."

"Drinking?"

"What do you want, Alice?"

"How about you and I make a trip out to the Massey place, right now?"

"I thought Robbie and Ranbir were —"

"Maybe they need some help, another couple pairs of eyes?"

"Sure."

She'd known he'd say yes and could sense the slight excitement in his voice.

"I'll meet you there in about an hour. I have something to do on the way."

Twenty minutes later, she was back in the basement of the police station, wishing she had asked Mercer to join her there first. She just hated this fucking place. She could swear there was someone lurking in here again. Okay, there was someone lurking in every damn place like this. A man. A big man. Sometimes she wondered if this paranoia was not simply a girl thing but rather came from what Alex had done to her. She'd deserved that. No, she hadn't. That was stupid. She had *not* deserved that. No one did. And if she could find that prick now, she would cut his balls off. What a trade. Luke for Alex. Worst trade in the history of the game.

There was a tool room down here, and she was pretty sure that what she needed was in there. She unlocked the door and peered into the dark space, then felt around for the string and pulled down to turn on the light bulb. There it was — among the old truncheons and shields and shovels.

A metal detector.

THE TRIP OUT to the Massey place didn't take long. She drove even faster than usual, late fifties and early sixties tunes on. She wondered what else her phone would find from that era. Was Gordon Lightfoot too young? Ronnie Hawkins and his groundbreaking kick-ass young band had been cool. She wanted to feel as if she were cruising around in this area sixty-plus years ago, maybe excited about a date, perhaps dressed up to go to a hockey game, maybe angry the way someone might have been at one or all of those people who'd disappeared back then, wanting to veritably kill them. Most young people in these parts had likely been listening to Elvis in those days. But again, she didn't want to hear the Americans. It had to be only music from here, that northern sound, whatever it had been. Before she left town, the Diamonds' song "Little Darlin'" was bouncing from the speaker. There was an innocence to it, a little humour too, fun falsettos. Somehow, she knew a few words and sang along. But she knew the next song even better, an oldie that you still heard every now and then. Paul Anka, now gone south and tanned and Americanized for so long, was belting out "Diana." She looked down at the screen — 1957, it said — and sang along. Anka was telling Diana that he loved her with all his heart, pleading with her to stay with him. As Alice listened, she realized something she'd never known about the song. It wasn't so innocent. It seemed to be about someone in love with an older woman. *A boy and a woman?* Deceptive darkness under the surface innocence. She remembered hearing somewhere that Anka's first hit songs had come out when he was only fifteen or sixteen, even though he had the powerful voice of a young man, and remarkably, he had written them too. This sneaky song had come from his northern imagination, born and nurtured here.

Mercer arrived at the same time as Alice, but when they got out of their cars, there was no sign of Robbie or Ranbir, just their cruiser.

"What the heck are you listening to?" he asked as she pulled up next to him, the strains of "Lonely Boy" still soaring in her car.

"Just getting in the mood," she said as she got out and walked around to the trunk. She lifted out the metal detector.

"All right!" said Mercer.

"Relax, Yankee. We'll only use it if we have good reason."

"We already do."

"What do you mean?"

"Those things can detect metal through concrete if it isn't too deep; even this dinosaur little model you have should be able to do that."

Alice hadn't known that.

"You're right. Good point. The crate had some metal in it."

A few moments later, they were in the basement, the metal detector strapped to Alice's arm, the plate hovering over the dug-out area. Nothing. Then she swept the rest of the basement floor with it, all of it. Nothing again.

"Well, maybe I was wrong. Maybe your metal detector isn't so great over concrete."

"Or maybe there aren't other bodies under here, at least none buried in crates."

"Let's go in here," said Mercer, motioning toward the crude wooden door leading into the fruit and jam cellar. "Probably dirt floor in there."

Alice popped up the simple wooden lock and was about to go in when she realized how dark it was in there.

"Find a light for me, Detective Mercer," she said, motioning for him to go in first.

He went in and found another old bulb with a string and pulled down, lighting the tight little area, walled with wooden shelves stocked with all sorts of jams and canned fruits, some of it glowing through the glass in the jars in lurid purples and oranges, like little brains floating in liquid. The room had an earthen floor odour.

Alice lowered the detector plate and started scanning. If there was anything below this sort of surface, the detector would pick it up immediately. But there didn't seem to be anything here either.

"How about over here?"

Mercer pointed to a darker area between the shelves near the wall. Alice moved in that direction, and a faint wobbly beep began to sound and then grew stronger and clearer. Mercer pulled his penlight out of his pocket and shone it at the business end of the metal detector hovering a few inches above the dirt, approaching the wall. Alice stopped suddenly. There were three tools there, leaning against the wall.

A shovel. And two axes.

Alice moved the detector away from the wall and back toward the floor. The beeping grew fainter. She turned it off.

"Nothing beneath the surface here," she said, still looking toward the tools.

"Two axes," said Mercer. He stepped forward and took the larger one into his hands. "Old ones. Very old."

"The second one is lighter," said Alice.

"Yeah," said Mercer, "lady's size."

They looked at each other.

"Let's go out and find Robbie and Ranbir," said Alice. "Bring the shovel."

They found two sets of footprints, the first as they were heading toward the barnyard and the second as they were going around to the back of the barn. From there, they could see the prints progressing toward a fence and then through a gate and up the hill into a field beyond. From where they stood, they could see two figures way up there and objects sticking out of the ground, like large stones or statues. The sun was beginning to descend, seeking darkness in this dark time of the year. Had this strange thaw not happened, any January ascent of this hill would have been difficult, but enough melting had taken place to allow them to walk without being nearly up to their waists and needing to put their hands down on the surface. Their boots sank only a few feet into the wet snow.

As they drew near the summit, they could see that the figures were Robbie and Ranbir moving around in a small graveyard, gravestones and memorials sticking out of the snow, some grass even evident up here where the sun had escaped the northern winter for a while and acted like it was in a different hemisphere.

"Hey!" cried Alice.

Robbie and Ranbir turned, both looking startled.

"Oh!" said Robbie. "It's you, Sergeant Morrow. Ma'am." He tipped his cap to her. "And Detective Mercer. Hello, sir."

"Hugh, Robbie, just Hugh."

"Sorry, sir."

"Captain America!" cried Ranbir. "'Nice to see you out on the land." He looked at what they were carrying. "Whoa! A metal detector. And a shovel. You guys come prepared. We didn't know we were allowed to dig."

"What do we have here?" asked Alice.

"Family graveyard."

Alice turned to Mercer. "There're a few of these around on the old farms. People were allowed to bury their loved ones on their property in the old days, and these things get grandfathered. You can still bury family this way some places. Maybe Evelyn will be planted here in the spring, who knows?"

"Here's Harold Massey's," said Robbie, motioning toward a grim, square gravestone, grey granite, obviously newer than the rest.

Alice and Mercer walked over to it and read the name and the dates, indicating that Harold Massey had been put underground here on this hill some sixteen years earlier. There was an inscription: *And the dust returns to the earth as it was, and the spirit returns to God who gave it.*

They just stared at it for a while, feeling the warm wind on their faces, the sun beginning to set toward the horizon. Alice and Mercer looked out over the landscape at the same time. It was beautiful. Tough and snow-covered, but beautiful.

"Anybody buried in here not a Massey?" asked Mercer.

"No, sir," said Robbie.

"But," said Ranbir," we did find something curious over here." He started walking toward a cluster of trees sticking out of the field like an oasis, not even a stone's throw from the graveyard.

"Yeah," said Robbie, moving toward him. "Bring the detector and the shovel. It's kind of weird."

They all walked over. There were half a dozen trees, all of them tall, old growth, but in their midst there was nothing, just bare ground, or at least less than a foot of snow.

Mercer was immediately intrigued. "This is interesting," he said. "Looks like it's been cleared out. Like a burial place for someone, or even a few people. Unmarked."

"Maybe babies," said Alice in a low voice, "not even named. Maybe they wanted to bury them near the others, though."

"Or maybe this is just an open spot in a tiny woods," said Ranbir. "You two have quite the imaginations. Or you're working too hard."

"Do you mind clearing back the snow, Robbie?" asked Alice as she strapped on the metal detector.

"Not at all, ma'am." He took the shovel from Mercer and quickly cleared back the snow. Then Alice stepped forward and set the detector plate a few inches above the ground. They soon heard a faint beeping.

"Oh my god," she said under her breath. She lowered it more. The beeping grew slightly louder.

"Could be a piece of a farm implement broken off and settled into the ground," said Ranbir.

Alice swallowed.

"Would you mind digging a little, Robbie? Start right here where the signal was the strongest." She pointed to a spot with the detector, and the beeping grew louder again. "Just dig there; you don't have to make a wide hole."

The frozen ground had softened a little. It was still hard work, though. Five or ten minutes later, almost two feet down, Robbie's shovel hit something with a ping. Something metal.

"Hold it," said Mercer. He got down on his hands and knees and dug at the ground, and soon he was outlining the shape of something. He worked for another minute or two and then stood back. They all stared.

It was two metal bars on a shipping crate.

No one spoke as the four of them took turns digging for the next half hour. The sun set, and everything grew dark. The three who weren't digging held flashlights. When the whole crate was revealed, they all took hold of it and hauled it out of the earth.

There was something inside.

Human remains. Another skeleton.

"I stand corrected," said Ranbir quietly.

Alice could tell without examining it closely that it was a woman's remains. The skeleton was shorter than the one in the basement, wider hips relative to the rest of the body. She guessed this human being had stood just a little north of five feet. She thought of where the four of them were standing. Less than a stone's throw from the Massey family graveyard. She thought of the physical description of Violet Massey in the file. She had been five foot one.

Alice looked out over the dark landscape, her homeland. She thought of all the ordinary people who lived here. She thought of her own secrets. And she thought of those terrible words Mercer had used.

Serial killer.

13

The List

ALICE AND MERCER had been walking back down the hill for a while before either of them said anything. And then it was as if they were just speaking quietly into the night.

"That was Violet Massey," said Mercer.

"So, now we have two murders."

"Maybe three."

"Yeah …" Alice looked toward the barn and the farmhouse in the dark distance as if searching the empty buildings for a light that wasn't there. "But we can't be sure about what happened to Evelyn … and maybe this one wasn't —"

"No, that skull looked damaged, as if she'd been in a fight."

"A fight? Like being beaten to death?"

"Yeah, like that."

When they reached the barnyard, Alice turned to Robbie and Ranbir coming up behind them. "That's two human remains in animal shipping crates on the same farm. We really need to know more about Harold Massey. I know I just asked you to look into it, Robbie, but as soon as you know anything about him that might be useful, give me a shout. Maybe I'll ask Chief Smith to let you have tomorrow morning to do all that."

"That would be great."

"What?" said Ranbir. "And miss a day with Elwin Most?"

"Like getting paid time and a half," said Robbie.

"We have the list of Evelyn Massey's friends, and you can be sure that now we'll be asking every one of them about her husband."

"But why would he want to kill his sister?" asked Mercer to no one in particular. "Why would he beat her to death?"

"Maybe she found out about what he'd done to the guy in the basement?" said Robbie.

Alice moved toward the cars, and so did Robbie and Ranbir.

"Would it be a thing around here for a brother to be concerned that his sister would tell on him about something like that?" asked Mercer. "How close are families in this community?"

"Close," said Alice as she reached for her door.

"So?" continued Mercer.

"But not close."

"That doesn't make any sense."

"That's correct." She got into the car and closed the door. "Emotions are a complicated thing around here."

"She looked after Harold's financial books too, didn't she, for the farm?" asked Mercer. "Maybe it had something to do with that? A money thing?"

"Now you're reaching," said Alice. "It was just a family farm. Listen, I've had enough for the day. I'm wiped. I have visions of a bubble bath and a book in my head. See you three later."

"We'll get this all written up and inform who needs to be informed," called out Ranbir as he got into his cruiser, thudding the door. Then Robbie's door closed too, like an echo in the cold night.

The two police cruisers pulled out of the yard, Alice in the lead, spinning her wheels a little as she started moving and then went flying up the lane. The other car followed, leaving Mercer standing next to his Ford Escape as if still full of questions.

Five minutes later, not long after Paul Anka's "Put Your Head on My Shoulder" from 1959 had played and "Puppy Love" from 1960 was partway through, Alice's phone rang. She looked down at the caller ID, then answered.

"I'm done for the day," she said.

"You know, I have a bathtub at my place too."

"Nice try. I'm going home." She hung up.

Alice wasn't going home, though, at least not for long. Her mother and father were out of town today and tomorrow, visiting her aunt and uncle a half day's drive away. And she was thinking about going out instead, to the suburban club she'd been to quite a few times lately, half an hour toward the city. Each of the last two times she'd gone, she'd come back with someone. The last guy had been a little violent. Maybe that wasn't the right word. Aggressive, once she'd given him the okay. She often liked that in men. As if she deserved it. But Hugh Mercer wasn't like that. Ever.

She looked down at her phone again.

He answered on the first ring.

"Yeah," she said, "I think I'll take you up on that. But I'll need food."

"I can do that."

"And that bubble bath."

"Uh ... you may have to bring the bubbles."

She laughed out loud, and it sounded strange in the car, not because she never laughed but because she rarely did it with a man.

"I'll change and see you in about an hour."

She had never gone to his place dressed in civilian clothes. Nor had she ever worn perfume. But she put on something nice and found a small bottle of the only scent she liked at the bottom of a drawer. She quickly washed her hair.

On the way out to Mercer's, she didn't play any music. Instead, she started thinking, and soon her thoughts turned to Violet Massey, the victim of a fight. With a man? *Brutally beaten to death.* Wow. What would that be like, knowing you would lose as soon as it started? The terror of that. The utter fucking frustration. And why did Hugh think that's what had happened? She looked out into the cold world racing past her, though there wasn't much to see, nearly opaque darkness in a vast nothing, just shadows of things, their reality disguised, her headlights illuminating so little, just what was directly in front of the car. Then she thought of the other missing people from way back then and the face of the one they had decided to research. Caleb Carruthers. The good-looking young man. She remembered the weird feeling his face had given her … that she had seen someone who resembled him recently. Then it hit her.

It was Blair Massey-Khan.

MERCER'S HOUSE APPEARED warm and inviting as soon as she saw it from the top of his lane. She paused there for a moment before she went down. It looked like a home. Or, at least, it seemed that way to her.

"Wow," he said when he met her at the door. "You look great." He had something playing on his phone through the speakers in the background. It wasn't from up here or from the late 1950s or early 1960s. It was soul. American. "I have a surprise for you."

He took her upstairs to the bathroom, the one with the view out over the fields. The big tub was thick with bubbles, and on the edge sat two little pink bottles with pictures of the princess and queen of Arendelle from *Frozen*. She laughed again.

"That's all I could find. Barely beat you back here!" he said.

"Take your time. I'm cooking up a storm downstairs."

It would be ribs, done on his barbecue just outside his front door. She didn't have to guess. But that would be fine.

During dinner, despite the problem of keeping the thick sauce from their fingers, licking it off and laughing about it, neither of them could resist looking at the list of Eveyln Massey's friends that Sal had sent Alice.

There were five names — four women and one man. Alice and Mercer knew the couple — Delilah and Ebb Morton, whom they had interviewed during the Becky Prior case and who lived at the end of Mercer's sideroad. Mercer instantly said he was shocked to learn that Delilah had reached the age of ninety, that he'd put her somewhere in her mid-seventies and he was a good judge of age, a skill that came with his job. Alice didn't know the other three women, though she had heard of all of them, longtime residents of the area, one merely eighty, another in her nineties, and the last almost Evelyn's age. All of them other than the Mortons lived near the Masseys.

"What do you think of bringing them all together and interviewing the whole group in one sitting?" asked Mercer. "They can draw on each other's memories that way. It loosens people up too, to be in a group like that when they're interviewed. Sometimes it makes them say something they wouldn't say on their own. And around here, it seems to me, you really need to loosen tongues."

"Okay, makes sense. But I don't want Ebb involved — he'd be useless. Just the ladies, and maybe just Sal and I should talk with them. Just a woman thing. That might make them open up even more. No handsome young Yankee to impress them or put them off their game."

"Well, thanks for those adjectives, but I —"

"No, I think it's best that it's just women."

Mercer paused. "Okay."

They somehow managed not to talk about the case for the next little while, though their conversation wasn't overly personal. It never had been, until recently, until Mercer had started pressing her on some things. Instead, they talked of films they'd seen and music they liked, surprised at how different their experiences were — if a film or artist wasn't American, he rarely knew it. And yet, their tastes were somehow similar, deep down.

They went naturally up to his bedroom, and in the midst of things she almost said that she loved him, but she stopped herself, thank god. The morning brought the biggest surprise. Shock, in fact.

She was still there.

She felt the surreal winter sun on her face through his uncurtained window as she awakened, then she slid her eyes over and saw him, lying there with an arm around her waist. She liked his arms, strong and darker than hers. She liked how they looked against her skin. But not at that moment. My god, she was still in his bed!

She carefully slipped out from under his arm and got to her feet. She saw her clothing and underwear on the floor, strewn there the way she always left it as soon as things got interesting. She started putting on her clothes as quickly as she could and then made for the door.

"Aha," she heard him say sleepily, looking up at her from the bed, the covers pulled back now, leaving him invitingly naked.

Her heart pounded. "Uh, just leaving. Sorry."

He laughed out loud and couldn't stop laughing. "Sorry?" he finally said. "Sorry? Believe me, you have nothing to apologize for."

"Yeah, but I should be going."

"Why not stay? I have some sausages."

She looked at him and laughed.

"Very funny. But I'll make you a great breakfast. Promise. You being here now, this is progress."

"No, it's not," she said. She glanced at her watch. "Oh my god! It's ten o'clock! Sal will wonder where the hell I am!"

"Okay, so let's have a working brunch, then. Text Sal and tell her you are talking with me about the list she sent you. Hard at work — that's why you're late. Tell her that we're calling the people on the list and setting up the interview. You don't need to let on that we're meeting in person."

He got up and walked toward her. She could see a hug coming.

"Okay," she said and turned away. "I'll put together some notes about the list. You make brunch. Then we'll talk. Then we'll go into the station. Me first, then you at least twenty minutes later. Arrive separately."

"All right," he said, but she was already gone, descending the stairs toward the big kitchen and the little table there, pulling out her phone and her notebook. "Sal knows about us, doesn't she?" he called as he heard her footsteps reach the ground floor.

"That's not the point," she said to herself.

He barbecued the sausages too and put the eggs on a skillet on the grill as well, so he was in and out the door as Alice looked at the list again. Sal called in the middle of things, and Alice put her on speaker.

"Hello."

"Alice, what's up? It's nearly ten-thirty."

"Hey, Sal. I'm just doing some work on my own this morning, and talking with Detective Mercer about it, getting his thoughts."

"Oh."

"I've gone through the list, and I'll call everyone and set up an interview. We'll talk to all of them at the same time, maybe get more out of them that way. We'll dump Ebb Morton, he'd be useless anyway, just have the women. And just you and I will talk to them, maybe get more from them that way too."

"Okay. Makes sense. When are you coming in?"

"Soon, just grabbing some early lunch so I'll be ready to roll. Hopefully we can talk to the women today. I'm thinking we'll see if we can meet them at the oldest lady's place, so she doesn't have to go anywhere."

"Edwina Shields. Good idea. She's in a wheelchair. Or in and out of it. Husband dead, kids long gone from the area. Lives alone."

"Wow. Her too?"

"Tough old gals. Though I hear she's a very sweet lady."

"Can't kill them with a stick, as I believe you said."

"Talk soon. Say hi to Mercer for me."

They looked at each other a little guiltily as Alice hung up, then both shrugged their shoulders. It was hard to tell if Sal had known he was there and listening in.

Alice made the calls while they ate and was able to arrange for all the women to come to Edwina Shields' farm in the late afternoon. "What a nice group of ladies," she commented after everything was arranged.

"Even Delilah?"

"Well, other than Del, though she's not so bad, just a little crusty."

Delilah Morton had been brusque when she and Sal and Mercer had talked to her during their last case. Delilah wasn't her real name, just a nickname that had stuck. It made Alice wonder if she had been a bit wild in her day. Alice also recalled that Del Morton had told them that her family was related to the Carruthers family, which was a curious fact, though lots of families were related in this community. Delilah knew all about Alice's past too. That was another good reason to keep Mercer out of this.

ALICE KISSED HIM when she left but didn't linger. And then she found herself looking in the rearview mirror a lot and even glancing around as she drove through town, taking a different route home than she normally did, somehow worried that someone would see her coming home from a beautiful night with a man she cared about.

Once she was in her uniform, her mind was focused again, all business. There was so much to do — they needed to hear what Robbie had learned about Harold Massey, have a fruitful interview with the women who had known Evelyn and Violet all their lives, and then maybe even see, if she had enough time, if they could find an actor who had disappeared in this area about sixty years ago. Oh yeah, she remembered ... and consider why Blair Massey-Khan looked so damn much like Caleb Carruthers.

14

Six Foot One

IT WAS PAST noon, and the three police officers were talking in Alice's office when Mercer arrived. She tried not to make eye contact with him and merely nodded her head and said, "Detective Mercer."

"Sergeant Morrow," he replied as he sat down.

Neither of them looked at Sal, so they couldn't tell if she was smiling. But they heard her start speaking.

"I think it's wonderful that the two of you were able to get together so early this morning. On the phone, that is — or texting or Zooming or however you were working together, working *so* well together too, I might add, to set up this meeting with all those ladies for this afternoon. Bravo."

"Yeah," said Alice, "well, thanks for that, Sal." She turned to Robbie. "Now that we're all here, I wonder if you can let us know what, if anything, you've been able to discover about Harold Massey?"

Alice was looking forward to what Constable Robbie Trew had learned because she knew he would have done his homework and would have a lot to say one way or the other. He was like that. Young, anxious to please, a new breed for a cop, with a different outlook on things. His ideas could be kind of political sometimes, maybe even a bit naive, but she didn't mind that. He wanted to make a difference. His roots also went deep into this community, even though he was wasn't exactly like most of the others..

"Quite a bit, actually, though almost none of it from our databases or looking him up online. Harold Massey never had so much as a speeding ticket and did almost nothing that gained him any real attention, certainly no negative attention, in the old newspapers or in media of any sort. But my grandparents put me in touch with a few people who knew him, not when he was young or anything but once he'd been married to Evelyn for a while. He apparently finished school after grade ten so he could work on the family farm, which he eventually inherited from his father. Very successful farm, as you know, had a hundred head of cattle at one point, both beef and dairy. Had a big orchard too and sold to all the local grocery stores. His farm was kind of the envy of everyone around. He never seemed to go through hard times when the economy or the price of animals or milk would wax and wane. He was a churchgoer, an Orangeman, chairman of the school board in the early sixties for three years, that's one term. Apparently a good, kind man, people say, never said a bad word about anyone, nor did anyone ever appear to have a beef with him. He was apparently awfully proud of his wife, Evelyn, liked to kind of show her off, would buy her fancy dresses and jewellery. Though a couple people I talked to said she was a bit embarrassed by him socially, that he could be awkward, would never dance with her, and his clothes always looked like he was bursting out of them. A big man, said to have been as strong as an ox. Apparently, in the old days, men used to wrestle for fun, get down off the hay wagon loads and do it, and arm wrestle too. I talked to several people who say he never lost a match, even broke bones on other men, almost by accident because he was so powerful. He played hockey, defenceman, tough as nails they say, and played ball too, a catcher. People claim they never once heard him complain about anything."

"Interesting," said Alice.

"Good job, Robbie, excellent job," added Sal.

"Okay," said Mercer, "let's put all that in our minds and take it with us as we piece other facts together."

"Oh!" said Sal. "I have several things to tell you too! I have been a busy bee ... Well, I had extra time on my hands this morning, you know." She looked at Alice and Mercer, who both glanced away. "First of all, I called Gloria and Gwen again, because I forgot to ask them yesterday about Violet Massey and about all our other missing people. They both said they couldn't remember their Aunt Violet, understandable when you realize that they were ... let's see." She looked down at her notes. "They were ... barely one and three years old when Violet disappeared. They said the family view of Violet was that she was a very strong-willed lady, a sort of matriarch even though she never married, very protective of the family name and of her younger brother, whom she felt was kind of naive about women. Both Gloria and Gwen say that not much was ever said about her in the family in their hearing, which they attributed to the fact that she disappeared."

"Because there was something ominous about it?" asked Mercer.

"No, they didn't say that."

"And what about the other missing persons? Did any of those names ring a bell with them?"

"I'm coming to that, Detective Mercer." She gave him as much of a look as Salma Haddad was capable of giving anyone. "Gloria thought one of them, Shirley Ezinicki, was a teacher at her school when she was just a small child, but other than that neither of the sisters had ever heard of any of the missing people. Not a single one." She stopped and smiled.

"Okay, what's that look for?" asked Alice. "Spill."

"I looked into the newspapers from the 1950s and 60s, searching for plays presented at the Town Hall theatre — lots of those — or even a film shot here ... and there was one! In 1964. Not really a movie, but it was a pretty big deal to locals because nothing like that had ever been shot up here until then. It was a television thing, an episode of something made by this guy called Rod Serling, who was apparently a bit of a known man back then, made freaky thrillers, and he had this television series called *The Twilight Zone* that he always introduced in a manly voice over spooky music, adding to how intense and sometimes creepy the shows were. That's what was shot here, one of those. There were four main characters in this episode, set in a boring little town, of course, three guys and a woman. I looked up all the guys. All of them were, you know...." She looked at Alice. "Good looking for those days, I guess, but yeah, hot too, I'd say, for any time. And one of them was about twenty-nine years old, name of ..." She looked at her notes again. "Perry Scott. I've got a picture of him here." She showed it to them.

"Hmm," said Alice, nodding. "Lady-killer."

"Why are you telling us this, focusing on this guy?" asked Mercer, who was leaning forward a little.

"Because when I looked him up, I found some descriptions of him, biographical stuff, even his height, which was six foot one, and not long after he shot the episode here ... he disappeared."

15

What the Women Knew

IT TOOK A while for anyone to respond.

"So, now we've got three known murder victims, by name?" asked Robbie finally, looking amazed and almost frightened at what they were uncovering in his little hometown.

"Maybe just two," said Sal, staring down at her notes but not reading them.

"And counting?" asked Mercer.

That brought on another silence.

"Let's not get ahead of ourselves," said Alice after a while. "Let's stay calm." But she didn't feel calm, nor did she look it. *Three identified murder victims? Here?* And somehow, giving this victim a name, removing his anonymity, had made his violent death seem more real. She thought of the skeleton she had seen in that crate in the basement, the caved-in skull, the pulverized arms. "It seems like there is so much more about this that we don't know than we do."

"That's life," mumbled Sal to herself.

"But we do have locations and identities for all three bodies," said Mercer, "and we have two suspects."

He was relentless, thought Alice. He didn't take time to be shocked or sad, or at least he didn't show it. He was on it. On the case, on the cause of justice. After the culprits, the evildoers. She didn't know whether she admired that or not. Likely, she did.

"Harold Massey I can see as a suspect, I suppose," said Robbie, "big and strong and with possible motives, though no one who knew him figured him for anything like a murderer ... but Evelyn Massey? Really? I met her a couple of times, with my grandpa. Very nice lady. That saying about some people not being capable of hurting a fly would apply to her more than just about anyone I ever met."

"Do you think women are incapable of murder, Robbie?" asked Alice suddenly, and she was surprised at how aggressive it sounded.

"No," he replied quickly, "no, ma'am. It's just ... in this case ..."

"We have to consider all possibilities," said Mercer, putting his hand on Robbie's shoulder.

"Okay," said Alice, adamant that she wasn't going to pause here to reflect or to be sad or shocked. "Let's put together our interview with the ladies."

"Interviewees are as follows," said Sal. "Delilah Morton, age ninety. All of us know her from the last case. She can have some rather strong opinions, as you will recall — wrong ones. Though not exactly a neighbour of the Masseys, she is only about ten or so minutes away, which kind of qualifies in the country. Ten years younger than Evelyn, but knew her, attended the same rural church, had her as a Sunday school teacher, apparently. They were friends. Del often dropped by for visits as Evelyn aged. Remember, she also said she was related to the Carruthers family."

"Can't wait to see her again," said Mercer, rolling his eyes.

"Second subject, Margaret Hawkins, age ninety-four, also a Sunday school student of Evelyn's but only six years younger.

Margaret grew up really poor in the area, and Evelyn befriended her, supported her, became a kind of mentor. She and Delilah Morton would sometimes visit Evelyn together."

"Third interviewee?" asked Mercer.

"Patience, Detective, patience," said Sal. "I am not lollygagging." She paused. "Third interviewee is Edwina Shields, perhaps Evelyn's best friend toward the end, about her age, I think, maybe a year younger, and lives alone too, just like Evelyn did. Remarkable. Apparently, she and Evelyn were not close in high school, where they were only a grade apart, but grew closer as the years went on, especially as they both became older, lost their husbands, then became very elderly and tried to stay in their homes. We will be interviewing all these folks in her farmhouse, not nearly as fancy as Evelyn's, I'm told, but well kept. She is in a wheelchair, as I think you know, but gets around well and even gets out of it every now and then, carefully."

"And one more?"

"Hope Thomson, much younger than the other three, a mere child at age eighty. She's Evelyn's niece on her side of the family, daughter of a sister who had her rather young. Not unusual in these parts. She was Evelyn's only niece or nephew, so a favourite."

They talked for a few moments about what they wanted to ask and mapped out a plan for how to pace it and who to focus on.

"Great!" said Mercer. "I'll see you afterward? Get us men up to speed?"

"That would take some doing," said Sal under her breath.

"I've got some tunes lined up," said Alice, glancing at Sal.

"All right!"

"Maybe not such a bad thing that I'm not coming," mused Mercer to himself.

"THE CREW CUTS," said Alice once she and Sal were on the road and she'd gotten more 1950s songs playing. "Northern doo-wop, 1954. Turn it up!" Sal obliged. "Sh-boom, sh-boom!" came the smooth refrain from the all-male group, singing about how life would be a dream if they were loved by the woman they admired.

"They apparently had lots of hits," said Alice after the song ended.

"Really? With this stuff? That was top of the charts?"

"I know, eh? But a bit catchy, don't you think? Kind of clean-cut and inoffensive and bouncing along. This stuff came after the old swing music but before rock'n'roll. There's one called 'Earth Angel' from 1955 ... listen." Alice reached down to her phone as she sped along the road out of town and soon found it. "Earth angel," began the earnest voices backed with hokey harmonies, bopping and cooing in the background, singing about a fool being in love with a heavenly girl.

"That's a little better, I guess," said Sal. "I kind of like the lyrics, though, don't tell anyone."

They laughed.

When that song ended, Alice let the phone play more Crew Cuts, and the two of them hummed along, laughing out loud at times, until they neared their destination. Unlike the Massey farm, the Shields property was off the main county highway and down a couple of smaller roads. Alice estimated it would take five or six minutes to drive to the Masseys' from there. They turned down the lane. The house was much more modest, a white clapboard place set closer to a smaller barn than the Masseys'. The dwelling looked well kept, but the barn and sheds appeared abandoned, as if whatever animals had been here were long gone, as if a whole world had once been here but had now disappeared. A border collie ran out to loudly greet them.

Alice turned off the car but kept the music on. Their cruiser looked like it was sweating in the surreal sunlight, as if it were exhausted from the sprint Alice had just put it through. The music kept drifting out as the two of them flipped through their notepads, brushing up on how they wanted the interview to go.

A song called "Young Love" from 1957 came on, about the passion of falling in love for the first time. The barking continued in the background.

"I think we're scaring the dog," laughed Sal.

"A critic."

"Lovely words too, though, in a way. Naive and hopeful. I don't mind that. Wish there was more of that now. Imagine this playing around here when these folks were young and in love."

"And killing each other," said Alice.

"Yeah, well, that too."

They turned off the music, and the dog stopped barking and began wagging his tail. They got out of the cruiser and looked at the two cars in front of theirs. The first was parked in a breezeway — a very old pale-blue Rambler that had come off the assembly line more than fifty years earlier, though it appeared to be in good shape. Behind it in the driveway was a recent model black Honda Accord.

"I wonder who's driving the new one," said Sal. "I'm guessing the youngster, the eighty-year-old."

But she was wrong. The car had been driven by a man, and he was in the house with the four women. In fact, he came out to greet the visitors in the doorway, standing in his sock feet just behind a woman whom Alice guessed was the eighty-year-old niece. The man was solidly built, about a foot taller than the woman, almost looming over her, his face expressing a surprisingly intense interest in the police officers and their mission today. Alice put him at roughly the same age as the woman.

"Oh, good afternoon, ladies! I'm Hope Thomson, Evelyn Massey's niece. We are so pleased to speak with you both. My aunt was a lovely lady, and this is all very perplexing. We have to get this straightened out." She took their hands, one after the other, enclosing each of theirs in both of hers and patting them.

"And I'm Wilson Shields," said the man, nearly reaching over top of Hope to shake hands. "I'm Edwina's son. I rounded up all these gals and brought them here."

"Very kind of him," said Hope.

Edwina Shields' son? That didn't make any sense to either Alice or Sal. She'd married James Shields in the mid-1950s. This man seemed too old to be their son. He had that wrinkled and darkened soft skin under the eyes of people advancing through their elderly years.

"Won't you come in?" he asked. "Everything and everybody is waiting for you."

The interior was much more modest and compact than in the Massey house. Alice and Sal were ushered into the country kitchen, a smallish room with carpeted steps that led to a combination dining and living room. Up there, three other elderly women were sitting, all in dresses, all wearing glasses, one glowing at them from the head of an old-fashioned varnished table, a teapot near her right hand, the other two on either side of her. They were in chairs, and she was in a wheelchair. Alice and Sal recognized Delilah Morton on her immediate left and assumed the other woman was Margaret Hawkins, dear friend of Evelyn Massey, six years her junior.

"Oh dear, there they are!" said Edwina Shields, her blunt features framed by a healthy head of white hair, voice much sterner than her words. "Lovely, lovely to have you here. I don't get many guests anymore, and I'll likely have even fewer now that dear Evelyn is gone. Welcome! Sit. Sit! Make yourselves at home. We have tea and arrowroot biscuits and butter tarts."

Margaret Hawkins, a smaller woman with a smaller presence, almost birdlike, had put her hand to her eyes after Evelyn's name was mentioned and wiped them a little. Edwina had stared straight ahead when she said her dear friend's name, like a soldier. Her voice, though, was softer.

"Sergeant Morrow," said Delilah in her bigger voice, nodding to Alice, "and your friend, whose name I do not recall."

"Constable Salma Haddad."

"Oh, yes, dear, that's it, isn't it? Have you been in these parts long?"

"I believe you asked me that before, Mrs. Morton."

"Oh, did I? My apologies."

"Been here for more than three decades."

"Oh, yes, that's right. I recall that now."

"Married to a Meadows."

"Indeed? But you said your last name is …?"

"Haddad is what I use for work."

"I see." Delilah looked away and then up at Alice. "Well, sit, Alice, and make your friend put her tush down too. What have you been up to lately?"

It was asked as if Alice had been up to no good.

"Oh, you know, serving and protecting. We are hoping you and the other ladies can help us with this case too." She looked at Wilson Shields when she said *ladies*. It was going to be difficult to ask him to leave.

"Mr. Shields," said Sal as she sat and got out her notepad, "thank you so very much for bringing the ladies here and for greeting us at the door. Made us feel very welcome. Thank you so much! We will see you on the way out, I'm sure?"

"Oh," said Wilson Shields, who had pulled out a chair and was about to sit. "I guess you just want to speak to the ladies?"

"Indeed."

"Well, I'll make myself scarce." He stood up and pushed his chair back in. "Call me if any of you want anything." He looked toward his mother. "Are you okay, Mother?"

"Yes, yes, Wilson, don't fuss. I will be just fine."

He moved out of the room, almost reluctantly, it seemed, pausing once, as if considering returning. But then he took his cellphone out of an inner pocket in his sports coat and headed toward the kitchen. Alice and Sal waited to hear the outside door open and close, but that sound never came. They wondered if he had seated himself at the little kitchen table just a few steps down from the living room. He would likely be able to hear everything from there.

Their first question was a soft one, though it was offered in a loud voice. There were hearing aids on every one of their interviewees.

"You need to start them off slowly, gain their confidence," Mercer had said back in the office. That was rich, coming from him, thought Alice, Mr. Hit-Them-With-Something-Dramatic-With-Every-Other-Question. And what did he really know about talking to women? She felt divided about his advice. Mercer was an expert with a long career of working on homicide investigations at the highest level, so she needed to pay attention to his instincts and maybe even imitate how he went about things at times. But she also hated that idea. She wondered if maybe she should incorporate just a little of his MO but mostly be herself. These were her people, and her sex. *Go with your own approach*, she told herself, *but then hit them between the eyes every now and then.*

So that first question was tossed loudly and lightly around the table, a query about each of their relationships with Evelyn Massey and what they'd thought of her. The women's answers were predictable and added little to the investigation. Margaret Hawkins was in awe of Mrs. Massey, deeply thankful for her mentorship and friendship. Edwina Shields described Evelyn as a "darling girl and a lifelong friend whom I have known since we were in grade school, just one year apart." Delilah Morton thought she was a "great gal, though not perfect, no one is, but her imperfections were just little things." Alice made a mental note to go back to that. And Hope Thomson was indignant that they were "even talking about connecting Aunt Evelyn in any way to anything bad, let alone a murder." She called her the "best, kindest aunt anyone could hope to have."

Alice was glad to get that out of the way. And ready for a larger slice of her Hugh Mercer side.

"I just thought you should know that yesterday we found another body," she said as she wrote the last testimony about Evelyn's character in her notepad.

When she looked up, all the women were staring at her, and a couple of mouths were slightly open.

"On the Massey property," added Sal, coming in at exactly the right moment with the right tone, though Alice found her performance a little forced.

"Gosh," said Edwina. "Really?"

Alice looked back at her notes and added a period with some weight.

"We suspect the deceased was Violet Massey."

There was an intake of breath around the table, and as far as Alice and Sal could tell it came from every single one of the women.

Margaret Hawkins put her hand over her heart. "Oh Lord, that is awful. Truly awful. I can't stand to hear it. I remember Violet well. When she disappeared, it was a terrible thing."

"What do you remember about Violet?" asked Sal.

"She was a handful," said Edwina, not waiting for Margaret to respond. "I'm sorry to be blunt, but if you want to know the truth, she *was* a handful. Not always the most pleasant lady, rarely got a smile out of her, in great contrast to Ev. Violet never married, you know, a little plain as they used to say, and perhaps she was a little bitter. She had an apartment in town and operated our little town library. She kept a close eye on the Massey place, though, and the goings-on there. She looked after the family's financial books. She was protective of Harold, who was her younger brother and the only boy, the scion, you know, the inheritor. She approved of Ev, though. She thought she was a good catch for him. And she certainly had high standards."

"All of that's true," added Margaret, "but oh my gosh, you found her? Buried? Where? What happened to her?"

"We aren't at liberty to divulge any details, Mrs. Hawkins," said Sal. "I'm sorry."

"Next question," said Alice. She paused. "I'm sorry to say that husbands always come under suspicion when women are murdered."

"But Harold wasn't her husband, he was her brother," said Delilah, as if Alice were a fool. "And who says she was murdered?"

"I wasn't talking about Violet," said Alice, "though we certainly have to consider her death suspicious too."

"Too?" asked Edwina.

"Why? What was wrong with her?" asked Delilah. "Was there something wrong with the corpse?"

"Not at liberty to —" began Sal.

"If you weren't talking about Violet, then to whom were you referring?" asked Edwina.

"Evelyn Massey."

"But you said murdered, dear. You said a husband is unfortunately a suspect whenever a woman is murdered. You think Ev was murdered?"

All the women leaned forward and turned sideways a little as if cocking a hearing aid toward Alice and her response.

"There are some issues with how she died."

"And we are not at liberty to go further than that."

"Oh my goodness gracious," said Edwina.

Margaret had a tissue up her sleeve, and she pulled it out now, balled it up, and dabbed her eyes.

"So," said Sal, "you can see what we are dealing with. We found a body in Evelyn's basement, a man, deceased some sixty years ago. We discovered that foul play is not out of the question in Evelyn's demise either. And lastly, we found Violet Massey's body in a grave on the family's property."

"And there were other disappearances back in those days," said Edwina.

"Yes," said Alice. Edwina seemed like an ally in all of this. She didn't appear to be afraid to tell the truth. Sure, she had given Evelyn a glowing report, but so had the others, for the most part, and that appeared to be the truth about Evelyn. But Edwina didn't seem sentimental at all. She was a realist. Maybe that was why she had lived so many years, could survive here without her husband and family, living in a wheelchair. Something inside Alice felt a sort of pride in Edwina Shields and women like her.

"You are correct, Mrs. Shields," said Sal. "And we are deeply concerned about all of this and how it might all be connected. We need each of you, as witnesses of Evelyn's life, and Harold's and Violet's and all the people around them, including perhaps the man who was buried in the basement, to tell us the absolute truth about them. We want to know about any enemies they might have had, any dark secrets they themselves might have hidden, rumours you heard about them, what their childhoods were like, all of those things. We need all four of you to be honest with us, set aside reputations if you have to, and tell us the truth. You are our only lifelines to the past and maybe to what happened. So much more valuable than any data, any superficial facts."

Alice nodded. This had to be said. People around here were closed books. But for the investigation to get to the bottom of this story, she and Sal had to open them somehow.

None of the women said anything in response to Sal's comments. They merely looked perplexed, as if it were strange to suggest that either of the Masseys could have a single enemy or be involved in anything dark.

"Do you know who he is?" asked Edwina after a while.

"Who?" asked Alice.

"The man in Ev's basement?"

"Yes. We think we do."

"And you aren't at liberty to say?"

Alice and Sal looked at each other.

"He was likely an actor named Perry Scott," said Alice.

"Perry Scott?" exclaimed Delilah. "I loved him!"

"You did?" said Sal.

"Well, he was a very attractive man, in lots of shows on the television."

"I did too," said Margaret. "He was gorgeous. Perry Scott? Really? In Evelyn's basement? In Evelyn Massey's basement?"

"I remember reading that he disappeared," said Delilah, "not long after he made that Rod Serling thing here."

"*The Twilight Zone*," said Edwina.

"That's right. Good memory, Ed."

"Are you saying that she killed him?" asked Edwina. "Evelyn did?"

"No," said Sal, "we are not saying that, though we cannot rule out any possibility."

"Are you saying that Harold killed him? That Ev was having an affair with him and Harold found out and killed him? My lord, that's quite a tale."

"As Constable Haddad said, we cannot rule out any possibility. Do any of you have any knowledge of Evelyn Massey knowing Perry Scott? Did she ever mention him, or did you ever see her with him?"

"I'm sure she mentioned him," said Delilah sarcastically. "I mean, have you ever mentioned that Brad Pitt guy, Alice, or George Clooney? A woman mentions a man like that every now and then. Not that he was exactly like one of them. He wasn't that big a star, but we all saw him on the television from time to time, and we noticed. We weren't dead from the waist down in those days, you know."

"Del!" said Edwina. "That's a little forward."

"Sorry. You know me, Ed. I don't always have the biggest filter."

"That's okay, Del, but we have to respect the questions Miss Morrow asks us."

"Do we now?" Delilah gave Alice a bit of a look.

"Of course we do. And this isn't about Alice Morrow, anyway. The quality of her questions and her character isn't on trial here. Though ..." She turned to Alice. "I did hear it said, you know, through the grapevine, that your name was on an envelope that Ev left behind." Alice looked back at her without saying anything. "That was curious. None of my business too, I'm sure. Let's set that aside and address your very legitimate question, Miss Morrow, an important one ... which was if we think Ev knew Perry Scott or if we saw her with him or heard that she was running around with him ... and my answer is no. Any of you ladies know differently?"

"No," said Hope. "Never heard that. That would be incredible."

Margaret shook her head too.

"But I'm guessing you want to know about Harold," said Edwina. "Since his sister has been found dead and you're thinking his wife's possible lover was killed too, and put in their basement. Though that last bit indeed just kind of boggles the imagination. My gracious."

Love this lady, thought Alice, *we should get her signed up on the police service.*

"Yes, we want to know about Harold Massey in particular," said Sal. "And be honest. Please."

There was silence around the table for a moment. All the women shuffled in their chairs.

"I'll say it," said Edwina finally. "Not sure Ev ever loved him."

"Oh, I don't know," said Margaret. "She was a loyal wife … other than this weird possibility that you two have brought up."

"Oh, was she?" said Delilah. Then she paused. "Sorry. That filter thing."

Alice turned to her, remembering what she had said about Evelyn Massey having imperfections. "What do you mean by that, Delilah?"

"Well, I mean, Harold wasn't exactly Brad Pitt or James Dean, or Perry Scott for that matter, now, was he?" She looked around the table for confirmation, but none of the women said anything. "Come on, he was a bit of a bore. And though he wasn't a whole lot older than her, he might as well have been a couple of decades, the way he conducted himself. She had some spirit when I first knew her. One of those people who, as a younger woman, you kind of look up to. Beautiful, lots of pizzazz, ambition. Correct me if I'm wrong, but I think she dated quite a lineup of other guys before him, some interesting guys, sort of wild sorts. Maybe I shouldn't be shooting my mouth off. After all, Ebb Morton ain't exactly a movie star either."

"I don't think Harold was so bad," said Edwina, looking a little perturbed. "He was a big, strong man and a very capable one."

Delilah and Margaret looked like they wanted to say something but kept quiet.

"Yes," said Edwina after a while. "I dated him a couple of times, before the war. He was around five years older than me, but I was tall in those days, nearly his height, always looked older than my age. I was fully developed, you could say, physically. He treated me like an absolute gentleman, though. That would be my testimony about Harold Massey, an absolute gentleman. Yes, a physically powerful man, but I very much doubt he would harm anyone."

"What do you mean," asked Sal, turning back to Delilah, "about Evelyn dating some interesting guys? I think you even used the word *wild*. Because we actually have some evidence that she was not entirely happy in her marriage, in the romantic sense."

The women all looked at her without saying a word.

"We not only have suspicions that Evelyn Massey," added Alice, "may have had an affair with Perry Scott, but evidence that she had a serious earlier lover."

There was silence for a moment.

"Well," said Margaret after a while, "good for her."

All the other women smiled.

Then Edwina Shields said something that took the air out of the room.

"Caleb Carruthers," she said.

16

What Else They Knew

IT TOOK ALICE a while to recover herself, but when she did, she pounced.

"Caleb Carruthers is one of our missing persons."

"I was thinking that," said Edwina.

"Oh my lord," gasped Hope.

The other two remained silent, their hands over their mouths.

"But the fact that he went missing doesn't mean that someone murdered him, especially that Ev did it," said Edwina.

"Why would you say that?" asked Sal. "That last part?"

"Because, dear, she was deeply in love with him."

"That's, uh, true," said Delilah in a much quieter voice than she usually employed. In fact, it didn't even sound like her. Margaret Hawkins said nothing, her mouth a mere slit as if she were holding it shut, a sort of guilty look on her face.

Alice couldn't believe the bombs that were being dropped in this female conclave. And as much as several things that had already been said had shocked her, something else was shocking her even more. Not just the fact that Caleb Carruthers and Evelyn Massey had been lovers and that her good friends seemed to know about it or the fact that Blair had said that maybe she'd never stopped loving him ... but that both Evelyn's daughter Gloria, the pretty one, and most definitely her granddaughter Blair looked exactly like him.

"Can you tell me more about Caleb and Evelyn, Edwina, or any of you?" asked Sal.

Hope raised her hands slightly to indicate that she didn't know anything about it, Delilah sighed, and Margaret looked out the window.

"I think he was a distant relative of mine," said Del after a while. "I had a bit of a wild gene in me in my day too."

But that was it, no more offers of information for a few moments. There was an awkward silence.

"I suppose it's up to me," said Edwina.

"If you don't mind," said Alice.

"Well, they were an item in high school. He was a sort of wild guy indeed, but as handsome as James Dean. And that was the type he was too, a rebellious boy. I think she liked that, since she came from such a proper home where they had conventional expectations for her. She liked his looks too, I imagine."

Delilah nodded her head. "You know," she said, "you two wouldn't understand this, or at least not fully. But in our day, women had to lead lives of deception. There was a certain way we were supposed to act, certain jobs we were supposed to take on — mostly being secondary and being good wives — a certain decorum we were supposed to have, and none of it had anything to do with what was going on in our minds."

She stopped speaking suddenly. Alice had never seen Del Morton look vulnerable. But for a moment, she did. Alice thought of the fact that Delilah wasn't her real name but rather a nickname from her younger years that had stuck.

Edwina put her hand over Delilah's. "Evelyn was as smart as a firecracker and as beautiful as any movie star. But around here, that didn't get you anywhere. I was good in school too, very good. We both graduated high school with high grades. We were pals in a lot of ways. But neither of us went to university. My father discouraged it, and so did Ev's, said they didn't have the money. And they certainly wouldn't have allowed her to marry anyone like Caleb Carruthers. Well, she could have, I suppose, it wasn't impossible, but that would have been a very hard choice, and anyway, the way things went with him after high school, it just wasn't doable. She worked as a bank teller before she married Harold, held out for quite a while before she said yes to him. I think she was in her late twenties by then, a bit of a late start. I was a secretary before I married my man, so I started late too for those days, I guess. Though I have been happy with my life." She stopped for a moment and looked a little sad.

"Caleb Carruthers disappeared in 1959," said Sal, looking down at her notes. "By that time, Evelyn would have been in her mid-thirties with two small children. Is that another reason why you think she had nothing to do with his disappearance?"

"Yes."

"So," said Alice. "Just so we have a bit of a timeline on all of this. I'm guessing you and Evelyn and Caleb all finished high school around the end of the Second World War?"

"Not long before, yes, though Caleb never graduated. Harold was older. He went to war. He was a very brave young man. We heard that he'd been a good soldier, courageous, but he never talked about it."

"And you, Margaret, would have been starting into high school just after they finished, and you, Delilah, would have been in about grade four or five then?"

Margaret nodded.

"Yes," said Delilah, "though we were all in the same big school in town in those days."

"And you, Hope," said Sal, "you weren't born until just after the war and would have been a child when Evelyn and Harold married and started a family. You are about ten years older than Gloria and Gwen, correct?"

"Yes. I was over there at the Masseys' often, though. It was a favourite place for me to be as a kid. They were such a lovely family. I used to babysit."

"So, what was Caleb Carruthers doing between the time he didn't graduate from high school and when he disappeared in 1959?"

Margaret looked out the window again, and Delilah looked down.

"He was in jail," said Edwina.

Another bomb.

"For the whole time?" asked Sal after gathering herself together. "That's, what, fifteen years or so. What the heck did he do?"

Alice was feeling a little sheepish about not knowing more of Caleb Carruthers' past. It was likely there in his file. But there were just so many things to do. This case had so many parts to it.

"Not the whole time," said Edwina.

"He robbed a bank," said Delilah, "armed. Bonnie and Clyde style, though he didn't have a Bonnie, at least not one with him. Some of the kids around here were impressed. He was like Edwin Alonzo Boyd, a man some of the boys idolized, kind of a romantic bad guy, bit of an outlaw, broke out of the restrictions on life in our world. Yup, like Edwin Alonzo Boyd, if you know who I mean."

Neither Alice nor Sal did. But Alice was more interested in the timeline. She was also intrigued by the fact that Evelyn had been a bank teller. If you wanted to rob a bank, wouldn't it be helpful to have a girlfriend who knew something about them? But the women hadn't said anything about Evelyn providing him with information. Then again, they wouldn't, would they? People around here would keep something like that to themselves. At least outwardly. She thought of what Delilah had just said: ... *he didn't have a Bonnie, at least not one with him.*

"Mrs. Shields, you said he wasn't in jail the whole time. What do you mean?"

"I think he was in the Don Jail in the city from not long after the war when he committed the crime until the mid-fifties, and then when he got out, he came back here for a while, then he went away again, but he kept coming back."

"Let me stop you there," said Alice. "Did Caleb Carruthers reconnect with Evelyn Massey in any way during the times he came back?"

Edwina paused for a long time. "That, I don't know." She cleared her throat. "He seemed to have money at times, but I don't know how he got it. Then, yes, in 1959, if that's the correct year, he went missing. But who knows what he was up to, the crowd he was running with."

"So, it was while he was incarcerated that Evelyn married Harold Massey and started having children?"

"The first part. I think the kids started coming after that. It was an important choice for her to marry Harold, after being connected to Caleb."

Alice nodded. Blair, Gloria, and Caleb Carruthers' faces were all in her mind. Gwen did not look like her sister. She was also wondering if Caleb Carruthers had ever really disappeared. She could hear Sal sigh and glanced over to see her looking down at her notes and then looking back up at her. They were learning so much, and this case seemed capable of going in so many directions. What to ask next? Maybe it was time to retreat and consider the mountain of things they now knew, the myriad of possibilities. Or maybe it was time to do a little Hugh Mercer just before they left. Drop a bomb back at these women.

"I'd like to ask you all a general question," said Alice, "partly because of some suspicions I have but also because of what you said, Delilah, about women in those days living lives of deception. This is something to keep within the confines of this room." She could feel all the women tilting forward a little. "Do you believe that Caleb Carruthers is the father of one of Evelyn Massey's children?"

There was dead silence in the room.

"Well," said Edwina finally, "I once read somewhere, I don't know where, something that said that nearly thirty percent of the children in this world are not fathered by the men who are nominally their fathers."

Delilah Morton put a hand quickly to her eye and wiped, and Alice tried to picture her son, Ben Morton, and if he looked much like her husband, Ebb.

"That seems like a lot," said Sal. "I doubt that's true."

Alice knew she shouldn't let up. "That isn't answering my question, ladies. I would appreciate an answer." She said it as pleasantly as she could.

There was silence again.

"Excuse me!" said a voice from the doorway. Wilson Shields was standing there not looking pleased, appearing even older then he had before. "Don't you police officers feel like you've kept these ladies long enough? Your questions are upsetting for my mother, who has lost a dear friend who is under heinous suspicions, and yet you keep peppering her and her friends here with questions, veritably interrogating them. A few questions, fine. But this is shameful. These ladies are in advanced —"

"It's fine, Wilson," said Edwina, "don't fuss. The police officers are merely attempting to get at the truth. We all want that."

"How would the police officers like it," countered Wilson, "if I were to grill them, to grill Sergeant Morrow, for example, about her own life?" He stared at Alice.

Alice noticed Delilah, Margaret, and Hope all nodding, though barely perceptibly.

"Oh, Wilson," said Edwina, "that's not fair." She turned to Alice. "How are you, dear? You went through a great deal."

"*She* went through a great deal?" snarled Wilson. "How about Luke?"

"He was a lovely young man," said Edwina. "We all miss him." She stretched her hand across the table toward Alice. "Forgiveness is important. Intentions are important. And I believe your intentions were not bad. And you were a young woman, after all." Alice surprised herself by reaching across the table and taking Edwina's hand. It gripped hers firmly. "The questions Sergeant Morrow is asking us today need answers, and she and Constable Haddad need to put them to us."

"Thank you," said Alice. She gently pulled her hand back and stood up. She realized she was shaking. Sal stood up too, her hand briefly on Alice's back with a pat. "Thank you all. We may be in touch again."

"I'll be the judge of that concerning my mother," said Wilson.

"No, you won't, Mr. Shields," said Sal with a smile. "This is a police matter. Though we are so very pleased to have met with you. Thank you for the tea, ladies, and your time."

They almost backed out the door.

"I'll see them out," said Edwina, "we all should. Come on, ladies. This is our local police service. Let's show some respect, especially to women officers." She lifted herself from her wheelchair and took up two canes that were looped over the armrests. Wilson was immediately by her side and helped her move across the small, carpeted dining room floor down into the tiled kitchen and then to the outside door. She was hunched over as she struggled forward. Sal offered her hand to the other women as they followed, but no one took it.

Wilson walked with them toward the cruiser. When they neared it, he spoke to them in a hushed tone. "I'm sorry for being short with you, but I worry about my mother, and those other ladies, of course. Other than Hope, they are very elderly. They put on a brave face, but just about every one of them is facing medical issues." He paused. "My mother has leukemia. There is nothing they can do. She has very limited time left."

"So sorry to hear that," said Sal, "and we will bear that in mind. But you must know, we are not trying to upset them. We simply have to ask certain questions, and they are a lifeline in this case. Perhaps this is the last time we'll need to interview them."

"I hope so. Have a nice day."

Once Alice and Sal were in the cruiser, they looked toward the door and saw Wilson walking back toward the four women, who were all standing in the entrance watching them. Alice turned on the engine, and her phone picked up where it had left off. She glanced down at the screen: the Four Lads, "Standing on the Corner," from 1956. The song started with a jaunty melody and whistling, then the lyrics began, about a guy happily watching girls pass by on a street.

Sal and Alice looked through the windshield into the early-setting sun and saw the women watching them as if lit by stage lights, Edwina actually waving. Then they noticed that all of them were singing along with the words, the bouncy, happy tune reflected in their expressions.

17

Putting Some Teeth Into It

BEFORE ALICE AND Sal reached the road that led to the main county highway, they encountered a car pulled over on the shoulder. It took Alice a moment to realize that it was Hugh Mercer's Ford Escape. Before she had even parked behind it, he was out of the driver's door and approaching her. She lowered her window.

"So?" he asked.

It was past mid-afternoon and growing colder, the surreal warm spell's death imminent.

She felt like telling him how ridiculous it was that he couldn't wait to speak to her over the phone or back at the station, but she understood. If she had been in his shoes, she likely wouldn't have waited even this long. She would have been at the end of the Shields' lane. He nodded in fascination as she laid out what they'd learned, his eyes riveted on hers. She found herself staring back at him, locked into this story with him, and even though she was sharing detailed suspicions about murders, this contact with him, eye to eye, made her feel wonderful. It was as if Sal weren't in the car beside her.

"Wow," he said when she had finished. "That's a whole cluster of bombs. We have three suspects now."

"Harold Massey, Evelyn Massey, and Caleb Carruthers," said Sal. "If I may interrupt." Alice glanced at her and noticed that her partner was grinning at the two of them.

"Yeah," said Alice, "maybe Carruthers disappeared on purpose. He has all sorts of motive for these crimes, ones that stick out in this community. A criminal, one who robbed a bank armed. In love with Evelyn, whom he was being kept from, likely angry at the Massey family, and, if he vanished for his own reasons and was still alive and aware of what was going on in the early sixties, probably beside himself with jealousy when Evelyn was messing with Perry Scott too."

"Maybe he's *still* alive," said Mercer.

"If he is," said Sal, "then he's about a hundred years old."

"Well, so was Evelyn, and Edwina and Margaret are nearly there too."

"So, who killed Evelyn then?" asked Alice.

"Don't know, maybe herself," said Mercer.

"And the three other missing people? We need to find out if they have any connection to Caleb Carruthers."

"Good idea," said Mercer. He sighed. "I don't like the sounds of this Wilson Shields guy either."

"You're not saying he had anything to do with this?" said Sal. "What in the world could his motive be?"

"No. I'm just going with my gut here. Any time anyone seems to be obstructing an investigation, even in the slightest way, I'm suspicious. What's their angle? And you both think there's something off about his age, right? That's a flag. But that should be easy to check. If he's closer to eighty than seventy, then he would have been a teenager when these deaths started, not a small child. That would make him a very different sort of person of interest."

Alice's cell rang.

"It's Ranbir," she said and put it on speaker.

"Sergeant Morrow?"

"Yeah, Ranbir, it's Alice."

"We have a situation here at the police station."

"And what is that?"

"I believe I should not be telling you over the phone. This is sensitive information that one cannot be too careful about. It pertains to you, Alice Morrow, and the case of Evelyn Massey and the gentleman skeleton in her basement and the lady skeleton in the Massey family plot."

"Ranbir, for god's sake, just tell me what the fucking situation is!"

There was a long pause.

"No need for profanity, Sergeant Morrow."

"Tell me!"

"We have discovered an envelope."

"An envelope? What do you mean?"

"We did a final sweep of the Massey home, and an envelope was found in Mrs. Massey's bedside table. We have yet to open it. We are waiting for you."

"Why? Just open it and —"

"It is addressed to you. To Alice."

TWENTY MINUTES LATER, Alice, Sal, and Mercer arrived at the station, Alice in the lead. They found Robbie in her office sitting across from her desk, the letter resting on its bare surface like a message in a bottle on a calm sea. Sal smiled at Robbie, Mercer nodded, and they sat beside him. Alice went around her desk and fell into her chair with a sigh, then just stared at the envelope. Her name was written in the same handwriting that had been on the first one, old and shaky and, again, to her mind, kind of evil looking. Evelyn's hand.

"You read it," she said as she pushed it toward Sal.

Sal just looked at it for a few seconds as well and then picked it up and opened it.

"In the pigpen, northwest corner," she read, her voice growing shakier as she spoke.

ALL FOUR OF them were at the Massey property within an hour, now very late afternoon, the day growing darker. They had been told that the barn was empty and full of cobwebs, and it took them a while to figure out what part of the building had once housed the pigs. They tried the downstairs doors and found them bolted shut, so they walked around and up the hill at the back and entered by large doors that led them into the area where the hayloft had been on the upper floor. It still smelled of hay, and a few rotten bales were strewn about. It was freezing inside, and they couldn't find any lights, so they walked carefully on the plank surface using their flashlights, and Mercer nearly fell down a hay chute cut into the floor. They found a henhouse down a passageway, and a granary, and then discovered the stairs descending to the main floor. There, they were able to turn on lights and encountered the stalls where the cows and, in earlier days, horses had been kept. There was a small room off one long aisle where the milk separator had been and another with harnesses covered in frozen layers of dust. Then they found another passageway and worked their way carefully down it, again with only their flashlights guiding them. That passage opened into another room. They checked the walls and found a light, which Sal switched on. It illuminated that part of the barn.

"This is it," said Alice, nodding to the troughs that lined the front part of the pen near where the four of them stood in the passageway.

"You'd empty your pails over the fence into the troughs from here to feed the pigs."

"Harold would," said Sal.

The place smelled of ancient pig shit.

"Northwest corner," said Mercer.

"That would be over here," said Robbie, who had already climbed onto the top of the thick wooden fence and was about to drop into the pen, his eyes on the far corner.

As Alice looked upward, she noticed that she could see the dark upstairs of the barn through a square chute above, one Harold had likely tossed hay bales through, maybe the one that Mercer had nearly fallen into. *That would be a nasty fall*, she thought, looking down onto the hard concrete floor on which she stood a full storey below.

Robbie dropped into the pen.

"I'll wait here," said Sal, looking at the height of the filthy barrier that was between her and the pigsty.

Alice and Mercer both groaned as they got themselves up and over into the pen too. By then, Robbie was already bending down in the corner, his flashlight shining on the concrete wall and the floor.

"Nothing here," he said after a while.

"Wait," said Alice. "What's this?"

There was a crack in the concrete right where the wall met the floor, and chunks of concrete sat in the hole, as if placed there.

"Let's dig this out," said Mercer.

Robbie was instantly at it, pulling the chunks out. The crack was wider than it had seemed on the surface, and deeper. Robbie pulled more pieces out and then shone his flashlight into the hole he had created.

"Oh god."

"What?" asked Sal from across the room.

"There's something in this crack. Is this what I think it is?"

He pulled it out and, without examining it more closely, covered as it was in dirt, handed it to Alice.

She started to wipe off the soil but then cried out and dropped it on the floor. It clunked when it hit. "Sorry," she said and gingerly picked it up.

"What?" asked Sal. "What is it?"

Mercer shone his flashlight down on it and then took the object into his own hands, turning it over, fascinated.

"Teeth," he said. "Human teeth. A whole set." There was silence for a moment. They could all hear the wind whistling against the old barn windows. "Nice ones," added Mercer. "Male, I'm guessing. This guy had some attractive choppers."

Alice was thinking about Caleb Carruthers' photograph looking out at her from his file. His beautiful, toothy smile.

"We can't say it's him," she said.

"No, but we can think it," said Mercer. "I mean, the other missing people have no obvious connection to the Masseys — not that we know of yet, anyway. But he did."

She knew Mercer had taken a mental snapshot of Carruthers' toothy smile too.

"You've got human teeth in your hands?" asked Sal from the other side of the room. "Holy cow." They heard her take a deep breath. "I don't like pigs. They're not exactly stars in my religion. Unclean. You know, I've heard that if a pig found you unconscious, he'd try to eat you."

"But not your teeth," said Mercer.

"What?" said Sal. "Oh, I didn't mean that! Do you think that's what happened ... whoa."

The others climbed out of the pigpen.

"We need to see if there are any dental records for Mr. Carruthers," said Mercer, "or any DNA left on the gum pulp. Doesn't look like there's much, though, and this place has lots of leaks in it. Likely lots of water in here over the years, and dirt gathering in the crack where the teeth were."

"This doesn't look good for Harold Massey," said Robbie.

"Suspect number one now, it seems to me." Sal nodded.

"But he couldn't have killed his wife," said Alice, "unless he got out of the grave to do it."

"I'm really thinking that was suicide now," said Sal. "Seems more and more like it. Evelyn was distraught, feeling guilty in her old age, knowing what her husband had done but not able to say anything about it because it would bring shame on him and her family and herself. Shame too that she'd had those affairs. Her first note says as much. And then she wrote this second note so we would find more evidence in the pigpen."

"Why didn't she point the finger at Harold, then?" asked Mercer. "Or, in the highly unlikely case that she murdered those two men herself, admit that? Come clean, one way or the other?"

"Maybe she just couldn't bring herself to do that," said Sal. "Maybe it was too hard to actually put into words."

"So, you do the horrible stuff or know who did, but you can't say it?"

"Yup," said Alice.

"Sounds about right," said Sal. Robbie was nodding too. Mercer shook his head.

They walked out into the barnyard. The temperature seemed to be dropping by ten degrees every hour now. The wind was up. Everything looked black and grey, just the shadows of the farmhouse and their cruiser ahead of them as they made their way toward it. They all pulled up their collars.

Back in the car, Alice at the wheel and Sal beside her, the two men jammed into the back seat, they said nothing at first. As they went up the lane, Alice touched her phone, and the music came on again. "*Let Me Go, Lover,*" read the screen, *Hank Snow,* 1954. The twang of a slow-paced old country song played through the cruiser. The northern voice sounded authoritative, like a king of this kind of music. The singer pleaded with his lover to release him from the spell she had on him, which was slowly killing him.

They drove for a while with just the music playing, the cold, dark countryside passing by outside. Alice kept looking for Mercer in the rearview mirror, making sure that no one else noticed, and now and then he looked back. They didn't smile at each other when their eyes met. Their expressions were sad and serious.

Three murders, Alice was thinking. Maybe four. Bodies disposed of on the same property. Just skeletons remaining. And teeth.

Here?

18

Next Move

ALICE RESISTED MERCER'S offer to stay with him that night, and everyone reconvened the next morning at the station. The women had their doughnuts and coffee, and so did Robbie — in fact, they were all commenting on how much they were consuming and laughing about it. Sweet little balls of doughnut named after a famous singer and marketed as "bits" had just started appearing in the local restaurant, and everyone but Mercer was munching them down. He had forgotten to get any for himself on the way in and looked as if he felt a little left out and surprised that the room wasn't more sombre, given the events of yesterday. It took a while for the others to offer him any bits, but when they did, he said he was fine.

Alice had asked Sal to bring the doughnuts. And she had tried to encourage the banter about them. *Life goes on*, she kept telling herself. *Darkness roils somewhere inside all of us, but you have to try not to let it control you.* It was now evident that there had been a great deal of darkness in this community in the past. In fact, something terrifying — something she was steeling herself to confront. *Deal with it; get on with it*, she told herself. She was trying, every day, to do that with the trauma in her own life too.

"All right," she said once they had eaten nearly everything. Her mouth was still full as she began to talk. "The teeth have been sent for forensic tests. And Robbie, you're looking into dental records for Mr. Carruthers, right?"

Robbie nodded.

She sighed. "Next move?"

"Well," said Mercer, "we may never get any confirmation that those teeth belonged to Caleb Carruthers, but I think we all agree that they are likely his. Do we move forward with that assumption?"

"Couldn't they belong to one of the other three missing people?" asked Sal.

"Not impossible," said Alice, "but if that's the case, then they would have come from a woman in her twenties, a man in his fifties, or a male teenager. Did they really look like they belonged to anyone like that? Can't say definitely they didn't, I guess, and I'm certainly not a dental expert. But as we've said, we have nothing connecting any of the other three to these crimes. Not yet. We do have a lot that intersects with Mr. Carruthers."

"Speaking of the other three, though," said Sal, "don't we have a responsibility now, given what we're turning up ... no pun intended ... to look into what happened to them? I mean, Violet Massey's death came in 1958, Caleb Carruthers' in 1959, and Perry Scott's, if that's who we found in the basement, in about 1964. These other three" — she looked down at her notes — "Charlie Eaton, Albert Johnson, and Shirley Ezinicki, they were reported missing in 1960, 1961, and 1962, right in between the deaths of the people we're investigating, from this same area. If we're looking for the murderer of these first three or four people, then maybe finding out what happened to the other three, or at least one of them, will help lead us to the culprit ... or, I suppose, just confirm who it is."

"Can't disagree," said Mercer.

"Can't believe I even said what I just said ... all these horrible crimes," said Sal, almost to herself.

"So, which one do we look at now?" asked Robbie. "We can't do all three at once."

Alice sighed. "And we thought this was just the natural death of one elderly lady." She looked down at the missing person files still on her desk. "Let's do it chronologically." She pulled a file across. "So ... Charlie Eaton, age sixteen."

"Not looking forward to this one," said Sal. "That's my Mahmoud's age."

"And maybe the least likely to be connected to the other deaths. Teenagers go missing all the time. Drugs. Runaways. Even taken for sex trafficking," said Mercer.

"Yeah," said Sal, "but this is here, not New York, and it was 1960. It was a pretty closed society in these parts in those days, even more than now, as white as snow and a world unto itself. People here were farming, going to the odd barn dance or sock hop, or having what they would consider a very big day at the National Exhibition show in the city. They were listening to Hank Snow or, if they were really wild, the Four Lads and the Diamonds, but even then not seeing anyone like that live, just hearing them on a jukebox. Paul Anka was almost a rebel to people around here. That's the world from which this kid disappeared. That's what people were into."

"Or robbing banks at gunpoint," said Mercer.

"Yeah, well, that too."

"I think that what Detective Mercer is saying is that, again, we can't leave out any possibility," said Alice. "Let's see." She opened the Charlie Eaton file and perused it. "Yeah, sixteen years old, five foot four, about a hundred and twenty-five pounds — so kinda small — raised by a single parent, a father who is noted as a labourer here, and the kid has a record, minor crimes, shoplifting, the like. Too young to go to juvenile hall when he did those things, apparently. There's a scribble on this page that says 'troubled.' Another says 'loner.' He was in grade ten, and this disappearance happened in September, so he must have failed a year. He went to the old school in town, which had all the grades from kindergarten to thirteen in those days. He was caught smoking on school property more than once. Suspended for that twice." She looked down and read more. "Suspended another time for misconduct in class. And also suspended for offering cigarettes to minors, kids in grade one and two."

"Lovely," said Sal.

"What were the circumstances of him going missing?" asked Mercer.

Alice looked down and read for a few seconds. "Nothing to go on here, really. He just didn't come home one day after school. His father didn't report it until the next day. Hadn't noticed he was gone at first."

"I knew of an old Mr. Eaton, died quite a few years back," said Robbie.

"I did too, now that I think of it," said Alice.

"So did I." Sal nodded.

"If it's his kid," added Robbie, "then I bet the cops didn't spend very long looking for him, likely figured he deserved it or something."

Alice, Sal, and Mercer didn't say anything, though all three nodded.

"So, Charlie must have been a town kid," said Robbie, "since old Mr. Eaton lived in the east end, in one of those low-income apartment blocks."

"And the Masseys were country people," said Mercer. "What in the world would Harold Massey have had to do with him?"

"Nothing, you'd think … though we can't be sure yet," said Sal.

"What about Gloria and Gwen?" asked Mercer. "Wouldn't they have been in that school at that point?"

"Just starting out, I think," said Alice. "Gloria was born in '55 and Gwen in '57 or '58, so Gloria would have been in kindergarten."

"What about Wilson Shields?"

They all looked at Mercer for a moment.

"Well," said Alice, glancing down at her notes again, "Edwina married in early 1955, so Wilson had to have been born after that, which means he would maybe have been in kindergarten too."

"But remember, he looks older than that," said Sal, "a lot older. Ten years at least."

"That would put him in high school in 1960, around Charlie's age."

"Okay," said Mercer, "we need to confirm Wilson Shields' age."

"Easy enough," said Alice, and she turned to her keyboard and screen. She entered Wilson Shields' name. "Hmm," she said after a while. "Born in September 1955."

"Coulda fooled me," said Sal. "Is that really right?"

"That's what it says."

"But aren't we wasting our time on him? What could he have to do with this, really? The bodies are all on the Massey property, all connected to Evelyn, and especially Harold."

"Good point," said Robbie. Sal smiled over at him.

"Okay," said Alice, "just one more thing on him and I'll leave it alone. I think I can pull up some records here for the old school, find out when he was there." She started typing in information and then scrolling.

"It's just the obstructing thing," mused Mercer. "Did not like his attitude."

"That's weird," said Alice, "there's no record of him being at school. None at all."

"How about for ten years earlier?"

She looked back at the screen.

"Nope. This search is over decades. I looked for him by name. His sister is in here, about a year younger. And ..." She typed in more names. "Gloria and Gwen Massey." She typed in another name. "Oh! There's Dad and Mom. They were just starting school then."

"That's lovely, dear," said Sal.

"No record of Wilson Shields, though?" asked Mercer. "That's weird. I doubt you could homeschool in those days."

"Nope," said Alice. "And I know for a fact that the Shields family have always lived on the property we visited. They were never away."

"So, where the hell was he? This guy is kind of obstructing an interview, he looks ten years older than he is, and he's a phantom in the school records. Has he got a secret we need to uncover?"

"All right," said Alice, "let's talk to him. Sal, can you do a deeper dive on this too? See what you can come up with: Why in the world wasn't he at school? I'll talk to Mom and Dad about him, see if they remember anything."

"Sure," said Sal, "but I'm taking a half day later on. Michael isn't the best again."

"Shit," said Alice, "really?"

"Yeah, Aya is coming home on the weekend, so that will cheer him up, I guess."

"I want to go to the east end of town," said Mercer, who had paused for a moment and looked at Sal as if he wanted to say something, ask if he could be of any help, but apparently couldn't come up with anything. "Yeah, see where Charlie Eaton and his father lived, check out the route from the school to there."

"How about me?" asked Robbie.

"Um ..." said Alice and screwed up her face, "sorry, but you're back to your buddy, Constable Most, for now."

TEN MINUTES LATER, Alice and Mercer got into her cruiser in the parking lot beside the old station building.

"So, the, uh, second letter," said Mercer, "it had your name on it too."

"Got your seat belt on?" She started the engine.

"Alice, you can't ignore this. We are trying to conduct a thorough investigation and look into everything, and we're finding some awfully frightening stuff ... and we're leaving out the fact that two envelopes with inside information have been found ... *both* with your name on them."

Alice pulled out onto King Street Circle. "The old school was just west of here. It's been converted into apartments."

"Alice."

"Well, what do you want me to say? I didn't know the Masseys. I don't have a fucking clue why my name is on those envelopes, and it upsets me. Okay? If you can find a connection, go ahead."

"We have to actively search for one. *We*." He looked out the window. "I know there are things about your past that you aren't telling me."

Alice thanked God that she had been smart enough to keep him away from the interview at the Shields place, where Luke had actually been mentioned by name. Edwina had been so sweet about it. Saved her ass. It had been awfully kind. But what was Mercer insinuating? That things about her past were somehow connected to her name being on those envelopes?

"I'm not on trial here. I'm not being investigated."

"I didn't say you were."

"It feels like it sometimes. My personal life is my personal life. You and I have a connection of a sort." She felt her eyes welling up and cursed herself, holding her emotions back. "But that doesn't mean I'm required to tell you everything about myself. People need some secrets. You've got enough yourself."

"I told you mine."

He was right. She'd never been with a man who could argue better than this one. Usually, they were useless at it. Sometimes, he really pissed her off.

"I'll think about it," said Alice. "I'll think about why Evelyn Massey might have included me in all of this ... I promise."

"Thanks. Sorry."

She smiled when he said that northern word but turned her face away so he couldn't see. "Here's the old school, up here on the left." She pulled into the parking lot. It was a big brick building with a half dozen concrete steps leading up to a front door that still said Boys' Entrance. The girls' entrance was to the left.

"Put on some of that dreadful music. It'll really fit this place."

She couldn't suppress a laugh.

"Okay. Let's see."

She tapped on her phone and then slid the screen over to the music she now had in a playlist. A syrupy tune began, female voices crooning, "Sweetheart ... sweetheart." Then a bouncy guitar started. Alice and Mercer sat there looking at the school, imagining boys in crew cuts and sweaters and bobby-soxer girls with their bobbed hair in bows and skirts that reached the knees. The male lead vocal began, accusing a girl of two-timing him, the anger in the lyrics at odds with the benign voice and melody.

The screen on the phone read, *Bobby Curtola, "Don't You Sweetheart Me," 1961.*

"I'll bet everything at this place had a look of perfection on the surface in those days," said Mercer.

Alice imagined Charlie Eaton, runtish and lonely, far from perfect, coming down the steps out of the boys' entrance and heading along King Street, going eastward.

"Let's take the route he would have taken," she said.

She drove back through town and onto King Street Circle, past the police station, past the Shelter Café, and onto King Street East. There was a new school out that way without much architectural character, straight-lined, high-school minimalist. They turned onto Alice's street.

"He probably walked up our street and right past our house. That's the quickest way to the east end, to the subsidized housing up there, though it wouldn't have been subsidized in those days, just neglected. Oh, I should stop for a minute to talk to Mom and Dad about him and Wilson Shields. Coming in?"

"Yeah, of course."

They headed around to the back door, opening the fence gate first. It was a comfortable two-storey white stucco house with green gables. Mercer hadn't been here since Alice had invited him for supper … the time he had been stalking her, investigating who she was, who she really was. She hadn't appreciated that. Then he had revealed some important things he'd known about the Becky Prior case that he'd been keeping from her. She hadn't appreciated that either. She had taken him up to her bedroom and grilled him. But it had nearly turned into something else.

"Mom? Dad?" she called as she entered. "I'm home for a moment. I have someone with me. You remember Detective Mercer?"

Doreen Morrow came quickly toward them from the kitchen, fixing her hair and patting down her clothes, a short, lean woman in her early seventies, perfectly outfitted in a pair of slacks and a sweater.

"Oh! Of course. So lovely to have you home again, Mr. Mercer." She took his hand into both of hers.

"Thank you."

"Ralph!" she cried out, alarmingly loud. "Alice is here with a man. Detective Mercer!"

They headed into the living room, where Ralph Morrow, a former schoolteacher just like his wife, was ensconced in a comfortable chair reading a newspaper. The living room had a thick rug. Alice had taken off her shoes at the outside door, causing Mercer to follow suit.

"Perfect," said Ralph. "Good day, Mr. Mercer." He swept off his glasses as if to get a better look at the American.

"Good day, sir."

"You'll stay for lunch?" It was still a couple hours before noon.

"No," said Alice, "just stopping by with a few questions, Dad. For Mom too."

"Okay. Shoot." He set down his paper. Doreen sat in what appeared to be her own comfortable chair right next to him, and Alice and Mercer dropped down into the loveseat across from them, but a good couple feet apart.

"You were born in the early fifties, right, Dad?"

"February 25, 1951, said to be the coldest winter on record."

Doreen raised her hand. "And I came into this world three years later, January 25, 1954, likely just as cold, but I've never looked into it like Dad has."

"So, you would have been about nine in 1960, Dad. And Mom, you would have been six. You're just a couple years older than Gloria and Gwen Massey, right?"

"Yup," said Ralph. "I still can't get over this Massey thing. Evelyn? Evelyn Massey? With a body in her basement? You've got to be kidding me. Harold Massey a suspect? Come on!"

"I never said that, Dad. Never breathed a word remotely like that."

"Yeah, but you've been thinking it," said Doreen.

Alice closed her eyes for a moment before she spoke again.

"So, in 1960, you'd have been in about grade four or five, Dad, and maybe grade one or two, Mom?"

"Something like that, yeah."

"What we're interested in today," said Mercer, "is not so much hearing about Gloria Massey, who'd have been in kindergarten then, but a child named Wilson Shields. Perhaps not so much a child — we aren't sure of his age, actually — but he'd have been in school in some grade in 1960. And we're wondering about someone else too, a teenager who'd have been in grade ten back then, a boy named Charlie Eaton."

"Charlie Eaton, yeah," said Ralph, nodding. "He disappeared."

"Is that what this is all about?" asked Doreen. "Are you connecting that to this Massey thing? Word is you found another body on their property."

"I'm guessing it was Violet Massey," said Ralph. "Wow, this is getting fascinating."

Alice held her eyes closed for a few seconds this time. "Okay, Mom, Dad, please don't speculate about these things. You know I can't share police work."

"Right, dear," said Doreen.

"I just want to know what you might know about Charlie Eaton and Wilson Shields."

"Don't know a Wilson Shields," said Doreen.

"You don't? You must, Dad."

"Rings a bell, but not a clear one. Is he related to old Mrs. Shields — Edwina?"

"Her son," said Mercer. "Records say he was born in the fall of 1955."

"Records say?" asked Ralph. "That sounds like you don't trust them."

"Dad, stick to the questions please."

"Well, as I said, rings a slight bell, so maybe I knew him or of him when I was little, but I know for sure he didn't go all the way through school with me. I'd remember that."

"Curious," said Mercer. "You wouldn't happen to have any old school yearbooks?"

"As a matter of fact, we do!" Ralph pointed to a row of books at the bottom of a bookshelf behind Mercer, each with a colourful cover. "The Blue and Gold!"

Alice got up and walked behind the loveseat to the yearbooks, examined the spines to find the right years, and pulled them out. Then she went back to her father's chair and knelt on the floor beside him so he could see what she was looking at and started leafing through them.

"Okay, here's Charlie Eaton, grade ten, 1960."

Mercer and Doreen got up and came over, looking down over Alice's shoulder. Ralph leaned forward for a better view. Charlie Eaton looked back at them, hair uncombed, a blank look in his eyes.

"I'm surprised he's even in that yearbook," said Ralph. "My recollection is he disappeared the first or second week of school that year. It seems to me, if I'm remembering right, that he left school early that day too, in the middle of the day. Had a spat with a teacher, which was a common thing with him, actually, and he just took off, headed home likely. Never seen again. Very upsetting for the students when he was reported missing, I remember that too, that reaction, very clearly. Nothing like that had ever happened at the school before. Everyone was hoping he might be found. It probably didn't seem right to remove him from the school pictures."

Alice thumbed through more of the yearbook, looking at the younger grades. "There's Gloria Massey, kindergarten ... oh, there you are, Dad, in grade four!" Alice, Doreen, and Ralph laughed. "And there's Mom! Look, Mom."

"Wasn't I a cutie!"

"But ..." said Alice, looking back and forth through the pages, "where's Wilson Shields? He isn't in here."

"Look in the older grades," said Mercer.

Alice went through the whole yearbook, and there was no Wilson Shields.

"Maybe he was sick on picture day," said Doreen.

But Alice couldn't find him in any of the subsequent six years of yearbooks. And there wasn't one for any of the years in the late 1950s.

"Don't think they had them till 1960," said Ralph. "Maybe couldn't afford them till then, or maybe it just wasn't a thing."

"So," said Alice, looking at Mercer, "Wilson Shields doesn't appear to be in school in the 1960s." She turned back to her father. "But you think you remember him, a little?"

"Kind of, but I couldn't put a face to him. Don't know why."

"All right," said Alice, "we've got to go. Thanks, you two." Mercer reached down and helped her up, which made Doreen smile. Alice replaced the yearbooks, gave her mother a quick hug, and waved to her father before they went out the door.

"Come back anytime, Mr. Mercer!" they heard Doreen shout from inside.

BACK IN THE car, they just sat for a moment, Alice texting Sal to get her up to speed on what they'd just learned.

"Curious," said Mercer after a while.

"Yeah, but there's lots of explanations. Maybe Edwina didn't send him to school here for some reason. We'll have to ask him. He's a minor character in all of this, anyway."

"You're right, but I really do feel like there's something off about him. We have to get to the bottom of it."

"Okay," said Alice, "let's drive up the street here and continue along the route Charlie would have taken that day on his way home from school. Left in the middle of the day and vanished. Interesting."

She pulled out of the driveway and drove to the end of the street, then turned east and went over the railroad tracks. Soon they were passing low-rise apartment buildings, many looking battered and old.

"It's always been like this in this part of town. There hasn't been a new building here in ages, and this is where it's affordable for lower income people. That's why there's homelessness in our community now. They've built a new subdivision in the north end, but it's only for people with money, and for developers to make more money."

Mercer was looking out the window. "There's hardly anyone around."

It was true. The streets seemed almost deserted. They saw the odd person huddled on the little concrete porches on the matching old semi-detached homes, smoking in the freezing cold.

"Yeah. It's often like this in this neighbourhood. Especially in the middle of the day."

Alice imagined what it would have been like in September 1960, the first week of school. She thought too of what it said in Charlie Eaton's file. *He gets into a confrontation with a teacher that morning and leaves. He heads out. Someone said they saw him going east once he left the front doors. Likely toward home.*

Alice and Mercer looked out the car windows and didn't talk for a while as they drove through the sad streets. She knew Mercer was doing exactly what she was doing: imagining Charlie walking along here alone. Or had the young man even made it this far? And was he alone?

"So, it was likely a lot like this that day?" asked Mercer after a while. "Almost deserted? He'd have the streets basically to himself at that hour."

"Likely."

"So, if someone wanted to grab him, they could do it unseen."

"Why would they want to do that, though? Here? And *who* would do that here?"

"Somebody who had a beef with him."

"A pretty serious one, given that he then disappeared for good. Maybe he just ran away."

"I don't know who would have taken him, or why, I'm just speculating ... but, man, this would be perfect." Mercer looked up and down the nearly empty street again. "If someone saw him leave the school, followed him, was acquainted with him so they could get him into a vehicle, he could simply be nabbed without anyone seeing. Without any fuss. No yelling or screaming. He would vanish without a trace under those circumstances."

"All possible. But maybe we are just wasting our time. Where's our path to finding out who took him, if they did? It's more than sixty years ago. It's just like all the others. And how do we connect this to the others? This may have no connection at all."

"Well, maybe we can find a way to connect Charlie to our suspects instead of to our missing persons. Just directly to *them* ... to the deceased Caleb Carruthers, to Evelyn Massey, or better yet, if possible, to our number one guy, Harold Massey."

Alice's cellphone rang. She looked down at the screen, then put it on speaker.

"Yeah, Sal?"

"Located someone who worked for the school board when Harold Massey was chairman in the early sixties. Just got off the phone with him."

Alice could tell from Sal's voice that she was onto something.

"And?"

"We chatted for a while about Massey and his family. This guy got kind of emotional at times. He said Harold was a great man and his family was wonderful, and that he could not imagine them up to anything that wasn't good. I talked to him about Charlie

Eaton too, about him disappearing, and he said it had shocked the board and the whole community. I got your text about Wilson Shields while we were talking, and since we were wondering about Shields and his connection to all of this, I just kind of mentioned to this guy that while doing research into the Massey family, friends, and acquaintances, we'd encountered the fact that one of them, and I named him, didn't seem to be in the school yearbooks. So, at that point this guy grew very quiet. I even wondered for a moment if he'd hung up."

"Then what happened?" asked Mercer.

"Coming to it, Detective." She paused, almost as if to piss off Mercer. "When this guy's voice came back, it was a little shaky. This is a man in his late eighties. He'd been pretty composed up until then. He said he had a confession to make."

"A confession? What?"

"Coming to it, Detective." Another pause. "He said that all of Wilson Shields' records were expunged, and he doesn't know why."

"How could they even do that?" asked Alice.

"I don't know, I guess things were different in those days, if you knew the right people."

"The right people? Like the chairman of the school board?" asked Mercer.

"Yeah," said Sal, "when I pressed this gentleman, he said that he hoped he wasn't speaking out of turn, that he'd never told anyone this … but that the order to do this, to delete all Wilson Shields' school records, came from Harold Massey."

19

Wilson Shields

MERCER DIDN'T HAVE to convince Alice to drive out to the Shields farm — without warning Wilson they were coming this time. They both had a cop's unspoken instinct that Wilson Shields would be there, that his slightly aggressive, protective demeanour the last time they had seen him indicated he would be staying with his mother for a while. They grabbed a quick snack at a new shawarma restaurant just opened by a recent Syrian immigrant, Mercer getting the beef shawarma and fries, Alice a tabouli salad and baklava, and then she got the cruiser to the farm in no time, both of them eating and talking as they flew along, more Bobby Curtola music making Mercer cringe as he rode shotgun next to Alice.

Sure enough, Wilson's car was there, but when they knocked on the door, there was no response at first. Finally, they heard Edwina's voice.

"Coming!" she cried.

"Oh god, she's coming all the way out to us on her own," said Alice.

Mercer tried the door. It was unlocked, and they both entered. Edwina was wheeling toward them, only half way across the kitchen floor.

"Oh my gosh, I'm sorry," she said. "I was lying down on the sofa when you knocked, and it takes me a while to haul this carcass into the chair. But it's lovely to see you again. Alice. And to see you too, sir. Come in. Come, come!"

"We should have called first," said Alice.

"Oh nonsense, why do people do that all the time now? In my day, you just came by."

"We're actually here to see Wilson," said Mercer.

"And we're sorry to disturb you," added Alice. "This is Detective Mercer, helping out from, uh, another police service. We just thought we should speak to Wilson a little as well, see what memories he has pertaining to the Masseys. Is he here?"

"Oh," she said. "Wilson? Not sure where he is. Out on the land, probably. He's staying with me for a few days, you know, on account of this terrible Ev Massey stuff. Lovely boy."

"Out on the land?" asked Mercer.

Edwina smiled. "That's what we call it. Gone for a walk on the property. Don't know exactly where. You could likely follow his footsteps in the snow. It's getting a little fresh out there now, isn't it?"

The temperature had dropped a good twenty degrees overnight. Alice had been reminding Mercer to always bring his new toque and warm mitts whenever he went out, and he had them now. They thanked Edwina and headed out. The snow was packed in a path toward the barnyard and back, so they followed it, and when they reached the barn, they noticed that a couple lines of prints went around the building and past it toward a fence with an open gate that looked out onto the back acres. Only on a farm not in full use would a gap be left wide open like that. They followed the prints, curious about why there appeared to be more than one set, until they reached the crest of a hill. They stopped there, their breath forming big clouds in front of them, both of their faces red and stiff. Alice had on her fur-lined woolen police bomber hat with ear flaps. They could see the prints going down the hill and then veering toward a forest. They followed without speaking, but as they neared, unsure that they wanted to search this large wooded area for a long while to simply talk to a curious but possibly just marginal player in their investigation, Mercer called out.

"Wilson!" he shouted. "Wilson Shields?"

There was silence in the crisp cold air, the sort of air that seemed to swallow up sounds. They listened. Alice thought she heard something, movement in the woods. They walked closer, and as they entered the forest, they saw Wilson Shields coming toward them, rushing, in fact.

"Hello?" he yelled.

"Mr. Shields?" said Mercer. "It's Sergeant Morrow and Detective Mercer! We want a few words."

Shields kept moving toward them quickly, almost as if he were running from something. "I'll be right there! Wait for me where you are!"

He arrived in a few minutes, out of breath, and started moving out from the trees toward the field, but Mercer didn't want to follow.

"Can we just talk in here?" he asked. "There's a bit of a wind. I like the shelter."

He was right. The bitter cold was slightly lessened here at the edge of the woods.

"Okay," said Shields, but he didn't look happy about it. His eyes were shifty.

"We feel like we neglected you the other day," began Alice. "We should have asked for your thoughts about the Masseys too, especially Evelyn and Harold. You must have known them growing up."

"Yeah, of course I knew them, nice people."

"Can you expand on that?" asked Mercer. "You know what we're after here. Did they have any enemies? Anyone who might mean them harm, them and Violet Massey as well? And what did you think of Harold Massey? Ever see him lose his temper, want to hurt anyone? Any jealousy about Evelyn?"

"Look," said Wilson, and he sighed, "you are asking me about people who were adults when I was a kid. And once I was grown up, I was gone to university, and I've been working in the city ever since. I knew them, yeah, way back in the day, nice people as I said, but adults to me with adult problems. I don't know anything about their private lives or enemies they might have had. I don't have anything to contribute. Now, if you don't mind, I was —"

"What do you do for a living, Mr. Shields?" asked Mercer.

Shields paused. "Why do you need to know that?"

"Just answer the question, sir. You are being asked this by a police officer."

"An American." Shields turned to Alice. "Does he have the right to —"

"Do you want *me* to ask you?"

Shields paused again. "I'm a lawyer in the city, do mostly pro bono work. Helping those who can't help themselves?" He said it almost in a tone of reproof.

"That's admirable," said Alice. "Married? Kids?"

"No," said Shields quietly.

"What were you doing out here?" asked Mercer abruptly. "In the woods?"

Shields turned and regarded him. "What do you mean?"

"Exactly what I asked."

He shook his head and sneered. "I was walking *my* property, our property. I grew up here, you know. I love this land. Usually, when I come home, I just check on Mother and don't stay long. I try to come to see her every four or five days. I've got time to be out on the land this week, though, and she needs me to be around, considering what happened to her dear friend."

"You grew up here?" asked Alice.

"Uh, yeah, of course ... what kind of a question is that? Mom and Dad lived here from the time they were married in 1955, and he lived here before that, born on this farm. It's a very old Shields place."

"I understand your father passed a number of years ago," said Mercer, "so it's just you looking after your mother these days?"

"My sister lives on the west coast. She's about a year younger than me, visits, but rarely, maybe once every few years. Not that you need to know any of that either." He had been looking down. Now, he looked up at Mercer. "What the hell does this have to do with anything you're looking into?"

"Did you know Caleb Carruthers or Perry Scott?"

"No and no."

"How about Charlie Eaton?"

Shields looked uncomfortable. "Heard of him. I know he disappeared. He was older than me. Didn't know him."

"You went to school here?" asked Mercer.

"In town, yeah. Of course."

"Then why aren't you in any of the school yearbooks?" asked Alice, channelling her inner Mercer. She could almost feel the amusement her partner was hiding.

Shields paused for a long time this time. "I went to school here," he repeated.

"You know it's a crime to lie to the police, right?" asked Mercer.

"Do I have to say it a third time?"

"Okay, so you were in school here," said Alice. "But there's no record of your attendance. Why is that?"

"It's none of your business."

"Were you born in September 1955?" asked Mercer.

"Yes. I'm guessing you know that, so why are you asking?"

"Just confirming. And were you friends with Harold Massey, and did he have any reason to help you to —"

"I've answered your questions about the Masseys. You will recall that I'm a lawyer. You have no right to harass me. Or to bother my dear elderly mother. If you persist in —"

"If we find," said Mercer stepping up closer to Wilson Shields, so close that his breath, visible in the cold air, floated into his face, "that you had anything to do with any of this, in *any* way, we will find out. Your lack of cooperation is concerning."

"I have cooperated fully. I have responded to your questions. You just don't like the answers. Your probing is into my personal life, not into this case. Now, if you will excuse me?"

He didn't go back into the woods right away. He stood there until Alice and Mercer left and headed up the hill. Once or twice, they looked back and saw him standing there at the edge of the forest, until at one point they glanced back and he was gone, vanished like Perry Scott and Violet Massey and Caleb Carruthers and Charlie Eaton.

"We should say goodbye to Edwina, let her know we've left," said Alice as they neared the house. "Don't ask her anything about Wilson again, okay? It's not fair to her." Mercer nodded. This time, they entered first and then knocked on the inside of the door so Edwina wouldn't have to come their way.

"Hello?" called Alice. "Don't get up, Mrs. Shields, we'll come in."

"Oh, you're so kind."

They took off their boots and walked through the kitchen and up the couple of stairs into the living room, over to the sofa where she had righted herself to speak with them.

"Did you find him?"

"Yes," said Mercer. "You were right, he was out on the land, in the woods at the back."

"Oh!" she cried. "He always loved that forest. Why did you really want to speak with him again? Just about his memories of the Masseys?"

Alice felt like grinning. This old lady was as sharp as a tack.

"You know," continued Edwina when neither Alice nor Mercer responded, "these terrible things that you say happened, with that awful corpse in the fresh concrete in the Masseys' basement and dear Violet, wherever it was you found her, and these stories about Caleb Carruthers, they were before Wilson's time. He would have been just a little boy then, or younger." She laughed at that last thought, imagining her elderly son as a tyke. It was good to see some happiness on the old lady's face, thought Alice.

"Thank you so much for your help, Mrs. Shields," she said, and she gave Edwina her hand. The old lady took it in both of hers.

"You have been through so much, my dear," she said and held her tightly. "We all have our trials, though, don't we? You learn that when you live as long as I."

Alice didn't want to look at Mercer. "Thank you," she said quietly and pulled her hand back. They started to leave.

"Was he a bit cantankerous with you?" asked Edwina. "Not much help?"

"Yeah," said Mercer, "to be honest, he hasn't been very forthcoming."

"Well, he's had a time," said Edwina, looking sad.

"A time?"

"His own trials. You will just have to trust him. He was only a boy. Respect his privacy when it comes to, you know, personal issues. I would appreciate that too."

"What issues, if I may ask?" asked Mercer.

"No. No, I'm afraid you can't. And I hope that doesn't seem rude. Dear me, I'd hate to be rude to either of you. Either you, Alice, or a visitor in our area like yourself, Mr. Mercer. Certainly to the police! But it would be wrong to betray more confidences. Wilson is a grown man now, has been for some time." She laughed again, though this time perhaps a touch bitterly. "Wilson had issues, yes, personal ones. You ask about Harold Massey, well, he was very kind during those days. We didn't have much. Not like him and Ev. And he helped us financially during Wilson's issues. But no, I simply cannot betray my son, betray more confidences; that would have to come from him, though I assure you it is nothing you need concern yourselves with. And I know for a fact, an absolute fact, that Harold Massey had nothing to do with any of this. He was a marvellous man." She looked a little sad, though there weren't any tears welling in her eyes. Alice thought of how tough women had had to be in Edwina Shields' day, just like Delilah Morton had said. How strong.

"WE NEED TO find a way to talk to Wilson Shields at least once more," said Mercer when they were back in the car. "He may be a key to unlocking all of this. He knows something." Mercer looked toward the house. "And he doesn't deserve that mother of his."

"Bobby Curtola?" asked Alice as she settled into the driver's seat. "'Fortune Teller,' 1962?" Her hand was hovering over her cellphone.

20

The Last Two?

ALICE GAVE IN that night. When Mercer asked her to come home with him, she said yes right away, with as little emotion as possible, though she felt a bit of a thrill at how happy her answer seemed to make him. She also insisted, however, that they stop by the station on the way to retrieve the remaining two missing persons files so they could go over them that night. Mercer was delighted with that too. Fearing that he was about to barbecue something again, she got him to pick up some sushi at a new place on King Street Circle just a couple of spots over from the Shelter Café while she grabbed the files.

She led the way out to his place, resisting the excitement she was feeling, looking in her rearview mirror and enjoying how far behind his Ford Escape was at times. She had been amused at what he had said when they got into the cruiser to go home from the Shields place. He had put his hand on hers as she reached for her phone to introduce another tune and asked, "Could we maybe not play any music?" They hadn't talked much about what they had learned, or suspected, from their chat with Wilson Shields. They didn't need to — they each knew what the other was thinking. Or at least most of it. That kind of pissed her off about this man. But she kind of liked it too.

What he was turning over in his mind, she assumed, was a list of suspects with Harold Massey at the top, Evelyn lingering somewhere on it but highly unlikely, Caleb Carruthers bouncing on and off it, perhaps a suspect in a death or two but obviously not his own, though maybe his death had occurred because of his murderous actions, killed by the honourable Harold Massey? And how was Charlie Eaton connected to any of this, if at all, and what in the world could Wilson Shields have to do with it, and if nothing, then why was he being such a shithead about it? And what had he been doing out there in the woods? She also knew that both she and Mercer were aware that there had been more than one set of footprints going out to the forest.

They ate the sushi at the little kitchen table with the two files spread out between them, careful not to get any soya sauce or wasabi on the sheets, pointing at various details with their chopsticks.

This time, they looked at the last file first: 1962, Shirley Ezinicki. She of the terrible beehive hairdo and cat eye glasses. "Says here," said Alice, popping a California roll into her mouth but then continuing to talk, "that she was born in 1933, so twenty-nine years old. Single. Old maid for that time."

"She looks like a tight-ass," said Mercer.

"Nice."

"Just being honest, not on social media here."

"Yeah, maybe you're right. She doesn't look like a bowl of fun, though that's another reason you'd wonder how she could get into any trouble. Says she disappeared in June. Was renting a house in the country, hey, just like you, Mercer. In fact ..." Alice read a bit more. "Well, not too close to here ... but ... oh my gosh ... not far from the Masseys."

They looked at each other.

"Got some, uh, wasabi, right there," said Mercer and he wiped her cheek near her lips with his napkin. He had done that before when they were eating here. Alice wondered if it was a bit of a come-on, though she didn't mind.

"Thanks," she said. She looked down at the file again. "Disappeared without a trace, just gone ... It was one of the last days of school. She simply didn't show up that day. Search was done of her property, found nothing. Search was done of the surrounding area, found nothing ... not very thorough though, just a ground search."

"So, we have a connection concerning her to what we're looking into — she was living out in the country in the same area. Exactly how far from the Masseys?"

"About three k."

"What's that?" Mercer was impatient, not wanting to calculate.

"A couple of miles, five-minute drive, half hour or so walk."

"Likely about same distance to some of the others, to all of those ladies we talked to, right? Though a bit farther from the Mortons?"

"Yup."

"Interesting."

Alice dug out a piece of the spicy dragon crab roll with her chopsticks and held it near her mouth while she looked at the sheet again. "She taught the early grades, so kindergarten, one, and two. Oh, that means she might have had Gloria Massey as a student. Gloria said she knew Ezinicki was a teacher."

"She may have taught Wilson Shields too."

"No, he wasn't there, remember?"

"But he said he was."

"That's not what the records say."

"As adjusted by Harold Massey. Shields has a sister too,

remember, he said she lives on the west coast and doesn't come home often, a bit younger? Maybe she was in Shirley Ezinicki's classes too."

"Maybe. Let's bear all these things in mind and look at our last guy."

She glanced across and saw Mercer also poised with a crab roll hovering near his open mouth, in imitation of her. She smiled and ate hers, and he ate his.

Dr. Albert Johnson was fifty-one years old at the time of his disappearance in 1961. They examined his photograph again, a respectable-looking man with a moustache and glasses and an air of fatherly competence, as innocuous as they come, a small-town doctor.

"How many doctors would there have been in town in those days?" asked Mercer.

"I'm guessing maybe two, at the most."

"So even if there were two, this guy would likely be the senior guy, unless the other one was pretty old, so there's a good chance he doctored folks in the countryside around here, the Masseys and all the others. Suspects, missing persons, them all. Probably birthed many of the kids too."

"Good point."

"What about the circumstances of his disappearance?"

"Uh, vanished in July 1961. Was out on house calls."

"Man, that *was* another time. Who was his last call?"

"Let's see." Alice looked down and read for a while. "Oh my god," she finally said.

"What?"

"It was Delilah Morton."

Alice tried to read Mercer's thoughts, and she could tell he was doing the same. Neither of them was a fan of the brash Mrs. Morton, entering her nineties but able to pass for seventy-five.

She had been hard on Alice during interviews, both recently and during the Becky Prior case, and definitely seemed to harbour a secret or two. There was reason to believe, as well, given the name that had stuck with her, that she had been a bit of a handful in her younger days. Alice recalled some of Delilah's biting comments during the group session at the Shields farmhouse, some of which she had shared with Mercer.

"Cops talked to her?" he asked.

Alice looked down at the file again. "Yeah ..." She read a bit more. "Says she was upset, knew nothing helpful. She said he had seen her about a 'women's issue,' that's what it says here, and that he had seemed fine when he left and told her he was done for the day." Alice read more and in the near-silence could hear Mercer drumming his fingers on the table. "His car was found at the end of her sideroad." She looked up at Mercer. "That's Ben and Beth Morton's place now." She went back to the file. "Delilah told them that once he left she hadn't watched him drive away and that the spot where his car was abandoned was obscured by a couple of old maple trees and a good third of a kilometre away anyway. His car wasn't noticed until later that evening when Ebb came home from an Orange Lodge meeting he'd left for shortly before Dr. Johnson had arrived. That was it, the good doctor was never seen again, not a trace of him."

"And this is just past the end of my sideroad, so not that close to the Massey place but out here in country nevertheless."

"That's correct."

"Which means, as we suspected, he was likely the Masseys' doctor, too."

"Well, we don't know that, but probably, yeah. We need to confirm."

"So, now we have a connection to Harold Massey for every

single one of these disappearances, either direct or indirect. And he has a connection to our reluctant Mr. Shields too."

"Yeah, though maybe we can say the same thing about Evelyn. If she were a man, wouldn't you be just as suspicious of her?"

"Maybe. But she isn't, and he is the more direct connection to several of these people, not her."

"But she wrote the notes."

Mercer paused. "Yes. There's that."

"Is it a male thing to think that women are nearly incapable of murder? Especially serial murder? And yet, you guys sure as hell think we are guilty of a lot of other things, pretty devious things."

"Touché," he said, though his pronunciation wasn't remotely French.

"You know what they say about a woman's wrath."

"How about this woman?" he said, nodding at her.

"Which one?" she asked, though she knew whom he meant.

"The one across the table from me right now. You told me you'd think about why those letters, from a woman, were addressed to you. It's part of the case, not an unreasonable thing to ask of you. We could do that now, together."

She gazed at him for a while. "I'm ready for bed," she finally said.

"Oh, that's so unfair."

THEY RARELY TALKED much in his bedroom afterward. But this time they did, at least for a little while, before he drifted off to sleep, though their conversation wasn't about them, of course, or about her secret.

"So, you've got five people disappearing in five years in this community," said Mercer, "and no one is thinking something is terribly wrong?"

"I guess they were spaced out over those years, and anyway, no one here would ever suspect that they were connected, or think there was a ... uh ..."

"Serial killer. You can say it. But why wouldn't anyone suspect that? I mean, even consider it a possibility?"

"We just wouldn't, not here. That doesn't happen here. It's not who we are."

"Isn't it?" Mercer sighed. He stared up at the ceiling as if continuing this line of thought was pointless. "We need to find out what attracts Wilson Shields to the forest on his property."

"Probably just likes to walk there, like he said."

"I agree, probably, but it's something I want to check off our list. Just find out what he's doing. Who knows, maybe he's meeting someone? And if it's just a walk in the woods every now and then, that's fine; that helps us set him aside as a possible person of interest."

"There was more than one set of footprints going out and back."

"Yeah, and every one of them his."

"He's going there often."

"Yup."

"I don't want to alert him in any way or to upset Edwina, so we can't just drive out there and tail him. And yet, if he's up to something, we need to know about it." She paused for a moment. "But there's a back way."

"Huh?"

"You can access the Shields family's property from a back road. It runs along the far side of their forest. I can get Robbie to go out there. He'd be overjoyed to get away from Constable Most again, even if it means staking out a whole forest in the freezing cold. He can just wait there camouflaged by the trees, not far from where we saw Wilson. Just wait like a deer hunter and see what he sees."

"I like it."

"Thought you would."

SHE WAS ABLE to get away that night without him knowing again, though she almost didn't. She woke up at around two in the morning and found herself wrapped up in his arms, her own around him this time too. For a moment, she savoured it, listened to him breathing, thought of the trials in his mind, his regrets, his hopes. Troubles, like her. But she slid out, got up, and made her way downstairs in her phantom northern way.

Robbie will be on this by the time you are awake, said her note. *Hope your dreams were sweet. Had to go. See you tomorrow.*

She drove home crying, thinking not of Mercer but of Luke. Nights at the farmhouse made her do that. She was thinking that perhaps the worst thing was that she'd never told him. Alex had asked her, and she'd said yes. It had seemed at the time an irresistible thing. She had wanted to call Luke many times, but she had told herself that he would have known anyway, that word would have been out, and it would just involve pain, horrible pain for him, and what was the point? Later, she had wanted to call him immediately afterward, after what Alex had done. But she hadn't done that either. When she'd heard the news the next morning, it had all just seemed so stupid, that was the worst part. Stupid on his part and on hers. Stupid on Alex's too. But she didn't give a shit about him anymore.

She thought of Mercer then. He was just like her. She knew it. Just like her and not like her at all, but that was perfect. He loved her. She knew that. Whatever she felt, though, she was keeping down like the boy with his finger in the dike.

When she got home, slipping past her parents' room like a teenager, hearing one of them turn over —and she knew which one — as if they were aware she was there, she got into bed but couldn't sleep. Then, for the first time, she let herself think about why her name was on those envelopes. But that didn't last long. She was worried that she knew why. So she stopped. But she couldn't sleep either. There was a short story collection called *Runaway* on her bedside table. She read it until the sun rose.

21

In the Woods

THEY HAD ALREADY finished their morning meeting, Sal there bright and early like an angel with more doughnut bits and coffee, Mercer late and bedraggled and displeased and unable to get Alice to make much eye contact, when Robbie called. Earlier, the sight of ambitious young Constable Most alone — strutting around the station, his nearly shaven head on display, his leers at the few female police officers barely hidden, his patriotically tattooed arms on display below his black-and-blue short sleeves — had amused Alice and Sal to no end. He looked so lonely, so in need of an audience. Alice had plucked Robbie from his grasp before Most could partner with him on the early shift, and Robbie had rushed out to the far end of the Shields place, parked his unmarked car on the back road, and been on the job before you could say "freedom."

Alice turned on her cellphone's speaker.

"Sergeant Morrow?" Robbie's voice on the other end was quiet but sounded tense.

"Constable Trew."

"Reporting from the Shields family's forest, ma'am."

"We can barely hear you. Can you please speak up?" Sal interjected.

"My apologies, Constable Haddad, but I have the person of interest in view."

They all leaned forward.

"What's he doing?"

"It's hard to say, Detective Mercer. He came into the forest not long after I arrived. That was pretty early. I'm camouflaged behind a large maple tree and under a grove of bushes of unidentified nomenclature. There's a valley in here in the forest, and I'm halfway down on the back road's side. There's a creek running through the woods at the bottom of the valley, and our person of interest crossed that water toward me and is now walking back and forth on this side of the creek no more than one hundred metres from me."

"That's just a bit over one hundred yards," said Sal quietly.

"That's correct, Constable Haddad. Thank you for keeping Detective Mercer in the loop."

Alice wanted to laugh out loud, but she held it back and didn't look at Mercer.

"And our person of interest appears to be casting his eyes toward the ground, walking back and forth over an area about a dozen metres square."

"No need to convert," said Mercer quickly and through his teeth toward his two colleagues.

"Wait a minute ... he's dropped down onto his knees ... he looks like he's praying ... or something."

"Praying?"

"Yes, Detective Mercer. He has assumed a praying position, and he isn't moving."

"Okay, we're coming," said Alice, "and we're bringing shovels."

Alice drove the cruiser even faster than usual, Sal riding shotgun and Mercer crammed into the back seat once more, the soft sounds of Oscar Peterson's magnificent piano in 1959 playing in their midst, his fingers lightly dancing on the keyboard, all three of them listening instead of talking, as if they were worried that they somehow might be heard — and perhaps also to calm themselves. When they arrived at the snow-packed back road and parked behind Robbie's vehicle, he was nowhere to be seen, and it worried them. They couldn't see or hear him as they entered the forest, either.

"Maybe we shouldn't have sent him alone," whispered Sal.

All three of them had shovels.

Alice was thinking about their concern that Wilson Shields was meeting someone out here. But if so, why was he praying? Was he in some sort of cult? She was praying too now, praying that she would soon see Robbie Trew's handsome young face looking back at her.

The forest floor rose slightly upward, and they tramped through it, last night's snowfall gathered in a pure white bed on the ground, the grey air frigid. They reached the crest of the hill and looked down toward the water. Someone was there, just this side of the creek, on his knees, looking down at something or someone.

Oh god, thought Alice.

But it was Constable Trew, and he was unharmed. In fact, when he heard them approach, he turned and smiled. He spoke up too, an indication that Wilson Shields was long gone.

"This is where he was. And this was what he was looking down at. I've cleared the snow away here, but it just seems like regular forest floor underneath."

"Let's find out," said Mercer.

Alice instantly wielded her shovel, driving her spade's point hard into the partly frozen earth, softened by the recent thaw, using her big police boots to power her stabs. Mercer followed suit, and when Robbie offered to employ Sal's shovel, she smiled and handed it over. They dug for ten minutes or so without finding anything, the digging a little easier as they got deeper, and then Robbie paused for a while, obviously wondering if they should stop. But then Alice hit something.

It wasn't a ping like the sound they had heard at Violet Massey's grave in the little wooded area up on the hill near the family plot on the Massey property, when Robbie's shovel had met the metal on the animal crate. It was just a clunk. A clunk and a crack. But it stopped them all.

Mercer snapped on gloves, knelt down, and felt around where Alice had reflexively pulled back her shovel. When his hands came out of the cold dirt he was holding a bone, cracked in the middle. Alice knew instantly what it was. And Sal gasped. But they let Mercer speak.

"Human," he said quietly. "Clavicle. Male, I think, young male, teenage."

They didn't start digging again for a full minute, and no one said anything, but then they all resumed, and before long they found a skull. When Mercer picked it up, he examined it for a moment like it was Yorick's and then said, "Likely from the same victim, nose broken." He gently set it down, and they started digging again, Mercer and Alice near each other and Robbie about five feet away. The two of them found nothing else, but Robbie soon located a few additional bones and another skull, which stopped them all in their tracks once more. Mercer went over to what Robbie had found, but this time, he merely outlined the remains with his boot and delicately extricated them, as if he, this tough New York homicide detective, had had enough of touching these gruesome finds.

"I think this victim is bigger. I think he's male too, but older. And the skull doesn't look damaged."

A teenage male and an older male. Charlie Eaton and Dr. Albert Johnson.

But no one said that. There was no proof, just facts they knew in their hearts. Secrets unearthed. *Where*, thought Alice, *is Shirley Ezinicki? Here too?* She looked around in the forest. They weren't digging anymore, and there were no sounds in the woods, only the freezing wind blowing lightly through the trees. Then they heard the howl of coyotes. One started, and then the others joined in, as they always did — an evil sound, but pathetic too, like nature crying.

"Is it just me, or does it seem like you never used to hear them during the day?" said Alice. Sal and Robbie nodded.

"Let's keep going," said Mercer, and he dug his shovel into the hard ground again, slamming his boot onto it with even more force, it seemed, than before, as if he needed to get deeper into the earth than his own strength would allow. "Who knows what else we're going to find."

"No," said Alice. She didn't shout, but it almost seemed like she had. She was looking at Sal, standing there without a shovel in her hand but appearing exhausted. A better word might be traumatized. Alice knew what her dear friend was feeling. She didn't know how many more bodies she could take either. What they were unearthing, almost daily now, just seemed wrong. Something was horribly wrong. She needed a break. So did Sal. And maybe Mercer and Robbie did too, though neither of them, she was sure, were about to acknowledge it.

"There's a pile of paperwork to do now," said Alice. "Not just about this. I've been avoiding important desk work for weeks." She sighed. "We need a break from all of this too." She stared down at the bones. "Some perspective." She glanced at Sal, who had now actually turned away from the site. "Let's get someone else to come out here and dig more." She held up her hand to Mercer when she saw he was about to speak, obviously in protest. "Dig a whole lot more." She looked back at him. His shoulders slouched, but then he nodded.

"You can't leave these skulls, these bone fragments, like this," said Mercer after a pause. "Unless someone were to stand guard over them until the other excavators get here."

"I will," said Robbie instantly, dreams of more time away from Elwin Most obviously dancing in his head.

"No," said Alice. "Let's bag what we've found so far. Mark the spots exactly. Constable Trew, could you go to my cruiser and get some evidence bags from the trunk, please? There's some tape, chalk, and evidence markers in there too."

The others sat plunk in the wet snow and didn't say anything until he returned. Then they marked the site, the graves, and left. They got into the cruiser and closed the doors. Robbie pulled away in front of them, disappearing on the forest road once he rounded the next curve.

"I'm guessing you'll call your chief directly about this," said Mercer in the back seat. "Ask for as many people as can be spared on this dig? Right now?"

"He's away," said Sal without looking back.

"Away? Does that even matter? I'd let him know even if he's in Cancun."

"Good guess," said Sal. "He likes to go there." She looked down at her watch. "But no, he's just away for the afternoon."

"How do you know that? I thought I saw his car in the lot this morning?"

"Because it's Thursday, and he has a thing in the afternoon every Thursday. He goes to a school or has coffee with citizens and shoots the breeze."

"Shoots the breeze?" said Mercer, his voice rising. "Where? What school? What restaurant? Let's drive over there right now and tell him. I'd like ten men on the job and right away."

"Men?" Sal's voice was quiet and a bit sarcastic.

"No," said Alice.

"No?"

'I think that's what she said," said Sal.

"Chief Smith doesn't like to be disturbed on Thursday afternoons," said Alice. "If he's not at a school or having coffee, if he can't get one of those scheduled, he sometimes just takes time to go home and be with his wife."

"I think it's nice," added Sal.

"Nice? Doesn't like to be disturbed?" said Mercer, and this time he was indeed loud. "We have human remains in that forest back —"

"And they aren't getting up and walking anywhere."

"Good point, Sal," said Alice. She started the engine.

They could hear Mercer sigh so loudly that it sounded like a word, and not a pleasant one.

"I'll let him know in the morning," said Alice.

"Good thought," said Sal.

"The morning!" exclaimed Mercer. "The morning?"

"Yeah, he likes to go to bed early, so there's no sense in even leaving him a message until tomorrow."

Chief Gordie Smith, somewhere just south of seventy, he of the encyclopaedic knowledge of heavy metal music and the cassette collection in his almost-always-closed office to prove it, didn't like to be disturbed, generally, about serious matters his police officers had to deal with on a regular basis. He often gave the impression that he was disgusted that such matters had to be dealt with and that there had been a day — his day — when such things had been rare indeed.

"I'll let a staff sergeant know," said Alice. "They'll send whomever they can out soon." She reached for her cell.

"I'll do it," said Sal. She took out her phone and made the call, politely asking the staff sergeant on duty if he could do "whatever he can" to send "as many officers as might be spared" to the site.

She described what they had discovered and what had to be done.

"Whoever they send out to dig needs to be cautious," said Mercer, leaning forward as if dictating what he was saying to Sal, "have a lookout, make sure they don't encounter Wilson Shields. But if they do, detain him."

"Didn't need to tell her that," whispered Alice as Sal started saying almost exactly what Mercer had worried she might leave out.

Mercer leaned back, and Alice hoped he was doing so sheepishly.

"Maybe we should just pick up Shields now," said Sal when she hung up.

"No." Alice shook her head solemnly. "It wouldn't be fair to Edwina. I don't want to take him in her home. That would be just so, so horrible for her. Think of what we'd be arresting him for. Serial murder, or at least hiding evidence pertaining to it."

"And," said Mercer, sitting back up, "we don't actually have any real proof against him, anything that would stand up in court, other than that there are bodies on his property. And if those bones belong to whom we think they belong, then these people disappeared more than sixty years ago. Wilson Shields was just a child then."

"So he says," said Sal.

"So the records say," said Alice, "and that's what matters. For now. No, we can't take him at this point."

"We should come back tomorrow," said Mercer, "late in the morning, once these sites have been more thoroughly dug. That will put us in a better position because we'll know what else lies beneath the surface, how many other dead bodies may be here."

Alice pulled the cruiser out onto the road, gunning the engine a little, as if to drown out even the mention of that thought.

No one said anything for a while as they drove along the back road through the forest, the tires crunching the snow beneath them.

"Tomorrow morning, we can stay in the forest until Wilson shows up," said Alice once they had gone a few miles. "Seems like he comes to the woods every day. We'll confront him then, far away from his mother but with full evidence of what's been covered up out there. Put him on the spot, shock the hell out of him, and see what he has to say."

"I like it," said Mercer.

"He knew they were there," said Sal so quietly that they could barely hear her. "Wilson did. The bones."

The others didn't respond.

Alice didn't have the heart to put on any music as they sped back to town in the grey of that noon hour. It just wouldn't be right to play Paul Anka or the Four Lads right now. Not even Hank Snow. Ronnie Hawkins and the Hawks, maybe, but perhaps they would fit too well! The sky seemed even lower than it often was in the winter.

Mercer went home after they reached the station, and Alice and Sal went to their offices and didn't say anything more about the case for the rest of the day, though they noticed when four officers left wearing heavy boots and carrying shovels.

Alice drove home at exactly 5:00 p.m., dreading what else they would know by tomorrow morning, what would be found either in the ground or, eventually, in the mind of Wilson Shields. In a way, though, if she were really honest, she was both dreading it and excited about it. She knew Hugh Mercer felt the same way. She watched an episode of another Scandinavian crime drama with her parents, Doreen exclaiming, "Dear me!" every now and then but never taking her eyes from the screen, and Ralph musing, "Seems about right!" a couple of times. When Alice got into bed, she imagined Hugh was with her. Just with her.

Luke's photograph looked down on her in the dark as she fell asleep.

22

A Young Boy's Nightmare

THE MORNING APPEARED to come quickly — so quickly that it barely seemed like she'd slept. She woke to the sound of a text but rolled over for a few minutes until she heard another text ping. She sat up in bed, conscious again of Luke's eyes looking at her, and read the first message. It was from the staff sergeant. The four officers had dug for hours in the forest yesterday and were back there this morning, young Constable Robbie Trew with them.

Alice checked the other text. It was from Sal.

Taking the day off. Sorry.

Both messages worried her. She wanted details in the first one. And the brevity of the second one was concerning. Was it Michael again? Sal had taken time off several days over the last few weeks. Alice loved Sal and her family and knew how dearly Sal loved her husband, so she prayed things were all right.

There had been no word from Mercer, but he was at the station before she arrived. They immediately headed for her cruiser. By the time they reached the Shields woods, the men would have had all of yesterday's daylight and some of this early morning's to dig, hopefully long enough to uncover anything else of interest that was beneath the forest floor. Alice and Mercer didn't say much on the way out to the countryside or play any music, just chatted a little about the skulls and the fact that neither of them held out hope that tests would reveal much more about them. The remains had obviously been in the ground a long while, so little or no DNA would likely be found, just as was the case with the skeleton discovered in the Masseys' basement. Both of them knew to whom those two skulls belonged anyway.

"The teenager's shows he took some sort of beating," said Mercer. "The nose is almost flattened. The older man's doesn't appear to have sustained any damage at all, not facially or to any other part of the skull, which is curious. Two different sorts of deaths? Does that indicate two different murderers? Or are both even homicides?"

The line of cruisers parked along the back road looked like a cop convention was taking place somewhere in the nearby woods: black vehicles on white snow.

"I hope people around here aren't too nosy," said Mercer, "and won't be calling up the Shields house and telling them there are a bunch of police vehicles parked at the far end of their property. We don't want Wilson to flee."

Alice didn't say anything. She knew that what Mercer was worried about was a real possibility. Word would have spread up the country roads quickly.

They almost ran through the forest toward the excavation site. When they reached the crest of the hill, they could see the officers near the spot, but none of them were digging, just leaning on shovels. When they got closer, they could see why. The officers appeared to be finished. They had unearthed a huge area, the length and width of several graves, and had dug deeply. There was a small collection of bones on a canvas sheet nearby.

"Constable Trew?" asked Mercer as they arrived and spotted Robbie. "What's up?"

Alice bent down and looked warily at the bones. There were only a few, but she knew they were all human. Several matched, but there were different sizes. A teenager's and an older male's.

"Detective Mercer," said Robbie. "Great to see you, sir." He turned to Alice and tipped his cap. "Ma'am." He was sweating in the subzero morning. "We encountered these items you see here, but that was all yesterday. We haven't found anything since then. I think this is it." The wind had come up, and they could feel it and hear it swooping through the forest.

Alice looked around in the trees. Where was Shirley Ezinicki?

"Have you posted someone at the edge of the forest on the fence-line?"

"Yes, ma'am. No sign of Mr. Shields so far." He looked over her shoulder. "Oh, maybe I've spoken too quickly. There's Constable Wong!"

They all turned and saw a young police officer running in their direction. He had gotten over the creek and was puffing up the hill through the woods on a beeline toward them. His face was lit up. As he neared, he called out to them in as quiet a voice as he could use without it projecting backward toward the edge of the forest from which he had come.

"He's coming!" he said. "He's coming!"

"All right," said Alice, "everyone down! Move back and get down, behind trees!"

"What about the bones, the open site?" asked Robbie.

"Leave them," said Mercer. "Just take your shovels with you. But spread out when you hide, so you are on all sides of him. We can't let him get away. He's not a young man, but he may try to run! And he may be dangerous. We have no idea if he's armed. Everyone be careful." He paused. "I would encourage you all to unholster your weapons and be ready." He glanced at Alice. "If that's okay."

Alice knew that back in the place Mercer and his countrymen called "America" that question wouldn't even have been asked. She also knew that Mercer wouldn't have asked it a few months ago. She appreciated that.

"Okay," said Alice. "But the use of firearms is our last, last, last resort. Only if he points something at you and seems ready to shoot. If he runs, we chase first. We'll get him."

The others nodded.

In a minute, they were all hidden, and a near-silence engulfed the forest again, just the frigid wind blowing once more. A few moments after that, they saw Wilson Shields approaching, his breath in big clouds as he navigated his way over the creek and then up the slight incline toward the site. He was toque-less and mitt-less in this cold January day, though his thick coat looked warm and had a hood, pulled back as it was. He did not appear to be armed. He seemed to be talking to himself as he approached, saying something indistinguishable about his mother, worry in his voice. His gaze was cast on the ground before him — he was so deep in thought that he barely appeared to notice his surroundings. It struck Alice how exhausted his face looked, with the deep creases in his forehead and the dark, sagging circles under his eyes: worn-out and trauma-wounded. It wasn't until he was about ten metres from the excavation that he actually looked at it. His eyes bulged, and an expression of shock came over his face, as if he were witnessing something horrific — a murder, a heinous act.

"Oh my god!" he cried.

Mercer stood up and came out from behind the tree where he and Alice had been hiding.

"Wilson Shields?" he said. "Remain calm. We have a number of officers surrounding you."

The others came forward now, all of them with their hands near their unholstered weapons, all of them looking nervous.

Shields took a step back, glanced in the direction he had come, and then eyed all the police officers. He looked like he wanted to run. "Okay," he finally said in a voice so quiet and so distraught that it was difficult to hear him. He also raised his hands over his head.

"No need for that, Wilson," said Alice. "Just assure me that you are unarmed."

"Why would I be armed?" he asked, as if this were an incredible idea. "I'm not hunting anything."

Alice nodded toward Robbie. He secured his service weapon in his holster and advanced toward Shields. "Sorry, sir," he said to him and patted him down. Robbie turned to Alice and Mercer. "He's clean," he said.

"Thank you, Constable Trew." Alice sighed. "You can all stand down. In fact, you can bag this further evidence and be on your way. We'll take things from here."

The men started doing as they were ordered.

"Step this way, please, Mr. Shields," said Mercer, motioning toward a group of large stumps not far away. "You no doubt suspect we have some serious questions for you. We can chat over here."

Good idea, thought Alice. *Get him out of the line of sight of these gruesome graves. It will help him answer things more soberly.*

All three of them sat on the stumps.

"I think it's time for you to be honest with us, Mr. Shields," said Mercer. "About a great many things."

Alice read him his rights, and Shields made no motion to indicate that he didn't want to answer questions. The lawyer in him knew exactly where he stood. In fact, he instantly responded.

"I didn't do this."

"Well, Wilson, it appears as though you were involved."

"I was just a boy." He wouldn't look at them.

"Were you?" asked Mercer.

Shields looked up at him. "What do you mean by that? These people in these graves died in 1960 and 1961. I was only about five or six years old then."

Alice went pale. "Wilson, what are you saying? Are you telling us that you know who these remains belong to?"

He wouldn't look at them again. "Yeah."

Alice swallowed. "Who?"

"Charlie Eaton ... and Dr. Johnson."

It took even Detective Hugh Mercer, formerly of the New York 1st Precinct Homicide Squad, a few seconds to gather himself.

"How do you know that?"

Wilson Shields sat on the stump, and his eyes shifted back and forth, as if searching for something in his brain. A memory? Perhaps a trauma? Or a lie?

"I saw him."

"Saw who, Wilson?"

"Mr. Massey."

"Harold Massey?"

"Yeah."

"Saw him do what?"

"I have always loved this forest," replied Wilson. "I started coming here not long after I could walk, I think. All alone. I played games that I invented, ran about ... really innocent and free. I know they say this land isn't ours, that it belongs to the Indigenous people who lived here before, and I think they're right. But that didn't matter to my little mind, and even now this just feels like home, especially in here. Like God is looking after me, God who doesn't care about what belongs to whom. God who loves us, loves me." He lifted his reddening eyes and looked around the forest. A tear fell onto his cheek, and he sighed and seemed to steel himself. He glanced at Mercer but then turned to Alice. "Harold Massey. Coming down the hill behind here with the tractor and the old wooden hay wagon, the fall of 1960." He looked in the direction of the graves. "I know the exact day. September 10, 1960. I saw him. I was playing back here. Well, I actually wasn't really playing that day. I had come here because I was very upset. Very, very upset. After what Eaton had done to me." He stopped and didn't seem like he wanted to go on. He dropped his eyes toward the forest floor and wiped them with a fist.

"Can you talk about that?" asked Alice. "That last bit? What do you mean by that part about what Charlie Eaton did to you? Or do you want a lawyer now?"

Wilson raised his eyes back to her, ignoring Mercer. "You know about trauma, Alice."

Alice froze and just stared at Shields for a moment. *Stick to your job*, she told herself. "This isn't about me. We all have issues of some sort."

"Secrets," said Shields, and he put his face into his hands and cried. They let him weep for a while. His shoulders heaved. Alice reached for a tissue in her parka and offered it to him, but he pushed her hand away and gathered himself, wiping his eyes with the back of his thick winter coat. "Charlie Eaton was a fucking pervert."

"What does that mean, exactly?" asked Mercer.

Shields raised his eyes and stared at Mercer for the first time, looking daggers at him. "He touched me."

"Can you —" began Alice quietly.

"I was *five years old!*" Shields shouted so loudly that it echoed in the forest, and Robbie Trew and his colleagues turned as they were walking up the hill away from the site to look back for a moment.

"When and how?" asked Mercer after only a slight pause.

"What were the circumstances? Did you tell anyone?"

"The circumstances?" snarled Shields. "The circumstances? Does it matter?" He stared down at the frozen ground. "It was ... in the schoolyard, first day of school, 1960. I was in kindergarten. I was waiting for my mother to pick me up. He drew me aside, around the back ... and he touched me. Then he told me to tell no one."

"Did you?" asked Alice.

"Not for a while, not for a day or two, then I told Mother."

"And what —"

"And then she told Harold Massey."

Mercer and Alice exchanged glances.

"She didn't tell your father?" asked Alice.

"No. That wouldn't have gone well. Not that it went well anyway. But maybe it would have made my parents' marriage even worse than it was already. Not that it was horrible, it was just, you know, not a love story. But who is to judge what the response to a pervert attacking a child should be anyway? Mother and Harold Massey had a thing in high school, even though he was about five years older. She loved him, always spoke highly of him, even after she was married. I remember seeing them having long chats at strawberry suppers at the church and at Christmas carol services. She could confide in him, I guess, more than in my father. And Harold was very capable. Mother and my father, they weren't ... I don't know what the right word is, intimate? But she never could have married Harold Massey. That wouldn't have been a fit, not for his family. He was a great man, at least in these parts, an honourable man. I think that's why he did what he did to Charlie Eaton."

"And what was that, Wilson?"

"I don't know. I just know that a few days later ... after that fucker touched me ... that I was out here in the woods, not playing, as I said, just crying. I hadn't been able to speak much since it happened. I lost the ability to talk for a while. Mother was almost hiding me from my father. I was here, just walking around ... and ... and ... I saw Mr. Massey coming down the hill with the tractor and wagon. He drove up to the edge of the forest, and then he carried Eaton's body, his face all bloodied, into the woods ... and he buried him ... buried him where you found him. Or at least where you found parts of him."

"Would you testify to that in court?" asked Mercer.

Wilson Shields looked even older now. "I ... I don't know."

"Because you want to protect Harold Massey?" asked Alice.

"I ... I don't know. He was a great man, honourable."

"You've said that," said Mercer, "but to my mind that doesn't jive with his actions. Those aren't the actions of an honourable man."

"What would you know about that?" snarled Shields.

Alice put a hand on Mercer's arm to tell him to be quiet, to let her take the lead for a while. "Wilson," she said softly, "there are *two* graves in the woods, and incomplete corpses."

"Yeah."

"You mentioned Dr. Johnson. What do you know about the second grave? Or the ravaged state of both remains?"

Wilson Shields paused for a long time. He put his face into his hands once more and rubbed, then he looked up toward the forest canopy and let out a groan. It took him a while before he could speak again.

"I watched Mr. Massey bury Charlie Eaton. And something about it made me feel better, better than I'd felt for a while. I felt my voice coming back. I came out from where I was hiding and let Mr. Massey know I was there. He ... he wasn't angry ... he didn't look guilty. He hugged me. He told me it was all better now, that I would feel better. He was big man, strong as an ox, and it felt wonderful. I felt protected. I could feel why my mother loved him. He told me that this was our secret. And I've always kept that secret ... until now. You have to understand why he did what he did. Can you not just let this go? Let bygones be bygones?"

"Sergeant Morrow asked you about the other grave," said Mercer. "Were you coming to that?"

Shields sighed again. "Yeah. But there's more to explain before I get to it." He paused once more. "I ... I ... uh, couldn't go back to school. Not here. So Mother arranged for me to be sent to another school, far away, on the other side of the city. A private boarding school, a good one, where I got a better education than I ever would have gotten here. I don't know what she said to my father or how she explained how she got the money, but he bought it. I vanished from here for a while, only came back in the summers."

"And Harold Massey helped you vanish," said Mercer. "No questions asked. Just went to a better school, far away?"

"He was, as I've said several times, a good man. He paid for my education, at least a lot of it. I think Mrs. Massey knew. She and my mother were dear friends. It was better for me that I disappeared. I could not have gone on here. I don't know if a five-year-old can commit suicide ... but I might have tried if I'd had to stay."

"And the other grave?" asked Mercer.

"I remember I came back out here to the woods a few more times that fall before I was sent away, just to look at the site, make sure Eaton was in there, could not harm me anymore. But I remember that it was disturbed a few times — coyotes, likely — and I brought a shovel out here. It was likely twice my size. I tried to bury what was left even deeper. That was not good for me, what I saw. The coyotes had taken parts of him away."

Alice felt sick to her stomach. *Toughen up*, she told herself. She looked toward Mercer, but he was staring at Shields, intent on the interrogation.

"When I came back the following summer, the grave was disturbed again, so I tried to get everything underground once more. I was too little to make much of a job of it. After that year, I suppose the coyotes had had enough. There were just a few bones and the skull left. Then ... just the summer after, actually, one day when I was trying to get everything underground again ... I saw more bones, the tip of another skull, nearby. The coyotes had been digging there too."

"Likely buried the previous year, 1961?" asked Alice.

"Yeah, I guess so ... I don't know. The coyotes had had their way with it too, and I buried those other bones as well."

"Why not just report it to the police?" asked Mercer. "That would have been the right thing to do."

"I don't think you are following what I'm saying ... nor do you give a shit, sir. Mr. Massey saved my life. He destroyed the pervert who'd harmed me. I could not give him up. I still wish I didn't have to. But you have cornered me."

"And you assumed Mr. Massey had killed the other person," said Alice, "in the other grave."

"Yes," said Shields, "and that he had good reason. That was the way I processed it back then, anyway."

"You said earlier, Mr. Shields, that you knew the other corpse belonged to Dr. Albert Johnson. How did you know that?"

"I don't, not for sure. I just assume it's him. I know he disappeared the year after Charlie Eaton did. A person going missing in these parts, everyone knows when that happens. The doctor disappears, then there's another body buried in our forest, and I knew the first one was Mr. Massey's doing. Buried side by side."

"Why do you think he would have killed Dr. Johnson, Wilson?"

"I don't have a fucking clue. Maybe he was doing something to little boys too. I don't know. But like I said, Mr. Massey would not have done it without good reason, great reason."

"That's not for you to decide, Shields."

Wilson stood up, then sat down, then stood up again and staggered a couple of feet toward the graves before he stopped.

"I was terrified ... also. Yeah, terrified of Mr. Massey too when I saw the other skull. Imagine a boy my age having to deal with that? To deal with *everything* I went through. I was terrified, traumatized, fucked-up, desperate. I know why you ask me so often about my age."

"Why, Wilson?"

He looked up at Alice Morrow with his bloodshot eyes, encircled as they were by darkened, sagging skin, all set in a creased face below thinning hair. "Because I have lived one hundred years in my seventy years on this earth. The things that have been done to me, the secrets I've kept, have aged me like a withering disease."

Alice looked back at him and pitied him. In fact, the expression on his ancient face nearly brought tears to her eyes. She arrested that quickly and glanced toward Mercer. He was examining Wilson Shields closely too, but he didn't appear to be pitying him. He seemed to be searching for something in this person of interest's eyes.

"I am not a suspect in any of this. That is ridiculous. You have no right to ... I am one of the victims. I might as well be lying under this ground!"

He fell back onto the stump and broke down and wept again, and they let him cry. It was horrible to watch, the sounds bursting out from him, heaving out and echoing through the grey-and-white forest.

"Your murderer has been dead for sixteen years," he said between sobs.

"Stay where you are, Wilson. Do not move an inch. Detective Mercer and I have to confer."

They stepped away from him and spoke in quiet tones.

"I don't want him to just go free," said Mercer.

"What would we arrest him for? Being brutalized by the actions of his elders?"

"For withholding evidence. Huge evidence. If what he's telling us is true, his silence, his complicity, kept the identity of a serial murderer from being exposed for sixty years! And we still have one victim unaccounted for. If Shirley Ezinicki was killed by Harold Massey too, then it happened after these two deaths we're dealing with right now. Wilson Shields might have saved her life."

"He was just a child then. A damaged child."

Mercer didn't appear to have a good answer for that. He paused for a moment. "I don't like this guy's manner either. I know he's upset, but he has all the characteristics of someone who is hiding something. Something more. He's nervous, not direct in answers, pausing, his eyes shifting."

"Can't that all be explained?"

"Maybe. But why is he telling us all this? He's a lawyer. Why didn't he just tell us that he had nothing to say to us and wanted his own lawyer? You know, get his story straight first. Protect himself. Instead, he just comes out with all this, as if he wanted the story he told us out."

"Story? He's devastated. That's pretty clear. Devastated and chronically traumatized. Don't you think? You've seen people who've endured the sorts of things he has."

Mercer nodded then sighed. "Yeah. Yeah, you're right, he seems like the real deal when it comes to that. No question. I just ... do you think he really could have reburied these bones when he was five or six years old? I don't know. I ... I think he has more secrets."

Their faces were close, and they were looking into each other's eyes. For a moment, Alice couldn't sort out her emotions. Again, she almost felt comforted, felt attraction, intimacy even in the midst of the terrible revelations they had just heard and the decisions they faced.

"Okay," she said, "let's keep him on a short leash. But let's not arrest him for anything, not yet. I'm not sure withholding evidence for some sixty years when you were a child when these things happened would stick. Maybe, maybe not. And anyway, perhaps it's better for us to have him loose. See what, if anything, he does next. What would charging and punishing Wilson Shields accomplish, anyway? Hasn't he been through enough?"

"All right," said Mercer, a look of admiration moving across his face and then disappearing into professionalism.

"I'll talk to him," said Alice.

She walked back to Wilson Shields, leaving Mercer standing a long way off.

"Wilson, look, I am sorry for what you have been through. But you should have found some way, somehow, to let the authorities know. You know that. I know you do."

"I just couldn't. I couldn't."

"You can go now. We will not detain you. But we will require you to call the station every day for the foreseeable future and inform us of your whereabouts, and you must stay in the vicinity so that we can reach you, in person, on short notice. As this case — these cases, really — wind up, we will need your testimony. And we may need to speak with you further as well."

She could see Wilson Shields swallow when she said that last part, something like the panic he had shown at times during his emotional confession resurfacing again. Alice didn't like that. "Okay," he said quietly.

"Go home and look after your mother."

"I will. Thank you, Alice." He took her hand and squeezed it. His hand felt even colder than the day.

23

Delilah

MERCER HAD ALREADY left by the time Alice turned around, hightailing it back through the woods toward the cruiser as fast as he could go. She had noticed him shivering while they talked and couldn't stop herself feeling a little amused as he raced away. She took her time, and when she finally appeared at the back road, he was standing next to the passenger side of the cruiser with his arms wrapped tightly around himself, rocking back and forth. His nose looked as red as the lead reindeer. She immediately began moving even slower.

"Very funny," he said. "Open the damn door and turn on the heat."

They got inside and started driving along the back road heading toward the concession road that led out to the county highway, the heat cranked up. Alice drove a little slower than usual on the snow-packed road. The bare maple and oak trees and the white-coated spruce and pine trees on all sides were like walls. A few houses peeked out every now and then, many of them new, built recently by escapees of the city. Once they returned to the county road and were heading east, they would pass the end of Mercer's sideroad in ten minutes. She'd made him come in the cruiser with her again, though, no driving of his own vehicle. That was partly a professional thing, partly personal. She hated that she wanted his company, that he felt like something more than company. She hated that last part dearly.

"So," said Mercer, "Harold Massey is our man, at least for most of this, and it's hard to believe that with so many homicides within such a short period that this is not all the work of one killer. No evident motive for him doing away with his sister, I know, but with all the other things going on, and with her within his reach, it's not out of the question. And he has big-time motives for killing Caleb Carruthers and Perry Scott —"

"And Charlie Eaton, it seems."

"Whose bloodied corpse he was seen burying in someone else's woods."

"Knowing that if it were discovered, someone else could be suspected. Or at least, not him."

"Strange, though, that he would bury a body on the Shields property, the home of Edwina, his former love."

"Maybe she wasn't, though; maybe most of the love was coming from the other direction."

"And yet, he helped her out, killed for her son, paid for his education."

"It doesn't make sense. Those two things — killing for her and then putting the evidence in her backyard."

"Maybe he hated her husband? Maybe he thought this could frame him if things got out?"

"Maybe. It sounds like he dearly loved Evelyn, though, was thrilled that she married him. He was happy with the way things turned out. Why, then, would he harbour any hatred for Edwina's husband?"

"And what about Dr. Johnson?" asked Mercer. "Why would Massey have killed him? The local doctor?"

Alice didn't answer. They were coming to the county road. She turned on her left-hand signal and brought the cruiser to a stop.

"And Shirley Ezinicki too?" she finally said. "Why in the world would he kill her? A young schoolteacher? And if he did, then where did he put her? She's our outlier right now."

They turned east and headed along the county road. For a long while, they both just thought, comfortable with the silence, aware that the other needed time to process what they were learning.

"All of the people in this story are in a sort of community out here, aren't they?" said Mercer finally. "I mean, they all know each other and live not too many miles apart — I mean, not too many kilo-metres, and —"

"Don't say *keelo*. Don't say *keelo* and then *metres*. Run it all together. Kilometres. Trust me."

"Pardon me. Pardon my American."

"I forgive you."

"But my point is that even though they aren't living right next to each other the way they might in town or even more so in a city, they might as well be, right? They know each other well, some are related, have entwined pasts, seems like they were even sleeping with each other, some of them."

"Getting over the fence, they used to call it."

"Here's an example," said Mercer. He was pointing toward his own sideroad, which was fast approaching just off the county road. "Delilah Morton lives right here at the end of my road. I know she's a bit farther away from the others, but she still —"

"Hmm," said Alice and turned so suddenly onto the sideroad that Mercer had to grab the door to not fall into her. "We need more answers," said Alice as she swerved. "And here's Delilah.

Good friend of the Masseys. Tough lady. Hard-ass. Perhaps with a slightly wild past. With interesting things to say about bedroom shenanigans out here, secrets. And ... the last person to see Dr. Albert Johnson alive."

"You want to talk to her now?"

"An American detective, homicide guy, lots of experience, once told me that when you are interviewing persons of interest, it's best to surprise them. Look, we were just saying that we can find motives for Harold Massey committing most of these homicides, but not Dr. Johnson's. I have the feeling from reading the reports that the local cops didn't exactly grill Del Morton; they likely knew her and were buddies with Ebb. Let's see what really happened that day in 1961 when she drew the good doctor all the way out here to check on her 'woman's complaint.' Let's put this tough old gal on the spot, the two of us, without warning her."

"All right." Mercer nodded.

They pulled up the steep driveway toward the sprawling one-storey bungalow — a house far too big for two people, especially two elderly ones.

"Wait a minute," said Alice as Mercer started to get out of the cruiser. "I have to get Sal up to speed. I'll just text; I don't want to call her since she may be sitting with her husband."

"Right," said Mercer, "good idea," and he waited while Alice texted Sal about the incredible things that Wilson Shields had told them."

Alice waited for a minute after she finished, but Sal didn't respond.

"All right," said Alice. "Let's go." They got out, approached the door, and rang the doorbell. Santa's sleigh still sat near the front window, covered in snow and ice, with "Merry Christmas" in lights across Santa's belly, nearly a month after the event.

They waited for a while, then Alice rang the bell again.

"She took a while when we were here last time, didn't she?" asked Mercer.

"Yup. Took her time. Knew it was me. Remember, she was spying on us from the window?"

"Don't see her there now."

More time passed, and Alice rang the buzzer again. It was loud, appropriate for the elderly folks inside, but still no one was responding.

Alice could see Mercer checking out the property, looking up and down the house, across the front lawn, and toward the garage, as he always did everywhere they went, surveilling places and people. The first time she'd seen him, at Connie's Home Style Grill in town, she'd noticed him examining her the minute he entered the restaurant, her with her head down pretending she didn't know he was there. She had known he was a cop, though, of some sort, and that he wasn't really interested in her as a woman — not at first, at least. Guys often weren't. But later, he definitely was. She wondered if he thought others didn't notice how he examined people and things. Standing there at the Mortons' entrance, he was craning his neck and looking toward their open garage door. Then he stepped off the front stairs and took one stride toward the garage.

"Look at that," he said.

Alice rang the doorbell again and stepped back too. Mercer had been looking at a pile of wood in the open garage and a big axe driven into one of the pieces, a thick chunk of firewood the width of a grown man's torso and nearly knee-high.

"Ebb must be ninety or more too, right?"

"I'm guessing, though maybe she robbed the cradle."

"Good for him, splitting wood at his age."

"Maybe it's his son, Ben. He's just next door, remember."

The door opened. "Hello?" cried Ebenezer Morton. He looked

a little confused because there was no one on the front step now. He stood there in the same outfit he had worn the last time they'd seen him — a warm checkered shirt with blue suspenders, jeans, slippers, and a farm implement company ball cap on his balding dome. Alice wondered if he ever changed his clothes or if he maybe had five sets of the same outfit. She also noticed his advanced age much more this time. Maybe because she was looking for it. He was puffing from getting the door, his breath in clouds in the bitter air, though he didn't seem to care about the cold.

"Good day, Ebb," said Alice and turned back up the steps.

"Oh, there you are, thought maybe a ghost had knocked on my door. What do you want? I was just getting a look at *Jeopardy* on the TV, and you folks are banging on my doorbell. Takes me a while to haul my ass out to here, you know. What are you staring at over there, young man?"

"Nice to see you again, Mr. Morton," said Mercer. "I was just looking at your garage."

"Why would you do that? Nothing in it of interest to the police. You ain't opening up the Elizabeth Goode case again, are you? That Yankee woman — no offence, young man, I know you're one too — was nuts, right off her rocker. But took care of her, didn't you?"

"Yes," said Alice, "we aren't here about that. Becky Prior was arrested some time ago. We want to talk to Delilah about the Massey case."

Ebb frowned. "Damn shame, losing the old girl. Not many of us left anymore. What the hell was she doing with a man's body in her basement, though? Hear they found Violet too, right there on the property. Christ, what's going on in the world? I suppose you won't be telling me how she came to be underground there. What the hell does Del have to do with this?"

"Likely nothing, Mr. Morton, but she knew Evelyn Massey well, and we are just following up on a few things, just crossing some T's and dotting some I's. She spoke to us earlier and was helpful."

Alice was pleased at Mercer's discretion, in fact surprised by it. No need to bring up Dr. Johnson's disappearance and Delilah Morton's connection to it with her husband. It would just upset him, though it seemed like it might be tough to upset Ebb Morton.

"Well, she ain't here, gone to town. Left kind of sudden-like, but you never know with women. Someone called. I think she said who it was, but I don't always listen the best, just filter out what doesn't matter, you know." He winked at Mercer. "Said she had shopping to do, so likely a woman friend who called, and she's spending my money." He winked at Mercer again.

"Thank you, Ebb. We'll talk to her later," said Alice.

"Were you friends with Harold Massey, Mr. Morton?"

Ebb paused for a second. "Sorry?"

Mercer offered the question again, louder.

"Harold? Yeah. Of course. Good man."

"That's it?"

"What else do you want me to say?"

Alice smiled. "Nothing, Ebb."

"He was a good worker, ran a tight ship on that farm of his, best farm for miles, had beef, dairy, pigs, sheep, hens, the whole lot, good family, good churchman, on the school board, hit a baseball a mile in his day, pretty rugged on defence in his time too, could put your ass right over the boards if you had your head down. Kids play with their heads down all the time now 'cause no one hits them. Harold woulda straightened them out." He grinned then turned serious. "I don't know what else to tell you. That's about it. Good man."

"So we hear," said Mercer.

"Listen, do you two want something to eat?" Ebb looked at his watch. "It's getting past noon, and I'm starving, and I bet you two are too. I could likely put together a peanut butter sandwich or something, maybe a beer, maybe have a butter tart in the fridge. We could watch *Jeopardy* while we eat."

"Uh, no thanks," said Alice. "We're good. On duty."

Ebb started to turn in to the house.

"See you're still chopping wood, Mr. Morton," said Mercer, motioning toward the pile in the garage, the big axe sunk deep into one piece.

Ebb laughed.

"Why are you laughing?"

"That ain't me."

"Oh, so your son —"

"Ben? No, it's Del."

"Delilah?" asked Alice. "She chops the firewood?"

"Indeed she does. Always did. Those gals in her day all did, not like these wimps of girls these days. Sorry, Alice, not including you, of course. But yeah, she used to help me milk the cattle, drive them in and out, bring in the hay, thresh the grain, chop the wood. And then she'd put on a meal every night, every morning and noon too. I couldn't cook a lick. Not a man's job, I say. Strong as an ox, my girl. I could arm-wrestle her down pretty quick back in the day, mind you, but she'd put up a tussle. I think she'd take me now. Look at the size of Del's backside sometime. I bet Ev Massey could chop wood too."

"I bet she could," said Mercer.

"Thank you," said Alice, glancing at her partner.

THEY DROVE INTO town thinking about what Ebb had just added, not bringing up additional ideas that now seemed like possibilities. Just possibilities, though, and they both knew that proof was what they were after. Facts.

Alice missed Sal and was worried about her, and her mind bounced around from everything that they were learning about the case to her good friend's situation at home, chased through the air in the cruiser now by the innocuous, jazz-inflected melody being played by the Moe Koffman Quartet, a flute-driven piece called "Swinging Shepherd Blues" from 1958. They drove into town past the two grocery stores, and then they both spotted the same thing — someone sitting on a park bench across from one of the stores.

"Delilah," they said at the same time.

She was alone on the bench, her head down but looking up every now and then as if waiting for someone. Alice pulled over and parked in one of the stores' lots, and they watched her for a moment, the flute's notes floating around as if trying to cheer her up. Then someone approached her. Not just someone, three people. Gloria, Gwen, and Blair — all three Massey women. They didn't appear to be feeling the cold.

"Let's join this," said Mercer.

"They look like secret agents or something."

"John le Carré and friends."

They got out of the cruiser and crossed the street. As they approached, the four women noticed them and immediately stopped talking.

"Ladies," said Alice.

"Good day, Sergeant Morrow," said Gwen. Alice didn't like the way she said her name, the mock formality.

"Just out having a chat?" asked Mercer. "Anything you'd like to share with us?"

All four looked down for a moment and didn't say anything. Finally, Gloria spoke.

"This has been very difficult for us. We thought we should meet and talk."

"Somewhere no one sees your cars gathered around? Where

you can get your stories aligned?" asked Mercer. "Some of you all the way in from the city."

"What are you accusing us of?" asked Blair.

Mercer turned to her. "I don't know. You tell me. Protecting someone? Your grandfather, Harold Massey? Protecting yourselves?"

"What do you mean by that?" asked Gwen.

"Well," said Alice, "we've uncovered a lot of things since we began this investigation. A lot of secrets. Just today and yesterday, there's been some pretty gruesome business. More bodies have been discovered."

Alice let that sink in. She and Mercer regarded them all closer, lingering on Delilah, who uncharacteristically looked away.

"Some of you have withheld things," continued Alice, "even by your own admission. Is there any other information you aren't sharing with us? We think we know who made some of these people disappear, who may have murdered them. And some of you will not be pleased about our conclusions. Horrified by them. We think we have our man." She looked at the Masseys. "But there are still things we don't know." She looked at Delilah again.

"Why are you gawking at me, Morrow? You of all people."

Mercer stepped between Alice and Delilah. "This isn't about Sergeant Morrow, Mrs. Morton. You, ma'am, were the last person to see one of our victims alive. We wanted to speak with you alone about it, so we dropped by your place. But now that you are all gathered here, defensive, acting as though you have nothing to hide, let's get it all out into the open, shall we?"

"All right," said Delilah.

"You're related to Caleb Carruthers, aren't you?" asked Mercer. "You haven't said much about that, even when we were asking about him."

Delilah sneered. "Oh my god, he's a fourth cousin or something, twice removed. Lots of people are related around here."

"Just tell us what happened that day, Mrs. Morton, the day Dr. Johnson disappeared," said Alice. "In detail."

Delilah glanced toward the others. The sneer had left her face. "I ... I called Dr. Johnson because I was feeling poorly. He had been my doctor forever, and he was Margaret's and Edwina's, and I'm sure he was yours too, Glor and Gwennie?"

"No," said Gwen. "Mother had a doctor in the city, a very good one. A Massey family doctor from way back. So she went there all the time, and so did we, and Dad too, I think."

"Really?" said Mercer. He glanced at Alice. "So your family has no connection with him?"

"No, none," said Gloria. "Didn't even know him, really."

"Go on, Delilah," said Alice.

"Well, that day, he drove out to my place. He had three or four calls, doctors did that sort of thing in those days, you know."

"Do you have any idea whom else he saw that day?" asked Alice. "Did he mention where he'd been?"

"I don't recall. One's medical concerns weren't to be spread about in my day. Not like now, with this online stuff, social media, people airing who they are and what they're about all the time. Women talking about private concerns. It's all unpleasant to me."

"Tell us how long he saw you, what the visit was like, what he was like, completely himself or nervous, that sort of thing, anything you noticed when he left and where he went."

"I think you know some of this. I'll bet it's in the reports."

Delilah was no one's idiot, thought Alice. She was not only older than she looked but a good deal more savvy. Alice wondered if she was harbouring other secrets.

"Did you see him alone?" asked Mercer.

Delilah glanced at the other women. "Well ... yes ... yes, he saw me alone, just the two of us. Ebb was in the fields doing something,

I think. No, he was away, at Orange Lodge."

"So, you called Dr. Johnson to come out to see you when your husband was away?"

"Yes, of course, I was feeling terrible ... and it came on fast."

"And how long did he see you, alone, just the two of you?"

"I don't like your tone, young man."

"I am not employing a tone. Please answer the question."

"Look ..." Delilah paused. "I suppose I'm going to have to say this or you will keep hounding me. Like I'm a suspect or something." She took a few seconds to gather herself. "I had my fun in my day, but then I settled down with Ebb. We tried to have children." She looked over at the Masseys. "But we couldn't. I couldn't. I wondered if it had anything to do with troubles I'd had, medically, in the past, to do with my ... social activity." Gwen and Gloria looked down, and Delilah continued. "So, I often saw Dr. Johnson, to see what could be done about making me more, you know, apt to have a child. We were using some medications, he had various ideas ... I didn't tell Ebb about any of this, you didn't in those days. That's why I was seeing the doctor, alone, when my husband was out. It didn't work, none of it. We adopted Ben when I was well into my forties."

They could barely hear that last part. Alice had never heard Delilah speak so softly.

"Thank you for that, Mrs. Morton," said Mercer, who appeared to have some sympathy for her but wasn't going to let it stand in the way of the answers he wanted. "But we need responses to particular questions. How long did Dr. Johnson see you that day?"

Delilah cleared her throat, put her shoulders back, and spoke up. "For maybe fifteen minutes ... perhaps more, maybe half an hour or so."

"Sun going down by the time he left?"

"No, no, it was June, I think, maybe early July, so long days, haying going on, I think, that's probably why I was thinking Ebb was in the fields."

"Did Dr. Johnson seem himself?"

"Yes, very much so. He was an impressive man." She glanced at the other women again. "But, yes, he was himself, not nervous, as you were probing about. I'd say he was happy when he left ... or maybe I should say ... at least, professional. His car was parked in the driveway next to ours, and he got in and drove away, and I watched from the front porch, waving at him, I think."

"Our report, Delilah," said Alice, "says you did not watch him leave."

"Well, you know all this stuff then, Miss Know-it-All, so why are you asking me, trying to catch me up? I've laid my heart out for you here. I probably didn't watch him all the way out the lane, just as he drove away, and then I likely turned back to the house. This was more than sixty years ago!"

"And you are aware, of course, that his car was found, empty, at the end of the lane, when Ebb came home from his meeting?" asked Alice.

"Yes. Yes, that's true. Obscured by the maple trees toward the end of the lane. It was horrible. They searched high and low for him, and no sign, just vanished."

"It says in the report that you were upset, but that's it, nothing about you having to be attended to, or weeping, anything of that sort."

"No, of course not."

"What do you mean by that?"

"One doesn't break down in difficult circumstances. My father taught me that. He was a taskmaster, but he was right. Folks nowadays show too much feeling, to my mind. What would have been the good of falling apart? The most important thing was to find him."

"But they didn't."

"No."

"And you do realize what I said before, that you were the last person to see him alive?"

"So I've been told."

"So what do you think happened to him?"

"I don't know."

"Speculate."

"You should have a lawyer with you," said Blair, clutching Delilah by the arm. "Don't say anything else. They can't ask you these sorts of things."

Delilah looked up at the two officers. Then she rose to her feet. Alice had forgotten how tall she was, taller than her and nearly eyeball to eyeball with Mercer. She indeed had a prominent backside too, as Ebb had noted.

"I did not kill Dr. Johnson. Why would I do that? Someone must have picked him up at the end of the lane, for whatever reason, someone who knew he was coming to see me. It was mid-summer. There would be no tire tracks in the snow. There'd be no tracks at all on our gravel lane."

"And what would their motive have been? This person or persons who picked him up?" asked Mercer. "Jealousy? Money? Hatred? Did he have enemies? You appear to have known him well, been seeing him a lot, perhaps been close to him?"

Alice thought that was a bit much, but she knew what Mercer was doing. Trying to get this hard-hearted woman, this tough lady, to be emotional again, maybe angry this time, and say something she shouldn't. But she was even tougher than he'd anticipated. She looked him right in the eye.

"I haven't the foggiest. But I will swear on a stack of Bibles that I had nothing to do with his death."

"Death?"

"Disappearance."

"How about a lie detector?"

"That too."

She maintained her stare at Mercer. He looked back but then relented.

"Okay," he said, "I think that's it. You can go, Mrs. Morton."

"We know someone else buried him, at least, and we know where," said Alice before Delilah could answer.

All four women looked back at her.

"Someone who is more than likely our killer," continued Alice. "We weren't insinuating that it was actually you, Delilah, but you must understand, there are still lots of things we don't know, what part different people may have played in these events, so we had to ask you these questions."

"Well," said Delilah, "I didn't play any part."

Mercer motioned for Alice to draw near him. "We have to talk to the Masseys," he whispered. "Alone. Now. Come clean with them. It's time."

"Come on, ladies," said Delilah, picking up her purse. Her face was pale in the cold day; not a smidgen of red had risen there from the bitter weather. "Let's go."

"No, not them," said Alice.

"They're coming with us," added Mercer.

"Where?" asked Blair, who looked frightened.

"To the police station. Just Sergeant Morrow and me and the three of you."

Delilah stopped for a second and looked back at her friends, who seemed frozen to the bench, but not because it was so cold.

"There was a serial killer among you," said Alice. "Among all of us."

"We are going to tell you three who he was," said Mercer.

"He?" asked Blair, and they could see her swallow.

"Why us?" asked Gloria, her voice quivering. "Why just us?"

"Follow us to the station," said Mercer. "Directly to the station. Speak to no one on the way."

"I must ask you all to brace yourselves." It was the least Alice could do: warn these good and decent women.

24

Hard Truths

BEFORE ALICE AND Mercer got into the cruiser, she texted Sal again, surprised and worried that she hadn't heard anything back after her last message. This time, she told Sal that they were taking all three Masseys to the station and that they intended to inform them that their father, or grandfather in Blair's case, appeared to be the lead suspect in their search for a mass murderer in the community's midst. It was a daunting task.

For some reason, Alice kept the car in view behind her, the compact little silver four-door Hyundai that Gloria drove, as if the Masseys might make a break for it as they moved through town. But Gloria drove like she was in a funeral procession, and it was hard to keep her in sight.

Alice reached the station without hearing back from Sal.

She and Mercer still hadn't eaten lunch, but neither of them seemed to care. She had considered slipping into the grocery store to get something quick. There were, however, much more important things to think about now than food. And if Mercer could run on adrenaline, then she sure as hell could too.

All three Massey women entered the building silently, looking as if they were about to be arraigned for murder themselves. Alice asked if they'd like anything to drink, and every one of them said no. They were then ushered through the front counter and into Alice's office. She didn't have the heart to speak to them in the little room where suspects were usually interviewed.

She was glad that Mercer was with her.

She took off her parka, put it on the back of her chair, and sat behind her desk, indicating to the three women to sit in the chairs in front of her. Mercer stood off to the side, leaning against the wall. She could reach out and touch him from there. This was her job, though. She had to do this. She had to lead and take responsibility no matter how harrowing these next few minutes would be. She was conscious of the dark circles under her eyes, her unwashed and less than luxuriant hair — dirty blond, the usual Alice look — and wondered if this one time she should have worn some real makeup to work. She hoped to dear God that she wasn't going to cry. There was no way she was handing this over to Mercer.

Why wasn't Sal answering her messages?

She cleared her throat. "Ladies, we've brought you in here today because our investigation into the deaths at the Massey home, the discovery of the body of Violet Massey on the Massey property, another discovery of human remains in the Massey barn, and the very recent unearthing of further human remains on a farm nearby, as well as some very disturbing eyewitness testimony, leads us to some extremely distressing conclusions."

She had been unable to look at Gloria, Gwen, and Blair, but now she raised her eyes to them and could see that none of them were looking back. They were either staring down or at the walls, terror in their eyes. She had never seen an expression like that on a human face. It was as if each one of them was utterly alone, solitary in a room of five people, all their pretense, their sense of safety, the role they played in life, the role we all need to play to stay sane and alive, was gone. There were no more secrets in their world, and everyone needed secrets.

Alice looked down at her desk again.

"We felt it was our responsibility to let you know what we have discovered and whom we suspect, since it will greatly impact you emotionally, and since we will eventually have to make this information available to the public, to the people of this community. We felt you needed to be out in front of this, somehow."

Alice looked up and saw that tears were running down Blair's cheeks, but worse than that, both Gloria and Gwen, women whom Alice doubted had ever shed a tear in public and perhaps seldom in private, had dropped their heads and were obviously desperately distraught, holding back their sobs and the shaking of their shoulders as if their very lives depended on it. Alice glanced at Mercer, who appeared indecisive, not a Hugh Mercer characteristic. Three women were now weeping in his presence, and the fourth woman was glancing his way. He reached over and pulled a tissue from a tissue box on Alice's desk and handed it to Blair. She slapped it away, hard. He didn't offer any to the other two.

"Let us tell you what we know," said Alice. "Perhaps … perhaps you will be able to point out where we are wrong."

Blair lifted her head and stared right at her, tears still on her cheeks, not wiping them.

"We are pretty sure," said Mercer, and Alice let him continue, "that the author of all of these crimes is more than likely the same person. That only makes sense. Why would multiple disappearances and almost certain homicides take place over such a short period of time in such a localized area if not because the victims were being killed by the same person? We cannot say this with absolute certainty, but it is highly likely."

"Couple that," continued Alice softly, looking back at Blair, "with the fact that one person in particular appears to be connected to all of these crimes, one person had the physical ability to carry them out, one person had real or possible motives in every case, and lastly, and most significantly, that one person has been identified by an eyewitness as burying two victims in a local forest."

Gloria and Gwen began to sob loudly. Blair kept staring ahead.

"We do not know why Violet Massey was killed," said Mercer, "but we do know it was a violent death at the hands of a powerful perpetrator, much stronger than her, and that she was put underground near the family plot, so by someone who knew where the Masseys were buried. We have discovered that the remains found in the basement of your family home were likely those of the actor Perry Scott and that Evelyn was having an affair with him, an affair that if suspected by Harold Massey would have given him a motive to kill Mr. Scott, one unlike any motive that anyone else could have harboured. We discovered Caleb Carruthers' teeth in the pigpen in the Massey barn, all that was left of him, right below a chute through which Harold Massey daily tossed feed to his animals. Caleb Carruthers was the great love of Evelyn's life in her younger days, perhaps the love of her entire life, and Mr. Carruthers appears to have returned to the area often. If Mr. Carruthers met with Evelyn, and Mr. Massey knew of it, this would have, again, provided motive for Mr. Massey to act."

Please do not say that we suspect he is Gloria's father too. Please do not say that, thought Alice. *That would be too much pain. Pain on pain.* She looked toward Mercer, and he stopped.

"And," said Alice, "and I am deeply, deeply sorry to tell you this ... as Detective Mercer alluded to, we have a witness who says he saw Harold Massey in the fall of 1960 transporting the dead body of Charlie Eaton to the forest at the back of the Shields property and burying it there. We are almost certain that Dr. Johnson was interred beside him the following year."

Blair put her hands to her face, and her mother and aunt wrapped their arms around their heads, faces down toward their laps. No one said anything for a while.

"Who?" said Blair finally, raising her head and looking defiant.

"What do you mean?" asked Alice.

"Who said they saw this? Who said they saw my kind, loving grandfather doing this horrible, horrible thing? Who is your eyewitness?"

"That's not something we can divulge at this point."

"I'd like to have him or her in front of me right now! They are lying!"

"But it makes —"

"They are lying, and that's really *all* you have to go on! All the rest is circumstantial!"

"But it fits a pattern," said Mercer.

"*Your* pattern!"

"No," said Alice, "it fits a —"

"*Shut up!*" she screamed at Alice.

"Blair, Blair honey, please don't speak that way to Sergeant Morrow," said Gloria through her tears. She took her daughter's hand and held it.

Alice Morrow suddenly felt guilty. It seemed to her at that moment that they might have the wrong man. Had Harold Massey, a serial killer, brought up a daughter like this? A daughter who would gently reprimand her own daughter for being angry at someone who had just accused her grandfather of such terrible crimes? It was an act of almost incredible decency, the decency that she knew was in the people of this area, regardless of their inner turmoil and secrets. Could this woman really be the daughter of an evil man? She glanced at Mercer, who looked perplexed too.

"You have no motive for Great-Aunt Violet's murder, none, and you only know that Grandma had a brief affair with Perry

Scott, not that her husband knew about it or had it within him to hurt Mr. Scott, much less kill him! I know my grandfather knew about Caleb Carruthers too, that Grandma once dated him, and I know he was fine with that — he understood it. I know he helped Charlie Eaton once or twice too. Why in God's name would he hurt him? And Dr. Johnson?"

Gwen raised her head, wiping her tears. "He wasn't even our doctor!"

"And what about Shirley Ezinicki?" said Blair, who was gathering herself and gaining strength. Alice and Mercer could see the intelligence in her eyes, the city marketing executive, as she grasped another defence and put it into words for them. "I've been reading about all of this since Grandma died and that awful note was found. I know there was another disappearance. A young woman named Shirley Ezinicki. A schoolteacher. I'm betting you have nothing to tie my grandfather to her. Nothing! Nor do you even know what happened to her. I know because you haven't even mentioned her name! Yet, you said yourselves that the perpetrator of each and every one of these horrible, horrible things was likely the same person! You said the killer almost certainly murdered every last one of them!"

Alice and Mercer were quiet for a moment as Blair stared at one and then the other.

"Your grandfather was the chairman of the school board," said Mercer. "You just admitted that he had contact with Charlie Eaton — and our eyewitness has convincing reasons why your grandfather would have hurt him. Shirley Ezinicki was a schoolteacher — a tenuous connection right now, correct, but a connection nevertheless, and we will know more when and if we discover more about her disappearance."

Blair stood up. She pointed a finger at Mercer, then at Alice. "All of this is either circumstantial or completely based on the testimony of someone whose story can likely be torn apart under scrutiny. I knew my grandfather! Anyone in this area can tell you who he was and what he was about! He did *not* do this! It broke his heart to even ship his beef cattle! He used to get into the trucks with them and pet them. He stopped shipping calves for veal and lambs for mutton because he thought it was so cruel."

Lambs? thought Alice, and she pictured the crates Harold Massey must have once employed to ship those animals.

"And what about my grandmother?" continued Blair. "From the information you've given us, it sounds like you find her death suspicious too. Again, you said the perpetrator of all these things is the same person! Did my grandfather rise up from his grave and kill her too?"

There was silence in the room again.

"Come on, Mom!" said Blair. "Let's go, Aunt Gwen! I don't accept a word these two have told us. I was honest with them, and they turned it against us." She glared at the police officers. "I am not uttering a single word about this to either of you again, and if you spread any horrific lies about my grandfather, I will find a way to destroy you!"

She left the room, and both her aunt and mother followed.

Then Gloria turned back toward the office.

"I'm sorry," she said, and she turned to go again.

"Gloria!" cried Alice. Gloria stopped and looked at her. "We are not saying that your father was unquestionably guilty of these crimes. But we have a good deal of evidence against him, circumstantial or not. We felt it our duty to inform you. We felt that was the decent thing to do."

"I understand," said Gloria. "This must be terrible for you too, very difficult for you to tell us." She motioned to leave once more but turned back again. "And I'm sorry about Luke. I really am. I want you to know that."

25

Salma Haddad

ALICE AND MERCER stayed exactly where they were for a long time after the Masseys left the room, Blair's passion still hanging in the air.

"I feel bad about this," said Alice.

"Don't."

"But she has a point, several of them."

"And so do we. Harold Massey remains our lead suspect no matter how angry that makes his granddaughter. It's only natural she would feel that way. Not uncommon." He paused. "That thing about shipping young livestock in crates was interesting."

But Alice could tell that he had his doubts too and that they had grown when confronted with Blair's heartrending defence of her grandfather. Neither of them wanted to say what they were thinking: Wilson Shields might be lying.

"I have to see Sal. I'm worried. She isn't answering my texts."

"I'll come with you."

She appreciated that. She also appreciated that he hadn't said a word about Luke after Gloria had mentioned him and left. And

Mercer could ask about him by name now. She knew too that Mercer's understanding, his current silence, meant she would have to take the initiative to tell him. And the time to do that was approaching.

SALMA HADDAD LIVED with her husband, Michael, and children, Mahmoud and Aya, in a split-level home down by the lake in an old part of town that was filled with similar houses. Michael Meadows had run his own little electronics shop for years but had closed it and retired a bit early recently due to health concerns, initially diabetes but then a minor heart attack that had left him without the energy he'd once had. He was subject to days when he felt weak and had trouble doing much, which angered him since he was still a relatively young man. He had met Salma Haddad, now his wonderful Salma Meadows, at a community event more than thirty years ago just after she began work as a constable in the police service, the only brown girl in town in those "thankfully long-gone days," as she liked to say. They instantly fell in love, and their love had never diminished. Their family meant everything to them, Salma even deciding once their children were born not to take any promotional exams to raise her rank higher than constable in order to have more time at home and fewer professional responsibilities. She often told Alice she would quit if she could, but she and Michael couldn't afford it.

Mahmoud answered the door, and when he saw his mom's good friend, his face lit up. He was sixteen and growing into a handsome young man. *About Charlie Eaton's age when he vanished*, thought Alice.

"Alice!" he said.

"Moud! How are you?"

"I'm good." He noticed Mercer behind her. "Hey, you must be

Detective Mercer. Heard lots about you. New York, eh? Homicide squad?"

"Yes, sir."

"Cool."

"How's your dad?" asked Alice.

Mahmoud's face fell a little. "Okay, I guess. He wasn't feeling well, and Mom took him into the hospital. Had another little heart attack, apparently. But he's, like, okay, I guess. They just say he has to be careful. He's in bed. Mom's here, in the kitchen, making him some of her special soup. He loves it. Aya's here too — just got home. She's here for a couple of days."

"Are you letting us in?" asked Alice. "Or keeping the cops at the door?"

"Oh, crap, sorry, come in. I'll get Mom."

They entered, and Alice threw off her boots and tossed her coat over a little banister that led up a few carpeted steps to the living room. She did it as if she were at home. Mercer followed suit.

A young woman with long, dark hair was sitting on the sofa watching television, her black leggings tucked under her, a university sweatshirt for a top, somehow looking elegant in her casual outfit. She noticed who the visitors were and turned off the television, got to her feet, and embraced Alice.

"Alice! So great to see you!"

"You too. I'd like to introduce you to Detective Hugh Mercer. Hugh, this is Aya Meadows, our top-of-her-class business administration student, on her way to an MBA and world domination."

"Pleasure to meet you, Aya."

"Hi, Detective Mercer. She is so biased."

Sal entered the room from the kitchen. She looked tired. "Sorry about not answering your texts, Alice, I'm a little distracted." She noticed Mercer. "Oh my gosh, Detective Mercer! Aya, you haven't even asked them to sit! Aya, get him something! What would you like? Tea? Coffee? You could have some of my soup. Maybe some —"

"I'm good," said Mercer, sitting, "and you are busy. We just wanted to see how you were doing, and maybe bring you up to speed a little, if you want."

"I've got some homework to do," said Aya. "It was nice to meet you, Detective Mercer."

"You too."

She went off down the narrow hallway. Mahmoud had vanished as well.

Sal sat on the sofa beside Alice, so close that she had to move over a little, closer to Mercer. "It's been a bad day," she said. "I guess Mahmoud told you. Michael had a little episode. He's fine, for now. But I wonder how long that will last." Tears were welling in her eyes. Alice took her by the hand. "He has been such a wonderful husband. Loved me from the day he met me and proved it every day after that. This Egyptian girl who came to this country as a child. You know, it wasn't easy for him at first, marrying me, and I made him wait a bit so he would be sure, but I never heard a peep from him about the things we knew some people said about us. In fact, I was always worried that he would assault someone if they said anything bad about me in his presence. It took me a while to agree to have kids. He wanted them from the beginning. And then we named them, and he said, give them Middle Eastern names, give them Muslim names, and ... he said ... 'I couldn't be prouder to have their names attached to mine.'" Sal wiped her eyes. "And he was all for me keeping my last name at work. I offered to just use his, but he said no, keep yours, right on your chest. This town needs it."

"And they did," said Alice.

"A lot has changed around here since those days."

"And a lot has stayed the same."

"But they're good people, here, most of them, only a few bad apples. Kind people," said Sal. "It's a special place."

"Weird people," said Mercer.

They looked at him and laughed.

"So, what happened with the Massey ladies?"

"They were pretty crushed," said Alice. "And … then … Blair made a good case for her grandfather. It left me unsure. I know there's a pile of stuff against him. We are wondering, though, if Wilson Shields could be lying, at least about some details."

"Why would he do that?"

"Good question, Sal," said Mercer.

"Because he has some skin in the game?" asked Alice.

"Of what nature?"

"Oh, I don't know, perhaps he helped Harold Massey? He certainly had motivation in the case of Charlie Eaton. Maybe he's just putting Massey into the crime to exonerate himself. Massey is long dead and can't refute anything Shields says."

"Okay," said Sal, "but then we have to come up with motives for Shields for all these other homicides. And if he isn't lying about his age, they're homicides he committed as a child."

"Maybe this was a group thing?" said Mercer. "Maybe they all know who did it, know that several people did it, and they are keeping it quiet. That would fit around here. Or maybe there are accidental deaths among these crimes, which would mean that not all our victims were even murdered. Maybe some were crimes of passion committed by different people. Or maybe all the people keeping this quiet agree the victims weren't intentionally killed or think they deserved to die because of some moral crime, like adultery. That would fit around here too." He rubbed the back of his neck and sighed. "Someone, who knows who, kills Violet Massey, that's what started it all. Maybe even Caleb Carruthers, since Violet had encouraged her brother to marry Evelyn, the love of Caleb's life. Then Harold finds out that Carruthers did this — so, tough and honourable guy that he seems to have been, he acts as judge and executioner for Carruthers, whom he may also have caught around his wife. Then he kills Charlie Eaton as well for what he did to his own old flame's son. Maybe Delilah is somehow involved in Dr. Johnson's death — seems like she could really swing an axe, and we know at least one crime was done that way, and she was the last person to see him. Or maybe she at least knows how it was done. Interestingly, he was a doctor, one who made house calls and knew intimate things about everyone around him, knew everyone's secrets, maybe was even having an affair or two himself. Maybe he discovered who the killer was, or killers, and he had to be silenced … I don't know."

Mercer came to a halt, glanced over at the women, and shrugged his shoulders. It was the look of a highly capable professional who was reaching his wits' end on a case.

"But the doctor probably wasn't killed with an axe," said Alice. "Remember, you said yourself that his skull didn't have any wounds."

"And that still leaves out Shirley Ezinicki," said Sal, "and Evelyn Massey."

"Right," said Mercer, still appearing a little lost.

"There's got to be something more we can do to try to solve this, though," sighed Alice, "having come so far with it."

"I don't know," said Mercer, "maybe this is impenetrable, unprovable. That happens sometimes. Maybe we just have to let it be. People around here seem so nice when you meet them, but sometimes it feels like everyone has secrets, and they aren't giving them up. It's like a community of friendly icebergs."

Alice and Sal both appeared to want to say something, but they didn't.

"It seems to me," continued Mercer, "that we have two things left to do, that we *can* do. We can look closer into the Shirley Ezinicki disappearance, and we can confront Wilson Shields again, tell him to his face that we suspect he is lying and see how he responds, see if he cracks in any way."

"Okay," said Alice.

"But I have to tell you, my money is still on Harold Massey."

"Interesting way of putting it," said Sal. She didn't add that it sounded like the American way.

"Yeah, he still seems most likely," said Alice, "and maybe we just need to know why and how he did all this." She stood up and shook her head. "Incredible, though, absolutely incredible. The whole thing." She sighed. "This is enough for today, more than enough. Let's meet tomorrow, with Robbie present too, and make some final decisions. We can't spend forever on this. Are you good with that, Sal? Will we see you tomorrow?"

"Sure. I think Michael will be okay without me."

"Are you certain?"

"Yeah, Aya is here for the next couple of days anyway." She paused. "But Alice ... there's one more thing we can do. Though ... I'm reluctant to even mention it."

"No, Sal, go ahead, of course."

"We ... uh ..." She glanced at Mercer and then back to Alice. "We should think more about why your name was on both of those envelopes ... shouldn't we?"

Alice felt an instant sense of betrayal and almost wanted to slap Sal and then immediately felt terrible that the thought had even crossed her mind. Sal was saying this because it needed to be said, not to be mean. She was saying it because she was her friend. Alice saw that friendship in Sal's expression. There was something pleading in it.

"You're right, Sal. That is another thing we need to look into."

They moved toward the door, and Sal stepped into the hallway and called down it. "Aya and Mahmoud, come say goodbye to our visitors."

They immediately came from their rooms.

Alice and Mercer put on their boots and coats and looked up to the top of the short flight of carpeted stairs and saw the two young people standing there smiling down at them. Alice took a couple of steps upward and hugged them both and then moved back. Mercer reached up and shook their hands.

"Aya, keep making your mom and dad proud at school," said Alice.

"I'll try."

"I know you will. And Moud, buddy, what's up with you these days? Hardest working man in grade eleven?"

"Yeah, made the basketball team, don't know if I told you that, so that takes up lots of time, and schoolwork, tons of it right now."

"Like what?"

"Working on an English Lit essay that's kind of cool because there's prize money for the best one. Some old guy donated it like eons ago for writing something about a local person from the past who made a positive impact on our community. I think I have an idea. Comes from this old white guy actually mentioning in his suggestions for topics that someone write about local Indigenous leaders and issues and how unfairly they were treated, even mentions that missing Indigenous women and children would be a good subject. Kind of inspired me. This old guy put this together more than twenty years ago! It's called the Harold Massey Essays."

"Oh my gosh," said Alice.

"Yeah, I told Dad about it just now, and he said Harold Massey was a really good man, influential in the community, and that he told him once that if anybody was ever mean to Mom and to us, to just let him know and he'd speak to them."

"I didn't know that," said Sal.

"Well, Dad said that Mr. Massey told him to never tell you."

"YOUR MONEY STILL on Harold Massey?" asked Alice as she and Mercer walked out to the cruiser.

"For god's sake, it's like we're suspecting Jesus Christ or the Buddha."

They got inside the vehicle, and Alice turned on the heat and adjusted Mercer's heated passenger seat so it was cranked right up. Then her cell rang. She looked down at the screen.

"Oh, it's Ranbir." She tapped it. "Hello?"

"Sergeant Morrow, we have a situation."

"Another envelope?"

"No, ma'am, not an envelope."

"What, Ranbir, what?"

"Someone to whom we believe you have been recently speaking about the Massey case has just …" He paused.

"Has just what?"

"Committed suicide."

Alice was glad she was sitting down because she felt like she was going to faint. Her mind raced from face to face in the Massey case, dreading who it might be. Blair? Gloria? Gwen? My god, after that last terrible meeting that she had put them through. Or was it Edwina after perhaps hearing more from her son? Delilah, stricken by their questioning? One of the other dear friends of Evelyn Massey? Suicide was not a good subject with Alice Morrow. Not a good one at all.

She couldn't speak.

"Who?" asked Mercer loudly from his passenger seat.

"A man named Wilson Shields," said Ranbir.

26

Death in the Woods

THEY RACED OUT to the Shields farm as fast as Alice could make the cruiser go. As explained in great detail by Ranbir Singh, Wilson Shields appeared to have done himself in with a hunting rifle his father had used to shoot varmints — like pigeons off the barn roof or groundhogs when they raised their heads above their homes in the fields. His mother still kept the rifle in a closet just inside the back kitchen door. Edwina had grown worried when he had not returned when she'd expected him from a second walk in the woods after lunch, and several hours later she'd asked a friend to go out and check on what was keeping him. He was found within a few metres of where he used to kneel and pray.

Alice hadn't been at many violent crime scenes. She'd seen some dead bodies and broken up a few vicious fights, some involving knives, and she'd observed the wounds those encounters had caused. And … in her last case, the one she'd worked on with Mercer, she had shot someone in an act that had saved a woman's life. This death wasn't like that. It wasn't necessary. Suicides were different. She hated them. And she dreaded looking at what Wilson

Shields had done to himself, likely just one accurate shot to the place where men always did it, directly to the head. The head, where all your troubles were, where humanity thought themselves into pain and worse.

She knew that Mercer would have no trouble with this, and that upset her too. He had likely seen these things, violent and bloody deaths, more often than he could count. She was adamant that she would not show a single trace of emotion.

It was growing dark by the time they got there. This was the darkest time of the year. They parked behind two other police cruisers, a fire truck, and an ambulance on the back road. Alice was relieved to see that these vehicles were here and not convened in poor Edwina's driveway. She spoke to the constable standing by one of the cruisers, a young woman who had been with the service for a year and whom Alice had great hopes for, since she had been trained as a social worker first and appeared to really care about the people she encountered while on duty. She explained to Alice and Mercer that nothing had been moved at the crime scene and the others were waiting for them to arrive.

There was a new photographer there too, a guy whose main goal in life, it seemed to Alice, was to sensationalize everything, even what were usually just little crimes and troubles in the community. He was taking photos of the line of vehicles and of the cold grey forest while standing on the road and looking anxious to get into the trees and get his money shot. This guy was a buddy of Elwin Most, who Alice was pretty sure fed him information. But the young constable was doing her job, keeping him out here.

Alice made sure she led the way over the snowbank and into the darkening woods and tried not to break stride even for an instant as they marched up the hill and reached the crest. But when she looked down toward the spot on this side of the creek and saw the body slumped over in the dim light, head nearly torn from the body, she almost turned around.

"Whoa!" said Mercer under his breath. "Good shot. He did that with just his hunting rifle."

It wasn't said in admiration or with any kind of repulsion, just a statement of fact. An American statement of fact.

They descended the hill toward Wilson Shields, nodding at the others, among them Robbie and his idiot partner, Most. Alice made sure she walked right up to the victim. He had fallen beside one of the stumps they had sat on when they'd interviewed him that morning to keep him away from the human remains and their graves. In fact, it seemed to Alice that in order to do this grisly deed, he had sat on the very stump he had been on just six or seven hours earlier.

Mercer came up close to her, his shoulder touching hers, as if to comfort her without making it obvious. Wilson Shields' teeth were shattered, and his mouth was caked with a huge bubble of blood, the back of his skull torn out.

"It looks," said Mercer quietly, "like he probably put the butt of the gun on the ground, the other end in his mouth, and fired from a sitting position." He looked around. "Funny place to do this."

"It's like he was trying to tell us something."

"Yeah," said Mercer.

"What?"

"Well, something about this spot, about the people buried in these graves and who did it. Why else kill himself here?"

"But he told us who did it."

"Yeah." Mercer looked over at the bloodied corpse. "But now you might argue that he appears to have been feeling a good deal of guilt about it all. Is he saying to us, since he knew we would be here right after he did this ... 'I was lying to you'?"

"Or maybe it was just the trauma of what was done to him as a child by one of the people who was put to rest in this very spot?"

Mercer nodded.

"Or maybe ..." Alice felt a chill run through her as this thought occurred to her, and it came almost involuntarily out of her mouth. "Maybe he didn't kill himself. Maybe someone else shot him, right here, for some reason."

They both looked around the woods, as if worried that they were being watched or that some other threat was imminent, both thinking of the possibility that Evelyn Massey had been murdered, not sixty years past but a little over a week ago.

"We can run tests on the rifle," said Mercer, "but no killer is going to be stupid enough to leave fingerprints behind on a weapon. They would either make sure just Wilson's prints were on it or take the gun with them. I wouldn't rule out homicide."

They looked down at the ground around the stumps. The snow there was absolutely filled with footprints: Wilson Shields' prints from his many trips out here and their own and other police boot marks from the last few days of investigations. It would be almost impossible to pick out prints belonging to any potential murderer.

Elwin Most sidled up to them. "Hate to say it, don't speak ill of the dead and all, but" — he nodded toward Wilson — "loser, really. Suicides are for fucking losers." He held up his hands as if to stop a rebuttal. "I know, I know, that's harsh, have some compassion, right, but you have to be tough in life. It's like these homeless people with their ugly tents in the park —"

"Unhoused," said Robbie, who, even though he was a good ten feet away, seemed to be listening to his partner as if embarrassed by what he might say.

"Yeah, yeah, whatever," continued Most, glancing over his shoulder as if to keep Robbie and his opinions back there. "Dress it up however you want. Life throws you some curveballs, and you have to deal with it. This guy" — he looked at Wilson Shields' dead body again — "obviously couldn't handle it. I feel bad for him, don't get me wrong, but I'm a self-help guy. You make your own breaks. Too many whiners and losers nowadays. If your skin ain't the right colour, if your gender doesn't suit you, if something way back in history affected you, then it's poor me. Come on. Self-reliance, no complaining, that's what I believe in. Lots of people who have big troubles and are screwed by life find ways to succeed, pull themselves up. Ayn Rand. You know her? The writer? She's a fucking genius. Read her and you'll understand all this. You can find quotations online. I'm a big fan — a follower, you might say. She's all about freedom, freedom of the mind. You should read her, all of you."

"Shut up."

"Sorry, Alice?"

"Shut the fuck up, Most. And it's Sergeant Morrow to you. Step away from the crime scene and ask Constable Trew to come forward."

"Trew? I'm the ranking —"

Alice glared at him, and he stepped back, motioning with a distinct lack of enthusiasm for Robbie to move forward.

"Sorry about that, Sergeant Morrow."

"Not your fault, my friend. Anything to add about this? Your thoughts?"

"Well, you and Detective Mercer know way more about these sorts of crime scenes than I do, so I'll leave any conjectures up to you. But I do have something I'd really like you to look into. I noticed it when we were first inspecting the scene, but I didn't say anything about it. Constable Most didn't notice it, thank goodness, though I'm not surprised — thinking too much about himself. But I wanted to just leave it until you got here. It's over this way."

He turned on his flashlight in the dimming woods and took

Alice and Mercer a few strides past the stump where Wilson Shields had died. He squatted, and they knelt down beside him. Then Alice saw it, a piece of paper, illuminated by the light Robbie shone, darkened by moisture, jammed into the frozen leaves and bramble at the bottom of a tree and camouflaged by the snow, a bit of blood on it. Alice took out some blue nitrile gloves, snapped them on, and pulled the paper out.

"Good stuff, Robbie," said Mercer.

"Thank you, sir."

"Hugh."

"Right, sir."

The paper appeared blank, but when Alice turned it over, she could see there was some writing on it in a shaky hand, but it was incomplete, just four words: *I didn't tell the*

"Suicide note," said Mercer. "One he couldn't bring himself to finish."

"Or an interrupted confession?" asked Alice.

"I think the next word might have been *truth*," said Robbie. "Don't you think?"

"Good guess," said Mercer.

"About what, though?" asked Alice. "About him seeing Harold Massey burying the bodies, about what Charlie Eaton did to him, about his age, about his involvement in the other disappearances?"

"Why is it," asked Mercer, "that the more evidence we gather on this case, the less sure we are of who we are looking for?"

They all stood up.

"Okay," said Alice. "Edwina likely knows by now, right, Robbie? It was a family friend who found him, wasn't it? She sent him out here to look for him?"

"Yes. He was in shock. Called 911 on his cell and was just sitting here in the snow when we arrived, facing the other way. Older man, at least in his seventies. He said he'd go back and tell her."

"Do we know him?"

"I don't think so. We took his name and number, and I didn't recognize it as anyone you've mentioned connected to this case. Just a neighbour, a friend, helping."

"What's your gut instinct about the chance that he might be involved in some way?"

"In this death? Zero. This guy was devastated. Called the rifle a shotgun and the barrel a shaft. Don't think he knew the first thing about a gun or how to shoot one. I have the sense that he wasn't a longtime resident — maybe a city guy who had moved out here nearby and become friends with Mrs. Shields. Seems like half the people living here now are from the city. I told him to call for emotional support for her, let her close friends know, see if she wants them with her. I've been in touch with some people on the social work side too."

"Good job, Constable Trew," said Alice.

"Well, it's the least we can do."

"There was a sister too," said Mercer. "Wilson said she lives on the west coast. She needs to know right away and be with her mother soon."

"I recalled that too, sir, and let Sergeant Singh know at the station. I believe he made the call. I'm guessing she might even be on a plane by now."

Alice wanted to give him a hug but resisted it.

"All right," she said, "we have to talk to Edwina, and soon, but not now, not today. We have to give the poor old dear some space. This is going to be so incredibly hard for her. Let's all convene tomorrow morning at the station, and then a few of us should speak with her. I'm afraid she needs to know everything we know. It might help her deal with her son's death too, give it a reason. We can present him as innocent in all of this; there aren't any facts that don't support that, not yet anyway."

MERCER PULLED OUT his little flashlight and pointed it downward, searching the snowy ground as they walked back toward the road. It hadn't snowed a great deal during the last few days while they were all tromping in and out of here. Now, however, as they reached the cruiser, gentle flakes were falling. They got over the snowbank and onto the road, Mercer sending his beam of light along the road's snow-packed surface. He cursed. "Too many fucking footprints *all* the way in and *all* the way out of the woods, and a million tire tracks from all these vehicles on the road."

They got into the car, and the instant Alice started the engine, he turned on the heat.

"Do you really think it's possible that someone murdered Wilson Shields?" Alice asked.

"Well, I don't think it's *im*possible."

"But Robbie said that the guy who found him was a highly unlikely suspect, and what he said in defence of that theory made perfect sense."

"I agree."

"So, what are you talking about?"

"Maybe it was someone else."

"Who?"

They were no lights on this back road. Alice turned on her headlights, and they pulled out, the whole world around them now a dark, wintery wonderland, with the flakes sparkling and looking almost silver the way they sometimes did at this time of year in this kind of dying natural light when illuminated by the intrusive beams of a car.

"Well," said Mercer, "which individual among the many to whom we have spoken would be capable of doing this? Of getting into a car, maybe packing a rifle, if they didn't use our victim's own gun on him, driving out here, knowing where to go, having the physical ability to slip in and out of the forest, and killing

Wilson Shields? Who among them would have the motive to do it? Remember, too, that Wilson was the only living male attached in any way to these crimes."

"What does that mean?"

"Well, I know you've been getting after us, me and Robbie, for not considering women as possible suspects, but let's be honest, Alice, most evidence, most research, tells us that it's usually men who do these things. Women serial killers are rare, to say the least. Men do nearly eighty percent of the murdering in America, I know that for a fact, and when it's violent it's probably even higher. More than three-quarters of homicides are violent, and that's what we seem to be looking at here, violent crimes — heinous, violent murders — covered up by the killer. That just shouts men to me."

Alice drove on for a while. *He's on about this again*, she thought. *It almost seems like he doesn't even believe it's possible that a woman could do something like this.* It nearly made her laugh, but she knew that was highly inappropriate.

"So, you think there's absolutely no way that a woman could have done this?"

"Depends on what you mean by *this*. If you are talking about the bulk of these crimes, then yes, I think it is highly unlikely. Not impossible, it isn't *always* men, but *very* highly unlikely. However, if someone did kill Wilson Shields … it was a woman."

That startled Alice a bit. *But they're all old*, she thought. Then it hit her.

Blair Massey-Khan.

"Blair," she said.

"Yup."

Alice found herself nodding. "She's the only one young enough to do this … to come out here, get over the snowbank and into the woods, handle a hunting rifle and utilize it. She's now the only one who is incensed about all of this, about our investigation."

"She's smart. She said herself that she was looking into all the missing persons cases on her own. She could have figured out the Wilson Shields connection. She knew that her grandfather helped him, that he was involved in all of this, even if just in a tangential way, the only person —"

"Wait," said Alice. "When we told her that we had an eyewitness who saw her grandfather carrying dead bodies to a forest location on a farm near her family's farm, did either of us identify that eyewitness's gender?"

"I don't know. It was a mistake if we did."

"She's got motive," said Alice as she turned off the back road and headed toward the county highway, her headlights illuminating a tunnel of light in the silvery snowfall and black distance. "A big motive, actually. We as much as told her that all we really have against her grandfather, other than circumstantial stuff, is this eyewitness's testimony. She bloody well shouted that back at us."

"And now that witness has been eliminated. Just after we told her that."

"And we're looking for Evelyn Massey's possible murderer too. Remember when Gloria asked Blair to go and get her grandmother's medication to show us? Did you have the sense that she knew where it was? Didn't she come back awfully fast? I have no idea why she'd want to kill her grandmother, but it seems like someone did, and again, other than Wilson Shields, Blair is the only person we've talked to in all of these investigations who seems angry, deeply angry, deeply upset about all of this. Almost unhinged."

They drove in silence until they came to the stop sign at the county road. It was now suppertime. Again, neither of them were thinking about food.

"Let's go and see Blair, right now," said Alice.

It didn't take long to get to the Massey place. The first thing they noticed was that Gloria's car, the silver four-door Hyundai compact, was parked beside another similar one, green in colour, and a gold Mini Cooper was behind them. That little car had been out since the silver Hyundai had returned.

Alice and Mercer got out of the cruiser.

"Note which car was out last," he said.

"Not something you need to tell me."

"Yes. Sorry."

"Well, let's ask this woman, incapable of a heinous crime as her sex is, what she was doing over the last few hours."

"I didn't literally say that — that part about being *incapable*. In fact, I'm the one who suggested she could have done in Shields."

He's got a point, thought Alice. *Good debater again. Hate that. Sort of.*

They had taken their time getting out of the cruiser, and their voices had likely been audible as they came up the walkway. It was slippery from the falling snow. Mercer had learned to wear proper footwear up here, but he still didn't always know how to set his feet as he walked in certain weather. Though the lights were on in the big Massey home, the family hadn't turned on the outdoor lights, so the walkway was dark and its surface dim. Alice was sure that black ice, invisible ice, was unknown in Virginia where Mercer had grown up, and was probably not a regular thing even in New York and New Jersey. He had taken the lead going up the walkway, and about half a dozen steps along, he slipped and fell backward, heading for another landing on his ass, in danger of striking his head. Alice thought for an instant about how someone like him, a warmer-climate American, likely never considered the inherent danger of just walking about in her world. She leaned forward and caught him, but he was a big, well-built man. His weight knocked her over too, and they fell together with a crash — she on her back, Mercer, turned slightly toward her, landing in her arms. They both groaned as they hit the concrete and ice, then they were silent for a moment. They were looking up at the black sky, a few stars twinkling up there in the huge dome that was present on black and almost clear winter nights, white snowflakes falling gently onto their faces from heaven, tickling them. They started to laugh. In fact, they giggled and couldn't get up.

A head appeared in a window near the front door, and an outside light came on. Alice and Mercer got to their feet, helping one another rise and facing each other for a moment, smiling. Then they heard the front door open. Blair Massey-Khan was standing there holding a hunting rifle. She pointed it at them.

27

Let Bygones Be Bygones

MERCER STEPPED IN front of Alice to protect her, and she had no idea how to feel about that. It both nearly moved her to tears and pissed her off. She hesitated for a second and then stepped in front of him. After all, she was the one wearing the police-issue body armour. Immediately, she felt his hand on her arm, gently pulling her back behind him again. It felt like, in the face of this grave danger, they were suddenly in some sort of comedy routine. She started to move in front of him again, distantly aware that taking a fatal bullet was something she might secretly be hoping for, but decided to settle for standing by his side, pressing her shoulder into his to let him know she wasn't moving again.

"Same calibre," she heard him whisper, his voice sounding alarmingly calm in this situation. Alice stared at the rifle. She wasn't an expert in ballistics, but she knew what he meant. Blair's gun was similar to the one found on Wilson Shields. The bullet that had passed through his head would have matched both weapons.

"Get the fuck off my property."

"Relax, Mrs. Khan," said Mercer.

"I'm not Mrs. Khan, Mrs. Mercer. And I know how to use this thing."

"We just wanted to ask you a few more questions," said Alice, her hands up and facing Blair, far from her own weapon. She imagined how much Mercer likely wished he was the one bearing the police service revolver.

"You've already asked enough questions and caused enough pain."

"Have you just recently come home from somewhere?" asked Mercer calmly, looking back toward the little car and then to her again. "I mean, since we spoke with you at the station?"

Blair said nothing, nor did she take a step backward or loosen her grip on her rifle.

"Because we have been out somewhere," said Alice. Blair glanced at her.

"We were examining the body of Wilson Shields, dead from a gunshot wound through the head. The bullet came from a hunting rifle. We are trying to decide if it was suicide or not."

"He's the one," said Blair.

"The one what?" asked Alice.

"He's the one who made up the story about Grandpa disposing of bodies." She looked even angrier as she said this.

"Well," said Mercer, "he is conveniently dead now, so no longer an eyewitness. Where were you between about two p.m. and four p.m. today?"

That would have been when we were visiting Sal, thought Alice.

"I told you to get off my property."

"Please answer the —" began Mercer.

Blair turned the gun slightly away from them and upward and fired a shot, taking the tip off the leader pointing toward the black sky at the apex of a huge spruce tree in the yard, as if she had intended to hit the target point-blank.

"Women in the country know how to fire a gun, Mrs. Mercer. Accurately. I've asked you to leave twice."

"Okay," said Alice. "We're going."

"But —" began Mercer, stepping toward Blair.

"We're going," repeated Alice, placing her arm in front of her American colleague. She turned him, and they walked to the cruiser with their backs to Blair. She could sense Mercer's tension, his resistance, but he came with her.

They got into the cruiser, and she could almost feel the steam coming off Mercer. She remembered what he had told her about assaulting that suspect in New York, how he had lost his temper.

"Relax," she said.

She could tell that he didn't want to but that he was trying, and she respected that.

There was a knock on the driver's side window.

Blair.

Alice hesitated then rolled down her window.

"I had to go back into the city to my office. Just got back maybe ten minutes ago. We've decided to stay here together for a few days, to be with each other." Alice could see on her face how devastated Blair was. "About five people can corroborate where I was."

"Thanks," said Alice.

"And I'm sorry to hear about Wilson Shields. He had a tough time. I wish he wouldn't have lied about Grandpa ... but he must have had a reason for saying that." She looked up into the black sky. "May his soul rest in peace. Grandma's and Grandpa's too, and all those other folks who lost their lives around here."

Blair was crying.

"Don't do that with the rifle again, okay? Any time."

"Okay." She sniffled. "Thanks, Alice." She looked over toward Mercer in the passenger seat. "Good night."

Alice started to wind up the window.

"Oh," said Blair, "one more thing." She paused for a moment. "I was thinking ... maybe Grandma wrote those notes because she knew about something terrible — something not of her own doing or of Grandpa's — but couldn't bring herself to say more. Felt guilty about what she knew, and she thought that you, Alice — after what you went through — you would be fair. That you should be the one to look into it. That you were just a fair person, period."

Blair turned and walked away, her shoulders slouching, the rifle limp at her side, looking like the last thing she ever wanted to do was use it again.

THEY DROVE UP the lane, their headlights cutting through the pitch black, the falling flakes sparkling in the glow.

"Still doesn't mean that she —" began Mercer.

"The city is in the wrong direction. She could not have gone there and come back and also gone over to the Shields place, walked into the woods, committed the crime, and arrived back here not long ago. I don't care how capable she is with a rifle. She has witnesses too, lots of them."

Mercer didn't say anything. He was one man who knew when he was wrong. *One* man.

They drove the rest of the way to town without saying a word, both of them stumped by these crimes, stumped by them in so many ways. They got to the station, and he kissed her in the parking lot. She barely kissed him back and quickly withdrew from his embrace. *This isn't a relationship*, she wanted to tell him. She knew he wanted to say more about the envelopes, ask her more, bring up Luke, but he was smart enough not to do that either. This man was making things hard for her.

"Tomorrow," was all he said, and she nodded. They were both starving, but she could tell that he knew he would be eating alone tonight.

She drove home, not thinking of Wilson Shields or Harold Massey or Gloria holding her hand so tenderly, or of Blair's rage or her tears, or even of the remains of the five lost human beings they had found scattered here in her polite and friendly community, her community of well-meaning icebergs. Nor was she even contemplating what leftovers she might find in her parents' fridge. She was thinking of a pair of cat eye glasses and a beehive hairdo. Shirley Ezinicki was staring back at her from her photograph in her missing persons file. And Alice was asking her, *What about you? What happened to you?*

SAL WAS BACK in uniform and armed with four tall coffees and a smorgasbord of doughnut bits as she entered Alice's office the following morning. They had all arrived at virtually the same time, but none of them looked particularly eager. In fact, they all appeared exhausted — Robbie from having to deal with Elwin Most throughout most of yesterday, Sal from her domestic worries, and Alice and Mercer from frustration with this unsolvable case. They knew so much but not what really mattered. They seemed to be getting nowhere fast. In fact, looking into this case and the cases that might be attached to it appeared to be accomplishing only two things: finding bodies and getting more people killed.

Alice had been in Chief Smith's office for a few moments before she'd come to her own. The police service had received reports from forensics, and the chief had wanted to go over them and the state of this case before she conferred with the others again. What he'd had to say, in his sleepy, friendly way, hadn't pleased Alice.

She started off the meeting with her colleagues by reporting to them about the confrontation with Blair Massey-Khan and then turned to other things.

"Okay," she said with a sigh, "we have received more reports from forensics, and everything seems inconclusive. They cannot confirm to any degree of certainty that the five human remains we've found belong to anyone in particular. Just a lot of probablies and near matches. They are still working on it; we *are* just dealing with bones here. They may eventually get somewhere with dental records, but there's nothing certain yet. They speculate about causes of death but emphasize that these are speculations."

"But we know who the five are," said Mercer. "Perry Scott, Violet Massey, Caleb Carruthers, Charlie Eaton, and Dr. Johnson."

"*Know* might be too strong a word," said Sal.

"I'm sorry, but I have to agree, sir," said Robbie. "We can't really say we *know*."

Mercer looked like he wanted to get up and leave. He repositioned himself in his chair. "And we have a pretty good sense that something wasn't right about Evelyn Massey's death, that's six people, and Wilson Shields either killed himself or someone did him in, that's seven, and who the hell knows what happened to Shirley Ezinicki. That's eight bloody people!"

No one replied for a while.

"We have no real suspects," said Alice finally. "None whom we could put on trial, and even if we could, our best one is dead — and, frankly, his guilt just keeps becoming less and less of a possibility in my mind with every new thing we learn."

"About his character, mostly," said Mercer.

"Character means something," said Sal. "It would be different if we had proof that he did these things, real evidence."

"So," replied Mercer, "what are you all saying?" He looked at the other three.

Alice sighed again. "Chief Smith had me into his office just before we started. He's suggesting we let this go."

Mercer looked like a child who had just been told there was no Santa Claus.

"What?"

"I'd say that's an order," said Sal. "He isn't a very forceful guy. If he uses the word *suggest*, then he really wants you to comply."

"What the fuck?"

"He's not saying," continued Alice, "that we don't acknowledge what we know. Far from it. All the reports will be filled out, families informed as to what we uncovered, but he's worried that we are casting suspicion on good people. He knows the Shields family, and he's kind of shook up about Wilson's suicide, especially on the heels of us 'hounding' him, as he put it. He knows the Masseys too, knew Harold well, they apparently curled together."

"Our chief is not a young man," said Sal.

"He said," continued Alice, "that it appears to him that we will never know exactly what happened concerning these past incidents. He used the phrase 'let bygones be bygones.'"

"Wow!" exclaimed Mercer.

"Maybe he's right," said Sal.

"What?"

"Yeah," said Robbie, "he might be."

"I can't believe that I'm actually hearing this!" Mercer stood up and walked behind the three chairs, his hands clasped around the back of his neck. "You three are okay with just letting this case, these cases, go cold again? Frozen now? Forever? We are talking about the murders of eight people!"

"We don't know that," said Alice. "In fact, we can't say for certain that *any* of them were murdered. And none of us said we were okay with it, as you say."

"And this is a beautiful community in which nothing like that, no murder, no crime, is ever committed, in fact where no harsh words are even exchanged? There are zero secrets."

"That might be a bit of an exaggeration, sir. Bad things happen here, people do bad things, no question. We all know that. I agree with you that there is likely foul play here with this case, these old cases, perhaps lots of it, but we have to be realistic."

"Realistic?" Mercer sighed. "Look, Sergeant Morrow and I were just confronted by a woman who pointed a rifle at us, two police officers, and she even fired her weapon. And she's the granddaughter of our main suspect. She's veritably providing us with evidence that the Masseys are violent people."

"That's likely not true," said Sal. "How would you feel if someone was telling you that your grandfather was a mass murderer, the dear man you loved and knew to be a good person. You'd be traumatized; you'd do things you wouldn't normally do. She's had enough. We need to be sympathetic about that. I think the Masseys are lovely people, from what I know of them. And you heard what Harold did for my family. I think he represents what most people are like around here."

"I agree," said Robbie. "My mom had her trials moving here from Jamaica and being a visible minority, and some people treated her like shit, but most didn't. I'm willing to bet that she was treated better here than anyone in her situation would have been almost anywhere else — certainly better than in the States, from what I hear. We all wish our lives were perfect, but life isn't like that. And some people, it's true, like my useless partner, are definitely ignorant. Some people have attitudes about others — about Indigenous people or immigrants or those down on their luck — that really, really suck. But to me, that's the minority. Most people are trying, really trying. That's the way around here. That doesn't mean there aren't bad people among us, but it seems like we are looking for one bad person. One *really* bad person. *One.* I wish we could find him or her, but it seems impossible."

"There is no one for us to arrest, Hugh," said Alice. "And the chief says he'd like to keep the full extent of this out of the media; at least, he doesn't want a frenzy about it. They've been speculating enough anyway, and our local ambulance chaser — you saw him out there on the back road. That photographer. He'd do anything for a story. That's what matters to him, not what's right and wrong, not people's well-being. A frenzy would not be good for the community."

"Evelyn Massey was murdered. Just a week and a half ago! Someone is out there still doing this."

"We don't know that either. She took too much medication. That's an easy mistake, especially at her age."

"And her notes? They are damn near confessions. If not about her own guilt, then about someone's. She knew exactly where two human remains were. Exactly! And she was the wife of our main suspect and grandmother of a woman who points rifles at the police! We can't just sweep Evelyn Massey's written statements under the rug." He stared at Alice. "Her letters to *you*?"

Alice didn't like the way he said that and was worried that he was desperate now. Was he about to bring up Luke by name? In front of everyone? It made her heart race. Why did she think that her name on those envelopes had something to do with Luke? She did, though. Her intuition was shouting it.

Mercer sat down and sighed. He glanced at Alice again and appeared to see the terror in her eyes, though she was working hard at hiding it. Alice Morrow was an expert about secrets. Then she saw his eyes soften a little. Man, this guy was a challenge.

"But," he said, much quieter, "we still have a missing person out there. This schoolteacher, the young woman." He looked at Sal and then back at Alice as if to appeal directly to them. "Dead more than sixty years without her family and loved ones knowing what happened to her. Missing women is a horrible thing."

"Missing anyone," said Sal.

"Yeah," said Robbie, "but you're right, sir, missing women is a big thing up here, probably everywhere. You have that dead-on. Especially from marginalized communities. I don't know if Shirley Ezinicki qualifies in that respect, but we need to do better on this subject. Searching for lost people, all of them, just gone, or buried in forests or bodies of water or schoolyards, of any colour or race, is really, really important."

It was the earnestness of his youth on its soapbox again, but that earnestness was compelling. It stopped them all for a moment.

"All right," said Alice, after a while, "what do you propose, Detective Mercer? Do we have any leads on who killed Miss Ezinicki, or what happened to her? Robbie, Sal, you were checking into her background, her friends, enemies. Anything to report?"

They both shook their heads.

Alice turned back to Mercer. She admired and was thankful for his passion, especially concerning this young woman, but she couldn't say that out loud, or even to him in private. "Where should we look for Shirley Ezinicki? I'm all for it, if you have any suggestions." Alice wasn't able to say that last part with much conviction.

Mercer didn't have any suggestions, of course, other than a ground-penetrating radar search of the Massey property and maybe the Shields family's forest and all the farms for miles around. He obviously hated that that highly unlikely option was all he could offer, and Alice hated putting him on the spot about it.

"The chief," she said, standing up as if to try to bring the meeting to a conclusion, "said we have many other things to attend to right now ... instead of looking into 'ancient history,' as he put it. He wants this homeless encampment dealt with. Says 'these people' are making an eyesore of our public park."

"These people?" said Robbie.

"Yeah, I know," said Alice. "I'm just telling you what he said."

"And where are *these people* supposed to go? Almost every one of them can't afford a place to live, and the places they were allowed to live in before have been shut down. I think Elwin Most wants them chased around until they just give up and die. He says they're all lazy and drug addicts and a threat to public safety. When he's feeling really generous, he says that just *most* of them are. I hate to sound like an old fart, but where's the love for these people? Where's the idea of unconditionally helping those in need? Unconditionally." No one had an answer for him. "Maybe," continued Robbie, "they can all go and live in Chief Smith's house. I hear he has lots of room."

"I have one suggestion left about the cold cases," said Mercer.

"Yes?" asked Alice.

"You may not like this."

"Try me."

"You said yourself we should do this. I'd like to talk to Edwina Shields again."

"That was before I spoke to Chief Smith."

"I think we should leave her alone," said Sal.

"I don't mean we should pester her or upset her. I am well aware of what she's been through — her age, and her condition. But maybe we can frame our questions in a certain manner, say we are there to commiserate with her, comfort her in whatever way we can."

"Which we would be doing," said Sal curtly.

"Yes, of course, of course we would, but maybe we could get her to really talk too? Maybe that would even be helpful for her, you know, almost a sort of therapy. Go back over all of this: about Evelyn, Harold, her son, all of it. She strikes me as an impressive woman — kind and compassionate. And truthful too, when you ask her things point-blank. Look, Chief Smith can hardly oppose an essentially compassionate visit. I just think that, maybe, she might say something, intentionally or not, that reveals something we hadn't considered before. I think it's worth a try. As a last resort. And the right thing to do."

Alice drummed her fingers on her desk for a few seconds.

"And her daughter will likely be with her by now," added Mercer, "for support. We could insist that she stay in the room with her."

"Okay," said Alice. "But just me and Sal."

"No, I'd like to go too." He paused. "Please."

Alice drummed her fingers a few times again. "Okay, but you have to promise me to be good. Don't pressure her in any way. If she wants to talk, fine; if not, we have to let this be, maybe let it all be."

"All right," said Mercer.

This time, Alice didn't really like his smile.

28

Edwina Explains

FOR THIS VISIT, Alice insisted that they call ahead, and Mercer readily agreed. A woman identifying herself as Andrea Shields answered the landline and in a hard voice immediately refused to allow them to speak to her mother, but then Edwina could be heard in the background asking who it was, getting a reply, and admonishing her daughter to be kinder, in fact to apologize and to "invite Sergeant Morrow and her friends out to the house at once."

In the cruiser, Alice asked her cell for more northern music from the fifties, but it messed up a little and found the forties. She let it play, thinking this era more appropriate to Edwina Shields and her high school days anyway. It was big-band music, dancing-to-an-orchestra stuff. It came floating out, clarinets and saxophones, trombones and trumpets. Alice looked down at the screen: *Guy Lombardo and his Orchestra*, "The Sweetest Music This Side of Heaven."

When they arrived, they were met by a rather startling sight — Andrea Shields, a strapping woman who appeared to be nearly six feet tall, splitting wood with a heavy, full-sized axe in the driveway. She was going at it with a grim determination and what could only be described as a sort of fury, shattering four or five big pieces in the time it took the cruiser to get from the end of the lane to the spot where she was working. She was wearing a pair of expensive-looking jeans and a short-sleeved brown shirt that appeared to be made of velvet, and her hatless white hair was cut short and slicked up and back, all this in the freezing cold. Her muscles bulged as she worked. Alice, Mercer, and Sal were well aware that this lady was nearing seventy.

"Good day," said Sal, exiting quickly from the passenger seat and extending a hand. "You must be Andrea."

"I am." She tossed aside her axe and didn't take Sal's hand. Instead, she reached down and began gathering up the wood. There were quite a few pieces, and none of them were small.

"Oh, I can help with that," said Mercer.

"Me too," said Alice.

"No need."

The three of them stood there for a moment and watched her pick up everything and balance it all in her bare arms. When she had every piece, she turned toward the house. "Come on," she said.

"Thank you," said Sal.

Edwina was waiting for them in the living room, hunched over on the couch, her walker and wheelchair at hand, smiling at them, though the expression looked a little forced. She attempted to stand when she saw them, rising partway up, but Sal quickly told her not to and took her hand and lowered her back onto the sofa.

"So kind of you, Constable Haddad," said Edwina. "Good day, Detective Mercer, and so lovely to see you again, Sergeant Morrow. My gosh, I'm still not used to you having that title. I hope you are well."

"We are," said Alice, wanting to include everyone and not be the centre of any of this in any way. "We are so sorry for your loss."

"Yes, indeed," said Sal.

"Well, it is kind of you to say so, and to come to see me."

As they spoke, Andrea dropped her pile at the woodstove, got down on her hands and knees, and fed several pieces into what was already a red-and-orange inferno.

"I so like to have a fire on winter days. You know, Jim had electric heat put in here not long after we were married, but a woodstove can't be beat. It's a sort of heat that is truly warm, somehow."

"I agree," said Alice.

"Andrea is a dear for coming home to be with me, all the way from the west coast, fussing over me, doing the things that Wilson did. It's good that our girl knows how to swing an axe too!" She offered a bit of a laugh, but it seemed forced as well. Alice had expected to see her changed, perhaps on death's door, her face puffy and drawn from weeping. But Edwina Shields seemed the same as before. Alice thought of Delilah Morton speaking of how tough country women of her generation were. *One doesn't break down in difficult circumstances,* she had said. *My father taught me that. He was a taskmaster, but he was right. Folks nowadays show too much feeling, to my mind. What would have been the good of falling apart?* In some ways, it made a lot of sense. Alice was thinking of how seldom there were tears in her own home, of how rarely she had ever hugged her father. It wasn't the way around here. But this lady seemed even tougher, more courageous, than all the rest.

Andrea was getting to her feet now and starting to leave the room.

"We'd like you to stay, Andrea, if you might?" asked Sal.

"Oh ... okay." She appeared reluctant but sat down on the sofa an arm's length or more away from her mother.

"In fact, maybe we'll start with you," said Mercer.

"Start with me? What do you mean?"

"Yes, please, Andrea, we are glad to have the opportunity to speak with you as well," said Sal. "Though our main purpose in being here is to just check in on you, Mrs. Shields, make sure you are doing okay."

"Thank you, dear. I'm fine. I could be better, but I'm fine."

"So, we have a few questions for both of you, if that's all right. Nothing difficult or probing, Mrs. Shields, but if you would be so kind, we'd like to go over a few things about the Massey situation and about your son, very briefly, very very briefly ... if it's all right, again. We thought it might even, in a way, be comforting, to tell you what we know, to get to the truth of things, gently. You, after all, said as much yourself. You seemed to be a big believer in that."

"Absolutely. I'm fine, like I said. No use in collapsing. What's the point? You can ask me anything. Yes, the truth is what matters. You cannot run from it. I think that may be the secret to my longevity."

"I don't think you should be —" began Andrea.

But Sal cut her off, not even looking at her.

"That is so kind of you, Mrs. Shields. No worries, there will be nothing distressing discussed. Sergeant Morrow and I will make sure of that."

Neither she nor Alice even glanced at Mercer.

"Now, first, to you," said Alice, turning to Andrea.

"How are you doing?" asked Sal. "Are *you* okay?"

"Yeah. Sure."

Sal is such a pro, thought Alice. *She knows her role here. She relaxes people. It makes them talk.*

"So, you don't get home too often?" asked Sal. "Understandable, given how far away you live. Gosh, that's nearly a six-hour flight, isn't it, and that's only a bit more than halfway across our great country. We live in such a big place!"

"Yeah," said Andrea. "It is difficult to get home often."

"What do you do there?" asked Alice.

"Do you need to know that?"

"Oh, Andrea," said Edwina, "don't be difficult, my goodness."

"I ... uh," began Andrea. "I worked in the forestry business. Learned about trees and loved them when I was a kid. The forest was always a great place of solace."

"Like your brother," said Sal in a kind voice.

"Yeah, I guess. I worked my way up in the government, public service. I was assistant to the Minister of Forests before I retired a few years ago."

"Wow," said Sal, "that's impressive. Likely not a lot of women could even aspire to that when you started out."

Andrea smiled for the first time. "That is absolutely true. Changing now, though, thank goodness."

"So, did you raise a family out there?"

Andrea wore a plain gold band on her wedding finger.

"No."

They waited for her to say more. But she didn't.

"I see."

"Ms. Shields," said Mercer, "I'm sure you are well aware of what happened at the Massey home and the fact that there have been some other unpleasant discoveries out here in this general area, including on your own farm, in the forest you loved so much."

"Yes."

"Any thoughts about any of that? Can you think of anyone who might have wanted to do the Masseys harm? Did they have enemies, people with long-term grudges? Your brother told us some unpleasant things, things that we would rather not speak of, especially in present company, but —"

"What did he say?" asked Edwina.

"Mother, the police officer suggested that it would be best left unsaid. And I will add that I do not have anything to contribute to any of this. I didn't know the Masseys well."

"Well, that's not true," said Edwina.

"I was only a child when all of this happened, and that was more than sixty years ago. I have been gone for a long time. I do not know of any enemies they had either, so there you go. I was as stunned by all of these discoveries as everyone else."

"Did you know Caleb Carruthers, Charlie Eaton, Dr. Albert Johnson?"

"No, not well, at least."

"I want to know what Wilson said," repeated Edwina, almost as if to herself.

"What was your experience of your brother, growing up?" asked Alice. "Because he told us these things, we feel compelled to know more about him. You obviously know, and I don't think I'm being indelicate to mention it between the five of us, that he had some difficulties growing up and that he went away to school."

"Yes. He and I weren't close, partly because he wasn't around much, only in the summers. And we were, you know, boy and girl. Though I liked to do boy things."

"She was a tomboy," said Edwina.

"My father was a difficult man at times. He was a very tough father."

Edwina didn't speak.

Alice wondered about the Shields family and what life had been like for the children growing up, what sort of mother Edwina had been. She seemed, in some ways, distant from her daughter. They appeared formal around each other, not touching or even coming near one another. Alice couldn't imagine them hugging.

"He was a disciplinarian, my father," added Andrea quietly.

"Just like my father," said Edwina, "who used to beat the tar out of us." Then she turned to the police officers and focused her gaze on Alice. "You are not leaving this house until you tell me what my son said." She paused. "I'm sorry. That sounds awful. But you cannot mention that and then not tell me. Don't worry, you can't hurt me. Not more than I've been hurt already. I have one foot in the grave, let's be honest." That last bit appeared to be an attempt at humour, but it fell flat. She tried again. "I will have to get rough with you if you don't tell me, hand-to-hand combat." That should have been funny too, but it wasn't. Edwina really wanted to know.

"Well ..." said Mercer.

"Detective Mercer," began Sal, "we are not here to upset —"

"No, Sal," said Alice, "it's okay. Mrs. Shields is right. We owe this to her."

"Thank you, dear," said Edwina. "You and I go back a long way, you know, Alice, maybe longer than you know. I feel a connection to you."

Alice felt like taking the old lady's hand. But she didn't. "Go ahead, Detective Mercer."

Mercer cleared his throat. "Wilson Shields told us that when he was a small boy, he saw Harold Massey carrying Charlie Eaton's dead body to the forest at the back of your farm and burying his remains there. He was sure that Mr. Massey did the same with Dr. Johnson."

Andrea gasped and put a hand over her mouth. Edwina just stared at them, a steely look in her eyes.

"That's nonsense," she said after a while.

"As you know," continued Mercer, "those remains were discovered there just a few days ago."

"Our Wilson had a rather large imagination," said Edwina. "He was always given to fantasies. He used to go out to that forest and make up games all the time and tell me the most ridiculous things about what he was doing, what he had seen, monsters that were out there, as real to him as the five of us sitting here."

"He described it all in some detail."

"Yes, of course he did. He was a wounded child too. As you know." She said this without emotion. "He was a good boy, though, despite what he went through. He used to take me to see Evelyn all the time, you know, over these last few years when I haven't been driving."

"Oh?" asked Alice.

"Yes, never complained, not one bit. Sat there with us old ladies most times, other days went off and came back."

"Did he help you with other things around here?" continued Alice. "Did, he, for example, know your medications, get them for you, help you with them?"

"Why would you assume I am on medication?"

"Well, I —"

"That was a joke, Alice, dear. Yes, he did that."

"What about with Evelyn?" asked Mercer instantly, following up on Alice's questions, wordlessly working with her. "Did Wilson ever help her out with that sort of thing when he was with the two of you?"

Edwina paused for a second, looking closely at Mercer. "Yes. I suppose he may have once or twice. Though, as you know, her daughters and granddaughter came by often, and she had help — a nurse who checked on her several times weekly, as I have these days as well."

"He sounds like a good son," said Sal, not glancing toward Alice and Mercer.

"He was, all told." Again, she didn't appear sad, though this seemed like a moment when she might have been, when she might have wept. "And that thing about Harold Massey. My, my, that is preposterous. It almost makes you laugh." Though, she didn't.

"What do you mean?" asked Mercer.

"Well." She sighed. "I suppose I should tell you more about Harold. About him and me. I'm the age I am now, that's life, nearly finished, caught in this suit of old skin and bones. I might as well just be honest with you. Why not?"

"Yeah," said Alice, "why not?"

"Mother, do you really —"

"Oh, hush, Andrea. What's the use?" She seemed to gather herself. "I didn't just admire Harold Massey — and many people did do that, certainly — and I didn't just go with him a few times when I was in high school. I was in love with him. For a long time. Maybe I still am. He was a man. You know, Alice and Salma — a real man. He was about five years older than me, but we had something between us. A sort of chemistry. I had a full woman's figure when I was in high school, one a man could admire, though I've always had this rather blunt face. I was tall and strong, and so was he. My gosh, so was he. I wanted someone like him. A reliable man, a powerful one, one with integrity. I hadn't had that growing up. My father was brutal. Harold was kind, kind and decent. He never would have hurt those people. I know that to be an absolute fact. He and I, we knew each other, you know, physically. It was wonderful, and I will never forget it. Harold Massey was gorgeous to me, those times when we were intimate together, irresistible. He was ... he was big all over." Edwina Shields beamed. "He was always good to me about our physical relations, gentle and generous. He was not a violent man. He *could* be, on a hockey rink or on the battlefield in Europe or throwing bales of hay a mile high in the haymow, but never toward anyone in regular life."

Andrea Shields had listened to her mother with her mouth

open. She looked shocked, as if, for an instant, she'd thought Edwina was going to describe her sexual encounters with Harold Massey in graphic detail. In a way, she had.

"But Harold and I weren't meant to be," said Edwina. "Evelyn was meant for him. She was a beauty, you know, and perfect for him, a perfect match. I wasn't. I knew it, he knew it, and his family knew it. It was just young love between us, though young love is precious too. And I loved both of them dearly: Ev and Harold. Both of them. I had my man, anyway, my Jim." She said this without emotion too.

Alice found herself filled with emotion, though. In fact, her eyes were filling with tears, and so were Sal's, she was sure of it, though she dared not look at her. Edwina was such an admirable lady. Tough, as tough as nails. She was enduring all of this like a soldier, as brave or braver than Harold Massey. Alice wanted to talk to Sal right now, talk about women, about what women go through, but especially what had been endured in Edwina's day. This old lady was showing both of them what courage was, and how much courage was truly in the heart and soul of women.

"I think perhaps we've had enough for today," said Andrea.

"I think you are right," said Sal.

"I will see you out."

They all stood up. All of them except Edwina. "I'm so sorry to just sit here like a lump of potatoes," she said. "But perhaps I won't see you to the door this time."

"Of course," said all three of her visitors at once.

"Perhaps I won't see any of you again, period."

"Oh, Mrs. Shields," said Sal, "don't say that. I'm sure there will be another time."

"I knew your Luke, you know, Alice."

Alice froze.

"Lovely boy."

"Yes," said Alice and nearly broke down. It was the first time she had said anything like that in public since it happened, the first time she had acknowledged her lost love and her pain, her deep pain. This old lady had a way of connecting with her. "I'll … I'll give you my cellphone number," Alice managed to say to her. "Call me any time." She fumbled in her chest pocket inside her body armour, pulled out her card, and handed it to her. Alice wanted to stay with her, just sit down and be with her all night. But they had to go.

29

Alice Morrow and Hugh Mercer

ALICE DIDN'T WANT to go home with Mercer that night, but she did. She felt almost as if she owed it to him because she knew this was the end, for so many things. That moment with Edwina Shields had confirmed it. *Let bygones be bygones.* Let the pain die. Harold Massey hadn't done this, and neither had Wilson Shields. Whoever had done it, whether it was one person or more than likely several, even six or seven, and why they'd done it, if they were accidents or crimes of deep and nearly justifiable passion, she wanted to leave it be. Leave the bodies be. Those poor souls would have been better off staying underground with their secrets in the first place. She wanted Luke to leave her be too. She wanted what she had done to go away, just be *her* secret, and she wanted Mercer to go away too. It would all be easier that way.

When they got to his house, she started to kiss him, frantically. And then she tried to pull him upstairs. That would solve everything. For now. And then she could cut him loose, and he'd stop being here — stop being an invitation to something deeper that she couldn't have anymore.

But he stopped her.

"No," he said. "We are going to talk."

"About the case?" she asked.

"Yeah, first."

Alice didn't like anything about that answer.

"Well, I think it's over," she said. "Completely now. You've had your interview with Edwina."

"Let bygones be bygones?"

"No ... We've done a lot of good work on it, work that matters, that will be on the record. And I wish we could solve it all. But this just kind of feels like life, where you don't really solve anything."

"You don't?"

"No."

"That's pretty disappointing. Kind of boring." He tried to make her expression soften, did that unmanly thing where he looked into her eyes, but she avoided him. "I have lots of things that I want to solve," he said.

"Good luck. Especially with this case. We have a better idea of who didn't do these things now than who did. If you're honest, you know that's true."

"But we can't just give up, can we?"

"You never give up on anything, do you?"

"You know, that might be true." That thought made him smile.

"Maybe this isn't a good idea."

"What do you mean by 'this'?"

"This." She pointed at him and then at herself. "Tonight. Maybe I should get going?"

He sighed. "Why are you so unwilling to explore certain things? You weren't willing to really consider why your name was on those envelopes, even when it might have helped us make progress on these cases ... and you aren't willing to explore us, you and me."

She didn't respond. In fact, she took a step back toward the door.

"And you aren't willing to tell me about Luke."

The sound of his name on Hugh Mercer's lips made her heart pound. She lashed out. "And you, sir, aren't willing to explore what you did to that poor young man back in so-called America — that innocent person you beat almost to death."

She could see him swallow.

"And you aren't facing what you did to your wife and kids," she added. It was like she had him down and she wanted to finish him. She might as well have been raining blows on him, trying to kill him.

There had never been a moment between them like this, and yet, in the terror of it all, Alice knew it was a good thing. Good, no matter what happened next.

"I want to face all of those things. And I will," said Mercer in a quiet voice. "And I will. But are you interested in doing the same? I don't want to let this case die, let these lost people just fade away without knowing what happened to them. I wouldn't want that for myself or for you ... and I don't want us to die either."

"Well," said Alice, the sound of his voice saying *Luke* still hanging in the air, panicking her that he might say it again, probe again, "I do. I think it's best you go home. You are here illegally anyway. It would be better if I didn't have to formally ask you to leave. Goodbye, Detective Mercer."

She saw the tears well in his eyes only briefly as she turned and went out the door, and it seemed like she was in her cruiser instantly, that she hadn't walked along his snow-packed walkway without a sound and moved onto the snow-packed driveway like a phantom or opened the driver's side door or kicked her police boots to knock off the snow. She was just instantly driving away, up his lane, trying not to look at the warmth and the safety and the potential for love in the lights glowing through the windows and the front door of his farmhouse.

Out on the county highway, she turned on her phone and asked for music. It was still set on the fifties, but when she swiped at it, her eyes blurry, she swiped the wrong way again. She'd gone backward in time the last time, but now she went forward a little. "1963" said the screen. A duo she'd actually heard of called Ian and Sylvia began singing: a strong male voice and a beautiful soaring female one above it, mingling, sad and northern. "Four Strong Winds," it was called. She tried to concentrate on the slippery road, snow falling again in the black night, ugly and beautiful in the headlights, that tunnel again, showing the way through the darkness. On her cell, the man and woman sang about their time together ending and the need to move on. It was back when this song was on the radio that all those people were disappearing around here, way back then, near the end of the run of deaths. It was the year before Perry Scott died. He had come up here to this polite, decent country and vanished, buried under concrete in a basement. The song was full of cold wind and loneliness, and it kept blowing from her cellphone into her car.

She heard Ian and Sylvia sing "Early Morning Rain" and a few other songs, all seemingly bittersweet, before she arrived at the station. Each one of them hurt, but she let them play, wanted them to hurt her as much as they could.

She dropped off the cruiser and took her car home. Thank goodness her parents had gone to bed. In fact, she could hear them both in their bed this time, her mother giggling, but it didn't warm her heart. Not in the least. She kicked off her boots and threw her coat on the hook under the Home Sweet Home sign and rushed upstairs. There, she sat on her lonely bed, Luke staring back at her again.

"Why was my name on those envelopes?" she asked him. "Did it have anything to do with you? With us?" She couldn't shake that feeling. Why else would anyone single her out? It was the one thing she was known for by so many people in this community. Were those messages, these cases, somehow connected to her pain? It made her think that Hugh was right. She needed to ask questions about it, that was her duty. And, yes, she also needed to resolve what had happened to Luke and what she had done. If she didn't, then she wasn't sure she could go on. Not just as a police officer, not just in her social life, not just with her friends, like the amazing Salma Haddad, or with others at her church or at curling or with the whirlwind of men and the one important one named Mercer ... she just could not go on at all. She would spiral toward a fate like Wilson Shields ... like ...

She looked up at Luke and spoke out loud this time.

"Okay ... okay ... help me with this, my love. The notes in those envelopes, addressed to me, were written by Evelyn Massey, or so it seems. I didn't know the Masseys. Not well, only in passing, only as a good country family living not far from town. So, why me?" She stared at Luke. "Why you? Why you and me?" She thought of her young love for a moment, thought about him intensely, the first time she had allowed herself to do that in years. She allowed herself to feel the pain. She thought of how they'd met in the second year of high school — he a tall, slim guy with an irresistibly shy smile who looked at her the first time he saw her as if she were an angel coming toward him. She thought of his nervousness around her. She thought of how she adored the honest way he spoke, the way he walked, how kind he always was to her. She thought of how ordinary he was, how his dreams didn't stretch beyond the town, how he wanted to stay here, be employed here, teach maybe, raise a family with her, how they talked about that so often, every day nearly, and every week and every month of every single remaining high school year, all the way to the end, their relationship seemingly eternal, both of them admired by everyone around them. She thought of how she loved that and how it scared her.

But they were a strange match. Alice Morrow had always been "a handful," as her mother said. She had a bit of a salty mouth, she'd flirted with guys before she was even a teenager, she was always a loud personality. She played hockey on the boys' teams and played with abandon, once or twice challenging guys to fights. She wore her jeans as tight as she could make them and sometimes changed into different clothes in the school bathroom so her mother wouldn't know. She knew all the songs on the radio, especially the rocking ones, and could sing all the lyrics, smoked dope sometimes. When she got her driver's licence, she drove like the wind. She was like the wind in many ways.

She sat on the bed and fussed with her rings: the snake one on her left middle finger — a ring she had bought before she'd met Luke and had hidden from her parents — and her other ring, the straight gold bar on her wedding finger, blocking it from ever having another ring there, bought after he was gone.

Luke had been so different from her. A rock. Sweet and never aggressive. So down-to-earth. But Alice had found more than his smile irresistible. She had initiated sex the first time they did it. And it had been wonderful.

Still, she had wanted more. She always led her class in marks and in nearly everything else, it seemed, and Luke didn't. He was happy to be where he was and who he was. She had often thought, secretly, of course, that she still wanted other guys. Most of them were idiots, and Luke was so lovely, but some of them made her yearn to know more about them. It was in the way they walked too, different from Luke in their confidence, their swagger, their vision cast into the future to places far away from this snowy town. She knew that some of them looked at her like they couldn't understand why she was going out with Luke Holm, gave her glances that said they'd like to invite her into their world, a world of excitement that might fit her dreams. When she watched those guys with other girls at dances, boys whom girls lined up to dance with, watched them leading their dates across the gym floor with moves like movie stars, moves she knew she had too, moves so much better than their girls, moves so different from Luke, who danced awkwardly as he glowed at her while they swayed in the pulsing lights … she wondered even more about those boys. Alex Hall was one of them. He was number one. Smart, the best athlete in the school, dangerous at times too in the way he looked at you, the things his smiles promised, a boy who looked like a man, a man among boys. There was no one like him in those days.

She sat on the bed and told herself to stop thinking about Alex Hall. She fucking hated him. She turned back to Luke and looked at his face, smiling at her the way he used to. He always looked like he had secrets, but good ones. She started to sob and worried that it was so loud that her parents could hear her. She stopped herself and wiped her eyes. Who was Luke Holm, really, to do this to her? She had never actually thought much about his past. Everything was always very present with him, right to the end. He was a town kid but had moved here from the countryside.

That was when it hit her. The Holms were country people originally, farmers of very humble origins, Luke had said. In fact, she remembered now that he had told her that they were from an area not far from where the Masseys lived. That thought hit her like a bullet. She remembered what Edwina Shields had said to her: *You and I go back a long way, you know, Alice — maybe longer than you know. I feel a certain connection to you.* The old lady had also said, *Sergeant Morrow, my gosh, I'm still not used to you having that title.* But the most important thing she had said had stayed with Alice like nothing else had clung to her these last weeks: *I knew your Luke, you know, Alice.* As she heard the brave old woman uttering those words, clear as a bell in her mind, she also remembered how the ancient soul had comforted her, consoled her when everything else about Luke terrified her. Edwina had lost her love too. Harold Massey. She remembered Edwina taking her hand and kindly asking her how she was, the warmth of her hand, the grip, as if she wouldn't let her go.

Alice was exhausted. By everything. She lay back and fell asleep in her little teenage bed, still in her police uniform.

SHE WAS AWAKENED by a phone call early in the morning, the sky still dark outside her windows. Fumbling for the cell on the little bed, wondering who she was and where she was, she began to emerge into reality and had a vague sense that it was Luke calling and then that it was Hugh Mercer. For an instant, that thrilled her. But when she looked down at the screen, she saw another name, one she hadn't expected.

Edwina Shields.

30

Unmasked

SHE CLEARED HER throat.

"Sergeant Alice Morrow."

She expected to hear Andrea Shields' voice, and it made her heart pound. Had the precious old lady died in the night?

"Oh, yes, dear. It's me — Edwina. Edwina Shields?"

She said it as if she had to remind Alice who she was, and it made Alice sad.

"Of course, Mrs. Shields."

"Edwina. Please call me Edwina, dear."

That warmed Alice's heart.

"Of course."

"You could even call me Eddy, as my dear friends and family always have."

For some reason, that rang a little bell in Alice's mind, but she didn't know why, and as she paused to consider it, Edwina continued, sounding more urgent than Alice had ever heard her sound before.

"I was thinking about all this terrible, unpleasant stuff you and that lovely constable lady — you know, the one with the dark skin who was with you — and that nice handsome American policeman, southern fellow, were discussing with dear Andrea and me, and I realized that there is something else I need to tell you, something very important."

"Can you just tell me now?"

"Oh ... no, dear, I can't." She paused. "There is something I need to show you too ... in our barn."

ALICE DIDN'T BOTHER with breakfast. She didn't comb her hair either or even wash her face, though that was something she often neglected to do anyway. When she was young, when she was with Luke, and of course that time with Alex, she had been so different. Her face had needed to be perfect. Her scent had too, the one that Luke had loved and that she still kept somewhere, deep in a bottom drawer somewhere in her room. Perfume was for unimportant relationships now.

It was breathtakingly cold when she stepped out the door. She wouldn't bother to go to the station to get her cruiser; she'd just take her own car. But she wondered if it would even start. The sun was trying to come up, and it was one of those days when saliva would freeze on its way toward the ground, one of those days when there was a certain atmosphere in the air, so cold that it affected sound. It was a frozen quiet. The only sounds were her car's engine and heater working hard, her police boots crunching in the snow, and the windshield scraper as she cleared the windows of ice.

As she drove toward the Shields farm, the sun still offering almost no light as it kept trying to rise in the grey day, she turned on some music again. The phone took her back to Ronnie Hawkins — the

Hawks and their dangerous American sound, which was played better by this northern band than anyone in the south. There was more than a touch of evil in it, and she turned it up.

She passed the end of Hugh Mercer's sideroad and wondered if he was still there. Had he had enough of her, finally? Had she chased him away for good? She guessed he'd be gone sometime today, back to the States again, this time to stay, back to his wife, maybe, or was that part of his past now? She thought of his secret. Would he return and face it? Would he admit that he had beaten that suspect? Or was it better to let bygones be bygones?

A while later, she neared the sideroad leading to the Shields farm and "Who Do You Love?" came on again — ominous guitar rocking, Ronnie's growling lyrics, so wickedly far from the Four Lads and the Crew Cuts that it made her grin. Nothing false about it, nothing fake. It was the sound of truth. She drove along the frozen gravel road, snowbanks piled high on the sides. The modest home, clapboard and in need of paint, and the old barn soon appeared in the distance, shrouded in grey.

Ronnie Hawkins was singing about being bad, wearing a snake as a necktie, living in a house with a chimney made from a human skull.

She went down the lane and pulled into the driveway. There was only one car there — Edwina's old Rambler in the breezeway looking like it hadn't been driven for decades. The old lady was here alone.

On the cellphone, Ronnie and his northern Hawks were asking Alice who and what she loved. She got out of the car and moved up the walkway. There didn't appear to be any lights on in the house, even though the morning was still grey. It looked dark inside. For some reason, she had put her cellphone in her parka pocket and forgotten to turn off the music. It rocked through her coat as her police boots crunched in the salt on the snow and ice.

In the song, night was falling, and something ominous was approaching. She swiped the music off.

As she knocked, she realized that she had told no one, absolutely no one, that she was coming here.

No one answered the door.

She knocked again and then went in. At first, it seemed as if the house was empty, but then she saw someone sitting at a table in the kitchen in the dim indoors, holding a flashlight. Its glow shone upward indirectly toward this person's face. Edwina. For some reason, she was wearing gloves. She must have been cold.

Alice turned on the lights.

"Mrs. Shields?"

"Oh!" she said looking up from her wheelchair, pressed up against the table. "Who is it?" Her voice sounded hard and threatening.

"It's me. Alice. Sergeant Alice Morrow."

"Oh my gosh, it's you, dear. You've come quickly."

"Yes, I came right away. This sounded important. Why are you sitting here in the dark?"

"I like to do that sometimes. And I have a flashlight, so I can get around if I need to. Andrea got me up this morning before she went into the city. She has a friend there, I think, whom she hasn't seen in a long while. Andrea never had many friends. I encouraged her to go. I told her to leave the lights off when she went so I could watch the sun come up. But it's a dark day, isn't it?"

"Yes, Mrs. Shields, it is."

"I thought I told you to call me Eddy?"

There was that name again. Alice had heard it before, long before Edwina had asked her to call her that.

"What did you want to tell me?"

"I think I'd best just show you." She manoeuvred herself back from the table and came around it toward Alice. "It's in the barn."

She headed toward the door.

"You're going out there with me?"

"Of course."

"I'll get your coat." There was a clothes closet just inside the front door. Alice moved toward it. "In here?"

"I don't need a coat. I'll be fine. I have a sweater on."

It was a cold mid-January day, cold even for these parts. At least Edwina was wearing gloves. But gloves and no coat?

"Are you sure? It's no trouble. It's freezing out —"

"Nonsense. And don't fuss. Open this thing, Alice." She had arrived at the door. She cracked her cane against it with two hard knocks, as if it were a code for access.

Alice hesitated. "All right," she finally said and stepped around Edwina to open the door. The blast of cold air made her shiver, but the old lady merely gazed forward and then moved herself out onto the walkway.

"Here. I'll push you."

"Nonsense. I'll be fine. It's electric."

Alice watched the old, gloved hands grip the handles of the wheelchair and direct it along the walkway toward the barn. The Shields barn was close to the house, much closer than the farm buildings were at the Masseys or even Hugh Mercer's place.

Alice put her hands into her pockets to warm them, and the tip of a finger came in contact with her cell and turned it on. The songs had moved on to January 1965, the winter after the death of Perry Scott. A song called "Shakin' All Over" by Chad Allan and the Expressions came bursting right through Alice's parka pocket. The lead singer was rocking into lyrics about his lover's body being close to his, how it gave him chills, made him shake all over.

"What is that racket?" said Edwina.

"Sorry. I'll turn it off." Alice pulled out the phone and swiped it off, then opened her car door as she passed it and tossed the cell onto the front seat. She knew that old song — other bands had covered it — and it always gave her the shivers, just like the lyrics said. She rushed forward again to catch up to the old woman who was advancing without her toward the barn, looking at the back of her yellowing white hair vanishing into the dim day in front of her, hatless in the frozen air. *Eddy,* thought Alice. *Why do I know that name?* Then her memory attached another word to it. *Aunt Eddy.*

"It's in the silo."

The snow was trampled down in a path where Wilson had walked so many times past the barn toward the fields and the forest beyond. The path went up an incline toward the big rear doors to the haymow on the upper floor. It was a similar setup to the Massey farm, though the building was much smaller and more dilapidated. The wheels of Edwina's chair slewed a bit as she attempted to go up the hill, and Alice got behind and pushed. The old concrete silo rose in front of them at the back of the barn, higher than the main building, a grey cylinder reaching up to the grey sky.

When they arrived at the big sliding doors, Edwina again banged her cane on the entrance. "Open this," she said.

Alice found the chain and hook that held the doors together, undid them, slid one door to the side, and then helped Edwina go up the little incline onto the upper barn floor. Like the Masseys' building, it smelled of old, rotting hay, of a time long gone. Even the open door, drawn wide in the dull morning, offered the interior little light. Edwina lifted her flashlight off her lap and turned it on.

"This way," she said, veering left and rolling across the cold planks of the upper barn floor toward a wall, the beam from her flashlight illuminating the way. Alice could see a ramp coming into view and at the end of it another door, wooden and narrow, very narrow, less than shoulder-width across.

For some reason, Alice could still hear "Shakin' All Over" playing in her head, even though her cellphone was lying silent on the seat of her car. She remembered the electric guitar, the great voice, singing about being aroused by someone, getting quivers and shakes through every bone in the body.

"Where are we going?"

"To the silo, like I said."

Alice was far from being a farm girl, but she knew what silos were and what they were for. Farmers stored silage in them — usually corn, sometimes grass or hay, packed into the silo during the harvest and then fed to the animals throughout the winter. Stinking, sometimes fermented stuff that pigs and cattle apparently found delicious. You loaded the feed into the silos from a combine harvester or simply off a truck, using an auger to get the feed way up there and then down into the silo's interior. But Alice was guessing that the Shields silo was empty now, since Jim Shields had been dead for decades and the farm and barn weren't operational anymore; only parts of the fields were rented out these days.

"Why the silo?"

"There's something in there."

"What?"

"Well ... you tell me." She had gotten up onto the ramp and now motioned toward the entrance with her cane. "Go on." Alice could see the old lady's breath, and her own breath as well, in the stinking barn air. She paused and then manoeuvred around Edwina and walked up to the door. It had a simple latch on it. She pressed down on it and opened the entrance. It swung toward her with a creak. She looked through the narrow opening between several steel bars that lined it horizontally and gazed out into space. A different sort of stink arose from inside.

"Where do I go now?" Alice asked. "What am I looking for?" She was facing away from Edwina into the silo, and her voice echoed as if it were bouncing into a huge upright tunnel. Alice could hear the old woman wheel up close to her from behind.

"Shakin' All Over" still played in Alice's imagination. Spooky and reverberating, it now sounded like the band was somewhere deep in the bowels of the barn.

"It's on the bottom of the silo, way down," said Edwina. "I think it's been there for many decades. I always thought it was something else, but when you got talking about human remains being all over the place, hidden and buried around here too, on this very farm, I suddenly thought of it. Those iron bars you see are ladder rungs. You have to turn around facing me and climb down. Please, be careful, dear."

Alice turned toward Edwina and saw that she was close to her now, her flashlight held in one ancient hand and the cane gripped in the other. She had never noticed how large Edwina's hands were before. They filled her men's gloves. The flashlight was tilted up toward Alice and the open space, but it also cast Edwina's features in an eerie glow. It was as if Alice could see her skull through her nearly translucent aging skin. There was that expression again: the emotionless one she always wore. Edwina Shields, it occurred to Alice, hardly ever expressed any emotion on her face. It was as if she were incapable of it.

Alice turned sideways to get through the narrow opening.

"Don't do that," said Edwina, "that's too dangerous. You are going to have to take off your parka. If you try to go through there with it on, you will fall."

"How far down is it?"

"A good ways."

She was right about the parka. Alice couldn't get through the opening dressed as she was; at the very least, she would damage her coat. *Well,* she thought, *it doesn't matter. I will be in and out of here quickly, and I'm warm enough underneath, and it likely isn't as cold deep in the silo.*

She took off her parka and instantly felt frigid.

"And that too," said Edwina, pointing her cane at Alice's thick gun belt, holster, and weapon. "You won't be able to get through with that on, and if you do fall, God forbid, or if your gun catches on something, it could go off. I know guns, and I know gun accidents. You do if you are born and raised out here."

Alice thought of Blair firing that rifle at the top of the giant spruce tree in her yard, nipping the top branch off like a marksman.

Alice hesitated.

"Just being safe," said Edwina, the glow of the flashlight still making her face look ghoulish.

"Okay," said Alice. She undid her belt and set it and the holster and gun down gently at the top of the ramp near the foot of Edwina's wheelchair. Then she backed into the opening and slowly extended her right foot through the bars, which were a good two feet apart, and slightly down and into the open space of the silo. Her hands were against the sides of the entrance. Her boot heel kicked something, a pebble maybe, and it shot into the silo and across it, pinging against the far wall and then skipping down and down and down until she heard it smack onto the concrete floor below. The sound echoed for a moment. She couldn't believe how far it appeared to descend. She guessed maybe thirty or forty feet. She hesitated then ducked down a little, her head now brushing against the bar above her, and felt for that first metal rung just below the bottom of the entrance. She couldn't feel it. She reached up and gripped the rung above. For a moment, she still couldn't feel the lower bar, and her hands tensed. She paused, smelling the stinking interior, feeling the dampness all around her, and looked up. At the open end of the silo at the top, under the grey sky, she could see a piece of equipment, steel and circular, with an auger on it. It looked heavy, dangerous, and medieval. She felt again for the ladder, and as she did she heard Edwina rolling toward her. When she looked up, the old woman was almost upon her, and she had her cane thrust toward her. The look on her face, now barely visible in the dim light, had little emotion but a grim sense of determination. Evil determination.

"This is for Luke," she said, and she drove the end of her cane into Alice's chest with a force that Alice never could have dreamed Edwina Shields possessed.

31

What Really Happened Long Ago

AUNT EDDY, WAS all Alice could think as she fell into space. *Luke's Great-Aunt Eddy.*

It was like nothing for a moment, like time had been suspended. It wasn't the 1940s, and Guy Lombardo and Hank Snow weren't on the radio; it wasn't the 1950s with Bobby Curtola and Paul Anka. Though maybe, in some ways, it felt like Ronnie Hawkins was singing now, as Alice fell down and down and down, timeless and spaceless, falling to her death. At first, she just let it happen. This made sense. She deserved this. But then Sal's face came to her, and Aya's and Mahmoud's, and her own mother and father, and she saw and felt Hugh Mercer trying to love her, and then she saw Luke, and finally herself. She tried to pull herself out of it. A split second had elapsed, but it felt like forever. She thrashed all four limbs toward the wall, and one hand smashed against a metal rung; it hurt like hell, but it spun her and slowed her a little. Now, at least, she wasn't descending head downward. She kept falling and falling, and reaching out for the walls, touching them at times, tearing the skin from her knuckles and spinning herself again, slowing her descent slightly. The worst part was not knowing when she would hit bottom, when she would die. She ejected that thought from her brain. Amazingly, she was becoming determined to survive. She tucked her head under her arm and shoulder.

And then the landing came.

She had never felt pain like that before. First in her foot, shooting through it, accompanied by a terrible bone-cracking sound. And then her legs buckled under her, or both broke, and the rest of her body hit the concrete surface. But her upper back, arm, and shoulder hit next, protecting her head. And then she lay there, groaning, in mind-numbing pain, her ankle, both her legs, her right shoulder, and her arm crying out.

For a few seconds, there was only the sound of her groans. Then she heard Edwina up above.

"It wasn't Harold Massey whom Wilson saw taking the bodies to the woods to bury them." She paused, her voice flat, like so many voices from here. "It was me."

All Alice could think of was that first time she had spoken in an accusatory tone to young Robbie Trew, aware that Hugh was listening too. *Do you think that women are incapable of murder?* she had asked the two men.

"Just substitute me for Harold, put my head on his shoulders ... and think of what my son told you."

Lying there down below, Alice thought of all the times she had been shocked to even imagine that *anyone* could murder another human being in this community, let alone that a serial killer could be working his or her evil.

"I killed them all, dear," said Edwina up above, "though I'm sure you think I am and was incapable of such things, that I didn't have the strength or the intelligence or the audacity. Think again, as you breathe your last breaths."

Alice finally looked upward. She could see Edwina standing there. Yes, standing. She had gotten up out of her wheelchair and was looking down at her, as sturdy as a pillar. Alice was shocked at how big she appeared, drawn up to her full height now, no longer slouched over in her chair or crouching when she tried to walk. Alice thought of Edwina speaking boldly of her relationship with Harold Massey and the sex she had with him. *I had a full woman's figure, one a man could admire ... I was tall and strong, and so was he.*

Edwina Shields had Alice's service gun in her gloved hands.

"I killed every last one of them," she continued, "and I will tell you how. I will tell you why I am killing you now too, how I set this all up so you, Alice Morrow, would be my final victim. They all deserved what they got. Including you, you bitch."

There was still no emotion on Edwina Shields' face. There never was any emotion there. *A psychopath hidden among us,* thought Alice.

"I didn't intend the first one, Violet Massey." Edwina's voice echoed in the silo. "It was 1958, summertime. I'd driven over to the Masseys' to talk to Harold. I knew Ev wasn't there, but I didn't know he was gone for the day too. I couldn't help myself, though I knew he would resist me. He was like that. Honourable. When I got there, the place was empty, but then Violet came out the front door. She was staying there while they were away, looking after their two daughters for the day, the last still in diapers. Violet told me to keep quiet because the children were sleeping and then she told me to clear off. She said she knew why I was there. She'd always been like that — pushy, protective of her brother. She led her family in not wanting him to marry me. It was like I was some sort of disease to them and especially to her. So then she came toward me, her eyes glaring at me behind those glasses of hers, her hair tied up in a librarian's bun. She'd never had a man, never been with one, or anyone else. She didn't know what that was all about — the love and the hurt of all that. And I just hit her. I could hit like a man — my father had taught me how to punch with a pair of boxing gloves in the barn and had cuffed me in the face many times. I could take a punch. I think I could have at least survived in a barroom brawl in those days. Yeah ... I struck her in the face. I broke her nose, busted her glasses, and she fell back and hit her head on a rock on the lawn — a big, ornamental one Ev had set up there. That was funny, in a way. She was dead before I even started kicking her. I didn't mean to do it, not the killing part. I took their tractor, sitting there in the barnyard with its the front-end loader still on for the spring manure, and I loaded her on, just like the manure, and I took her and one of Harold's shipping crates, for a coffin, up the hill to the Massey burial site. I knew where it was. I dug a plot among some trees near there and put her in it and left. I could hear the kids crying inside the house — little Gloria and Gwen — but I knew Ev and Harold would be back to tend to them before nightfall. They all said she had disappeared. Without a trace. For no reason. Left. It sure seemed that way ... didn't it? They didn't used to ask a lot of questions around here."

Alice knew that she would soon share the same fate as Violet Massey and all the others, and she would appear to have just vanished, but she wasn't sure how. She looked up at that medieval contraption at the top of the silo. She found herself thinking of Mercer. She wished she had not sent him away. And not just because she was about to die. She wished she had had the courage to embrace his love. To not punish herself anymore. She was going to pay for that. Pay for that and other things ... at Aunt Eddy's hands.

"It was easier after that," said Edwina up above. "It just became normal. The next year, when I dropped by to see Ev one day, she wasn't indoors, so I went looking for her. I found them in the barn in the haymow ... her and Caleb Carruthers, her bank robber boyfriend. I could hear them a long way off. Man, were they having sex. At first, I thought, well, good for her, but that only lasted for an instant. I didn't know Carruthers was even back, though I'd heard he'd been snooping around. Ev was enjoying herself that day, in a way that I didn't even know she was capable of. The things she said while they were doing it shocked even me. Both of them completely naked in the barn, not even hiding it ... hiding nothing. But then I thought of Harold, of course, poor Harold out there in the heat of that late June afternoon, likely on the back forty doing hay, likely having taken the lunch that she'd made for him and gone ... she knew he would be gone all day. I hated her for it. And I hated him even more. Carruthers. Putting the cuckold on my Harold. Good, sweet Harold. I climbed up into the mow, and they were so involved with each other that they didn't hear me. I walked across on the hay in that silent way you can on a mow and hid. I watched them. All of it. When it was over, she told him to dress and get going, that he had a long walk back up their sideroad. Someone must have been picking him up there, maybe some other crook he knew, maybe someone from the city. She said she was going to walk in the fields, see Harold. I knew that Carruthers had fathered Ev's first child. That was obvious, at least to all us women, though no one ever said a word. It made me hate him even more, though. I was blind with rage about that fucker, about what he had done to Harold. Ev wouldn't see my car, since she had headed off over the fields. It was perfect. There was a bale hook leaning against the wall where I was hiding, a thick iron tool that you used to hook bales and drag them, heavy as a short crowbar. After she left, and he was dressed, still stinking of her, and starting to walk across the mow, I came up behind him, silent again, and drove that hook into his neck, and then I pulled it out and whacked him across the back of the skull. He fell face forward and landed a few feet from the hay chute. It wasn't hard to push him into it, head downward, and he landed on his skull on the concrete down there amongst the pigs. You know, pigs will eat a human being if one of us falls among them and isn't moving. I knew that. Good farm girl. Carruthers 'vanished' too. The next day, I visited the Masseys and went out to the barn, to see the pigs, I said, since they had a sow that had just had piglets. I found bits of Carruthers' remains and his teeth. I wanted to hold them in my hands, like a little war trophy — proof that he was dead — and I stuffed the teeth in a hole in the concrete wall."

Alice felt like she was going to faint. The steel contraption high above her was fading in and out of her blurring vision. She was thinking again that no one knew where she was.

"Once you've done that once, and then twice, you get a feeling that you can do it again, that you can rid the world of bad people, or at least people who have been bad to you. It is a wonder I didn't do something to my father, after what he had done to me. But for some reason, I didn't. Charlie Eaton, though. He touched my son!"

It was the first bit of real emotion that had come from Edwina Shields. Her voice echoed in the silo.

"My Wilson was just a poor little boy, and that pervert took him out behind the school ... and he touched him! The boy told me in tears. He only told me. And the next day, after I had dropped the little fellow at the school, promising him that I would find a way to take him away from all of this, I was sitting in my car, just ten or fifteen minutes afterward, just sitting there, angry ... and out came Charlie Eaton, traipsing out the front door, having been sent home for whatever crap he had just done in class. I followed him until I found a moment in his dreadful part of town where no one was around, and I pulled over in front of him, right on the curb, and told him to get in. I told him I knew what he had done and that I would tell everyone. He had no choice but to come with me. And he didn't fear a woman, not the way he would have feared a man. So I drove him out to our place, and I finished him. He wasn't ready for it. For me. It wasn't hard. Jim was in town at the co-op getting feed, and I knew he'd go from there to a watering hole he liked. So I had this young pervert all to myself. But what I didn't know was that my Wilson hadn't been able to stay at school that day, and he'd asked to go home, and they had called me and gotten no response. So they drove him out here and left him in the house. They would do things like that in those days. But he wandered out after they left and walked to the back of the farm to the forest, where he had just started to go on his own. He saw me there, unloading Charlie Eaton from the hay wagon and about to bury him in the forest. I told him what I had done and said that Eaton would never bother him again, but that he needed to never tell anyone. I let him watch me put him underground. He couldn't go back to school, not after what had been done to him and what he had seen me do. So, I appealed to my wonderful Harold, the chairman of the school board. I didn't tell him everything, certainly not what I had done to Charlie Eaton, just the terrible thing that had been done to Wilson, that we were desperate that it be kept quiet, and that we had no money to educate him elsewhere. You know what he did. I love him still. But poor Wilson, he lived with all of that. You could see it every day in the lines in his face, the way it aged him. I think he found the other grave too, one day when he was out there. He must have known I'd done other things too, how the other disappearances connected to his mother, what I was capable of. He lived with it, never told anyone, though I must say I am angry with him, even though he kept my secrets, that he tried to blame it all on Harold. That was a bad boy."

Alice couldn't believe that she was still conscious. Maybe it was because she wanted to know all of this. She always wanted to know. Just like Mercer. She found herself wondering how Edwina was going to dispose of her body. She knew she had a plan.

"Let me see, how many is that?" asked Edwina. "Oh, yes, three. There were three more. Four, actually, if you count the last." She paused, fingering the gun, aiming it down the silo toward Alice. "They were all just scores I was evening. I mean, I had killed three people, why not a few more? Why not eliminate human beings who had been awful to me, just god-awful, who deserved to die? Take the doctor. That bastard gave me two caesarians. Two! I doubt I needed either one of them, but that was how male doctors often treated women in those days, like animals, cows. And they were almost all men. They needed to get the baby out, hopefully a male, and one might as well slice up the mother to make it happen. Let's not pause, let's not think of how we are maiming her. I have an ugly rip down my belly to my crotch. An ugly rip. Johnson did that. Twice. I knew he was at Delilah's that day. She and I had spoken on the phone in the morning, and she said she was getting him to come out to her place, that he had agreed to do it as his last call. I was alone at home again. That's always when I struck. I was not in a good mood. I drove over there. I met him at the end of Del's sideroad, told him I was poorly, and made him come with me. At home, I gave him tea and fed him. Oh, I fed him. Fed the butcher. Fed him the stuff we give to the rats."

Alice started to squirm. She wondered if there was some way to save herself. Could she struggle over to the ladder and try to climb? But she looked up and saw that medieval circle of steel up there again, and Edwina, gun in hand, towering in the doorway halfway up.

"And so we come to Shirley Ezinicki," said the old woman. "Do you know that that bitch failed my Andrea in grade one? Failed her! A child. She tried to destroy her and her self-respect, almost as thoroughly as Charlie Eaton had destroyed my Wilson.

Andrea was never the same after that. She was a different child. That's both my children, Alice. *Both* my children. Who fails a child in grade one? Tell me, dear. Who does that? It was vindictiveness on her part, I know. She just didn't like Andrea. Well, I didn't like her then. She was renting a place over the way, less than an hour's walk through the fields, which is nothing to us country folk. It was June then too, just the day after she'd failed my little girl, after she'd come home in tears. I asked Miss Ezinicki to come through the fields and meet me, talk about it, made sure I sounded friendly on the phone, told her I understood that these things sometimes happened. She was no match for me. And then I disposed of her in the most inventive way of all my victims."

She looked up. Alice looked up too.

"Do you see that contraption at the top of the silo? That is called an unloader. You can adjust it and lower it and raise it in the silo. Ease it up or down or drop it like a bomb. I dropped it like a bomb that day. A silo unloader spins around and picks up the silage and feeds it through an auger and fires it through the auger to the animals to eat. I put Ezinicki in here that day, tossed her into the silo. It had silage in it then, and I remember the sound of her body whooshing through the air when I dropped her in here, kind of like you did, dear, and her plopping into the stinking silage below. You hit much harder. No silage now, you know. I thought you would die, but no worries. This still fits the plan." She paused. "I've lost my train of thought ... Oh, yes. Once I had thrown her into the silage, I released our unloader up there, and it came down like a guillotine on her. I remember that sound too. A car crash sound. And then ... I turned on the unloader so she was fed through the auger, tearing her into little bits for our own pigs to eat. It was an Ezinicki meal like the Carruthers one at the Massey farm. They both deserved it, remember that." Edwina stopped talking. There was silence in the silo.

Alice then heard her own voice echoing in the cylinder. She couldn't believe she was speaking or that, somehow, she was still curious at this moment. She knew now how she was going to die. The unloader. Pieces of her body would be spewed out onto the barn floor or onto the snow outside. Something about that, though, didn't make sense. In her pain and confusion, she couldn't figure it out.

"What about ... Perry Scott?" she asked.

"Oh, yes, the beautiful Perry Scott. A stud of a man whom the ladies around here never would have dreamed they could have, even for a day or a night. But our Ev. You know our Ev. A beauty who could rival any he'd seen in Hollywood. That Ev was a restless gal. Though, really, two affairs in the fifty or more years she was married is actually not that many. Men are certainly allowed more. But she could pick them. A looker and then another looker for lovers, the first a bandit, the second a famous man. Only the best for our Ev. The worst thing about it, though, was that she bragged about the affair to me, couldn't help herself. Not that Ev was a boastful person, but I guess it was too much for her to not tell her best girlfriend that she had bagged Perry Scott, that she had had a Hollywood hunk in her bed, in the marital bed she shared with Harold Massey, when he was away another day. The fucking tramp. Harold! She betrayed him again, this time in their own house. He would never know. He could never know. So, I had to take vengeance for him. Harold was having a new concrete floor put into his basement. A nephew of mine was doing it."

Oh my god, thought Alice down on the silo floor, remembering Edwina using the words "fresh concrete" when she and Mercer had first talked to her about the body in Evelyn Massey's basement. She remembered thinking it was a curious phrase but nothing more. A police officer isn't perfect. *We always miss something.* Why oh why had she not asked Edwina why she had put it that way!

"I picked a day when Ev and Harold and their kids were away, and I got a message to Perry saying that I was a friend of Ev's and she wanted to see him that day. The filming had been finished a few days before. We arranged for me to pick him up somewhere that no one would see us. I took him out to the Massey place, told him that she was down in the cellar with a surprise for him. I knew where they kept their axes back then, right near the basement door. I followed him down, and I cracked his skull wide open. All the old ladies around here could swing axes, but none better than me. Then I hauled him into the basement where the floor was broken open and about to be filled in. I got another one of the crates that Harold used to ship pigs and lambs from his barn and put Perry Scott in it and covered it with a canvas. I told my nephew that there was one hundred dollars in it for him if he buried the crate in the concrete without asking questions. He likely assumed I had killed someone's big dog on our property or a neighbour's animal that had gotten loose or was threatening for some reason and that I wanted the evidence gone. Maybe he suspected something worse, maybe he even peeked, I don't know, but we were family. You keep each other's secrets. And there was cash involved. So, he buried our lovely Perry Scott beneath the Masseys' floor. Evelyn never knew. She just knew he had disappeared, and, of course, she couldn't publicly know anything private about Perry Scott, or his whereabouts, at any time."

Edwina's old voice, which had been projecting down the silo, grew quieter for the first time. Alice could barely hear what she said next.

"I lost my temper with that one. I'm not proud of it. Not one bit. But, you see, I was just so angry with him, and with Ev. I got some binder twine from the barn when I retrieved the crate." She paused and spoke even more quietly. "I tied that fucker's hands behind his back, those hands that had touched Harold's beautiful wife behind Harold's back, and I smashed those arms and hands with my axe. I was so, so angry." She stopped speaking for a while. It was silent, cold and silent, the sky still grey above.

"But," said Alice, almost shouting up the silo to be heard, gasping, "Evelyn wrote those notes!"

"You know," said Edwina, "I have never once been a suspect in any investigation into any of these missing people. I know, for certain, that you and your American fancy boy, that Yankee fool like they are all fools, and that brown foreign woman have never suspected me for an instant, even over these last two weeks. Even after bodies were found on my property. Even though I had plenty of motive if you stopped to think about it. Even though I visited Evelyn constantly, knew her secrets, hated her, knew about her medication, knew her handwriting intimately and had many copies of it. I was hiding in plain sight. In the best of disguises. A woman. And lately ... an old woman." She paused. "That last day of her life, I convinced Ev, her memory failing as it was, as we talked in her kitchen throughout the afternoon, that she hadn't taken her medication, several times. I helped her to about four times her limit that day. Cleaned out the whole pillbox. I made sure Wilson had us on our way home before it took full effect." Alice remembered shaking that pillbox when Blair had given it to her back at the Massey home, realizing it was empty.

Edwina looked up at the silo unloader. "But now, I will commit my final and perhaps greatest homicide. And for *all* the right reasons."

32

The Murder of Alice Morrow

"DON'T DROP THAT thing on me!" cried Alice. "I beg you!" She wished she had more poise, more courage at the moment of her death. She wished many things. She wished she hadn't accepted Alex Hall's invitation to the prom. She wished she couldn't imagine Luke's face when he heard she'd accepted, the pain invading it like an army. How could someone, a decent person, leave their boyfriend of several years, their good and decent and loving boyfriend, like that? She needed forgiveness. She wanted someone to forgive her before she died. She didn't know who or what. Maybe God. She thought of her night with Alex at the prom, the way he had come on to her in the car afterward, the way he had held her down, twisting her arms, the way she had fought him and barely gotten away. The shame she had felt, how she'd cried for Luke that night. And then word had come.

Suicide.

"Oh, I'm not going to do that," said Edwina, glancing up to the top of the silo. "You aren't thinking straight, not thinking like a police detective, though that's understandable under the circumstances." She aimed the gun down at Alice, who felt so weak now that she could barely move. Edwina closed one eye to aim. "This has to look like I had nothing to do with it. I cannot release the unloader, that wouldn't make any sense. No. Here is what happened." She sighed. "It is perfectly reasonable, and when I call the police station in about ten minutes from my phone in my house, I will sound breathless, an old woman with leukemia on the verge of death, shattered by the fact that she has just found the body of dear Sergeant Alice Morrow at the bottom of her abandoned silo. 'You see, the good sergeant called me and asked if she could come to my place and search my barn. She'd had a hunch in the night that there might be evidence somewhere in there, or at least the buildings on this farm had to be searched, given that two bodies had been found on the property.' You went out to the barn on your own. Surely, an old woman such as myself would stay in the house. But I heard a gunshot, and, terrified, I somehow wheeled out here and followed your tracks and found you where you lie now, a bullet through your head. You took off your parka to get through the opening into the silo, but you did not take off your gun belt. It must have caught on the ladder or in the opening and ripped, and you fell about forty feet to the floor of the silo, and your gun must have somehow fired." Edwina kicked the gun belt and holster over the edge, and it flew out into the silo and down, landing with a smack near Alice's head. "That is the only explanation. No one else was here. No one but a female someone, an old, barely-able-to-function female in the house, not out here. I will shoot you wearing these gloves, Alice Morrow, not a trace of my fingerprints on your weapon, though they have no record of my fingerprints on file anyway. I'm just being cautious, covering all the bases, you know?" She paused. "Besides, we don't have pigs to eat you anymore. If I used the unloader, how would I have ever explained the pieces of you left behind, spit out by the auger?" She paused again. "But before

I finish you, I want you to say that you are sorry to Luke. Beloved Luke. I used to dandle him on my knee when he was a child. There was no one finer than that boy. He was my favourite; I think I loved him more than my own children. To think of what you did to him. They all deserved to die. But none more than you."

"I am so sorry, Luke," said Alice, almost before Edwina had the words out of her mouth. She didn't care, actually, that Edwina had a gun in her hands. She wanted to say it anyway. She was sorry. Deeply, deeply sorry. She loved Luke. She had made a mistake. We all do. We make so many of them. Luke had too, apparently. He had not intended to die; he had just wanted to scare her, win her back. And he would have. An autopsy showed he had taken only a few extra sleeping pills, but they were too much for a slight heart condition he didn't know he had. So, he slipped away into that undiscovered country, away from her.

"You know," said Edwina, "I stopped killing sixty years ago. I didn't know you could do that. I thought that people like me just kept on going. But I stopped. And then, I started again, just this year. But despite that, Alice dear, I will die a much-mourned woman. A fine woman. I will die an example of the great women who populate this area: hardworking, decent, long-suffering, polite, and kind as hell. My secrets will go with me to the grave, as if they were buried underground with me. I have won."

Alice couldn't look up at the barrel of the gun. She was going to be shot with her own weapon, a police officer's shameful end. So many times over the years, in fact, ever since Luke had died, she had almost wished for this moment. It was part of why she had come back to this area. She had the brains, she had everything to be almost anything she wanted to be, and she had always dreamed of being someone special, out there in the great beyond. But after Luke died, after her graduation, which she had not attended for fear that she would have been booed from the stage, she'd decided to come back. She wanted to punish herself, to walk about in this community with her guilt on her forehead like a gigantic "A." She wanted to live in the community that Luke had wanted to stay in, where he had hoped that both of them would live and that she had secretly wanted to leave. But she also wanted to seek justice for someone, she didn't know who — anyone. Perhaps for Luke, perhaps for everyone who had been wronged. She figured she owed it to him. Perhaps catch an Alex Hall in the act. And if she should die doing these things, well, all the better — a police officer, hated like many of them are.

Hugh Mercer's face appeared in her mind — Mercer with his own regrets and his need for forgiveness, Mercer who seemed to love her, truly love her. And she, Alice Morrow, looking up at the gun, waiting for the bullet to come at her, loved him.

"I am a good shot," said Edwina, "I won't miss. I was always the best in 4-H. And this will be like shooting fish in a barrel anyway. A sitting duck. Then I'll drop the gun down on you."

Images of Blair Massey-Khan picking off the top of the spruce tree flashed through Alice's mind again. She wished Mercer could help her, but she knew he wouldn't. He was gone, back to the place he called America. She wondered, with her dying thought, if he would return here when he heard of her death and somehow … somehow … figure out what had really happened. The truth. They both believed in the truth, no matter what it was.

Suddenly, there was shouting at the entrance to the silo. But it wasn't Edwina Shields. "What the hell?" cried someone. It was a younger woman's voice. "Oh my god!"

The gun went off, but the bullet ricocheted off the far wall of the silo, and then Alice dared look up, opening her eyes wide in terror.

Salma Haddad was standing beside Edwina Shields, nearly half a foot shorter than her but with both her hands around the old woman's hands, having forced the gun upward at the last moment.

33

Hope

SAL HAD CALLED Alice's cell and gotten no answer. That struck her as strange. Why was her partner not answering her phone first thing in the morning? That never happened. Good cop and dear friend that she was, she acted. She tracked the location of the cell. The Shields farm. She was there in fifteen minutes. She saw Alice's car in the driveway and found no one in the house. But when she moved back down the walkway toward the cars, she heard voices in the barn and then saw the boot tracks and wheelchair ruts. Coming silently through the snow toward the big doors up around the back, she began to make out what was being said and then started to run. Inside, her steps still silent in the rotting hay strewn on the floor, unheard by the old woman above her own voice and the shouts and gasps of Alice Morrow echoing up the big concrete cylinder, Sal ascended the ramp and saw Edwina Shields pointing a gun downward into the silo. She was alarmed at the strength of the old woman as she wrested the weapon from her.

Then, Constable Haddad hardly knew what to do. Should she handcuff a nearly one-hundred-year-old woman? What danger was she to any others? She pocketed Alice's weapon. Her friend was groaning down below.

"Alice!" she cried. "Are you okay?"

"No ... no, Sal, I'm not."

"I'm coming!" She moved toward the ladder.

"No!" cried Alice.

"What?"

"Cuff her!"

"What?"

"Cuff her first!"

"Mrs. Shields?"

"Cuff her to a post somewhere or a door handle and don't leave her near any damn machinery buttons!" Alice was eyeing the deadly silo unloader up above. "Then call for help. Then ... come down. And don't give her your parka. Leave her in the fucking cold!"

When the other officers came, they didn't know what to do with Edwina Shields either. Keep the handcuffs on? Put her in the back of a police cruiser and take her to the station for questioning? Treat her like a serial killer or an elderly woman on death's door? Or do you leave her alone? Leave her in her house to die, as she surely would in a very short time.

Alice was another matter. She was gingerly carried up the ladder and put into an ambulance, Sal at her side. At the hospital, tended to by nurses and a doctor she knew, the report wasn't good: broken ankle, broken fingers, separated shoulder, and bruised all over, but she was alive, and she would heal — at least, her physical wounds would. She was kept overnight to make sure there was nothing wrong internally. Sal stayed with her that night, and the next day she brought Mahmoud and Aya. Alice's mother and father appeared too, anxious but trying not to show much worry, and before she went to sleep, Constable Robbie Trew arrived with his mom, since she had insisted he bring her. But there was no sign of Mercer. She wanted to ask Sal if she thought he knew, but she couldn't bring herself to inquire. Sal's silence on the issue, to her, spoke volumes.

In two days, she was back at home to rest, told by Chief Smith, via an email message, to take a week off or more, whatever she needed, and to stay at her desk for a while after she did return. She wanted to go into the station and speak to Edwina, who was now being held in a cell and scheduled to be moved to a hospital. She also wanted to talk with Andrea, console her, though she knew that almost nothing she could say would help. She wanted to speak with Blair too, and Gloria and Gwen, and Delilah and everyone else. She didn't know what she would say to them. Would she apologize? Would she try to console them too? In fact, she wanted to console everyone, the whole community. The news that was quickly spreading that a serial killer had been in their midst would be a psychic wound that would never go away. There was a guilt now among them, a stain, a doubt about themselves that would feel eternal. These were good people. Good, secretive, flawed people. But more good than anything else.

She wondered too if anyone would console her. Or if she deserved consolation.

There was still no word from Mercer.

After five days, she couldn't stand it anymore. When her parents were out, she showered, still amazed at the bruises all over her body giving interesting backgrounds to her tattoos, those desperate black initials, A.M. with hearts, the ones she had gotten after Luke died. She washed her hair too, somehow, and put on a little makeup, and found the perfume and put some on too. She somehow got into her coat, one sleeve empty, and hobbled out the back door in her walking boot. She wasn't supposed to drive. She was still as sore as hell. It was her left foot that had been broken, though, and her car was an automatic, so she didn't need that foot: She could press the accelerator and hit the brakes with her right, and she could drive with her left arm and sneak her right out from the sling to steady the bottom of the steering wheel.

It was another ridiculously cold day, though this one seemed the coldest in a long while. The sky was grey again, and thick, as if there were no ceiling up there, just frigid heavy air coming right down to the snow-covered ground. The whole place was in a deep freeze. That paralyzed quiet was in the air again, the only sound, it seemed, being the lonely, plaintive blast of the train that passed through town every now and then. She couldn't scrape the windows, so she just sat in the car for fifteen minutes with the heater and defroster and fan all on at full blast.

Finally, she eased onto the street and headed out of town toward the country. But before she got there, she passed the encampment in the town park with its scattering of tents where homeless people were trying to stay alive. If Elwin Most had his way, the police would be driving them all out of there, driving them to God knows where, to misery somewhere else. This place was the source of a great deal of debate in the community, and there were plenty of other people who called the encampment an eyesore and an embarrassment and wanted it gone at any cost. It bothered them to see these people in their midst. But as Alice passed, she noticed a line of people at one end near the largest tent, their breaths clouds in the cold air. They were carrying groceries and cooked meals and sleeping bags and pillows and heaters and parkas and toques and gloves. The line was long, very long. And as Alice watched, she noticed Robbie there out of uniform carrying a big stack of clothes, his mother with him with a Crock-Pot of food, and then Alice saw Blair Massey-Khan and her mother and aunt, and Delilah and Ebb Morton, and Sal's son and daughter, there on their own. Alice nodded, and a tear ran down her cheek.

SHE DROVE THROUGH the countryside, drawn toward Mercer's farmhouse as if she couldn't stop herself. Before she had left her house, standing there in her room with her freshly washed hair and her perfume in the air, she had sat down on her bed and looked into Luke's eyes again. They'd stared at each other for a long time. Then she'd stood up and taken the photograph down from the wall. She'd gripped one end to rip it in half but stopped. She'd kissed his face and put the photograph in her bottom drawer.

Despite the weather, the countryside didn't appear so cold today. The endless blankets of white seemed lovely. She knew too that beneath them, the secrets of spring were waiting.

She turned down Mercer's sideroad and was disheartened to see that there were no tire tracks in the snow. She drove all the way along it to his lane and parked just out of sight, again, and looked down at the farmhouse. It was mid-afternoon. She stayed there for hours, just staring down at the house, hoping for signs of movement inside it. But it seemed abandoned. In fact, it looked dead. All possibilities were gone from that house.

She didn't need Mercer ... any more than he needed her.

She fought back tears. She had come to finally tell him her secrets. All about Luke. And all about herself. Well, maybe not all, but most. And she had come to tell him that she hoped he wouldn't leave. *But what's the point now?* she thought, looking down on that empty home.

She stayed, though, filled with something she hadn't felt since she was in high school: hope.

And then, as darkness began to descend ... the lights came on.

She drove slowly down the lane and parked next to his car. Then she moved in her silent northern way along his walkway. When she arrived at his door, she didn't knock. She just went in.

Acknowledgements

THERE ARE MANY people to thank as I make my way from *As We Forgive Others* to *A Place of Secrets* in The Northern Gothic Mysteries, investigating my northern country, its giant to the south, and hopefully, human beings, period — my little contribution to a certain sort of gothic literature, exploring forgiveness in the first novel, secrets in this one.

I want to thank everyone at Cormorant Books for helping me make these stories as meaningful and real and hopefully compellingly readable as we can make them: publisher, Marc Côté, first and foremost, for his belief in me and in the whole project; Barry Jowett for his support and editorial genius; Sarah Cooper for her sleight-of-hand ability to manage everything; Marijke Friesen for her lovely cover designs; Gillian Rodgerson for perfect proofreading; and Sarah Jensen, Fei Dong and Katherine Zheng. Andrea Waters too, for a spectacular copyedit that made sure, among other things, that we got the complicated range of ages of all the characters and the dates right!

Also, thanks to my fearless agent Hilary McMahon for being by my side (and at my book launches!) and pushing me in the right direction, now and going forward. Thanks to Sergeant Janice MacDonald of the Cobourg (Ontario) Police Services, who read and gave me notes for the first novel's manuscript and read the second one as well. And a special thanks to my brother, Stephen Peacock, a man with an encyclopedic mind, who explained to me the sinister capablities of a silo unloader.

And finally, as always, thanks to my family. Though I thanked my son Sam for his early reading and encouragement concerning the first novel, I neglected to thank my daughter Johanna, a wonderful writer and scholar, who through her love of gothic literature, taught me and inspired me to investigate and feature it in this work, and Hadley, the beautiful singer and recording artist in the family, who sang several of the songs from the first novel at its book launch, and I hope will do so for this one, as well. Thanks to Ash and Mac for their support too. And last, but certainly not least, my wife Sophie, who over the years has read everything I've written and kindly did so again this time, amidst her busy schedule. I'm blessed to have her in my life.

The author respectfully acknowledges that this novel was written while he was living on land located in the traditional and treaty territory of the Michi Saagiig (Mississauga) and Chippewa Nations, collectively known as the Williams Treaties First Nations, which include Curve Lake, Hiawatha, Alderville, Scugog Island, Rama, Beausoleil, and Georgina Islands First Nations.

We acknowledge the sacred land on which Cormorant Books operates. It has been a site of human activity for 15,000 years. This land is the territory of the Huron-Wendat and Petun First Nations, the Seneca, and most recently, the Mississaugas of the Credit River. The territory was the subject of the Dish With One Spoon Wampum Belt Covenant, an agreement between the Iroquois Confederacy and Confederacy of the Ojibway and allied nations to peaceably share and steward the resources around the Great Lakes. Today, the meeting place of Toronto is still home to many Indigenous people from across Turtle Island. We are grateful to have the opportunity to work in the community, on this territory.

We are also mindful of broken covenants and the need to strive to make right with all our relations.